"We both know you are anything but a maid, so please stop the knee bending."

"Yes, my lord."

"And stop calling me that."

"Yes, my lord."

"I said stop it."

She kept quiet for a second more before lowering her gaze so he couldn't see the twinkle in her eyes. "Of course, my lord."

He surprised her by being quite resourceful, grabbing her chin with his strong fingers and forcing her to look him in the eye. "I said stop it."

"Yes, my lord."

"I mean it."

"Of course, my lord."

"Stop it before I do something we both will regret," he said, lowering his head until their noses almost met.

Feeling his breath against her lips stirred something inside her, and she couldn't hold back a shiver of delight. Mesmerized, she stared into his eyes, watching them as they turned warmer, burning into her.

"Whatever you say, my lord."

His gaze turned darker, hotter, and before she could think one straight thought he lowered his head until their lips almost touched. "What would you say if I do the unthinkable and kiss you?"

"Thank you?"

He stared at her for a second, as if in shock over her honest and direct approach. His normal coldness disappeared as he reluctantly smiled down at her. Slowly, he lifted one hand and put it around her neck, stroking the sensitive skin of her neck with his thumb.

"Remember that you asked for it," he whispered.

Praise for Jennifer Wenn

"Jennifer Wenn weaves a wonderful story…"

~Pauline Michael, Night Owl Romance (3.5 Stars)

~*~

"Very well-written…. The characters are so vivid. They seem about to walk right off the page."

~Maura, Coffee Time Romance and More (4 Cups)

~*~

"The plot, the characters, the love, loss, pain, and just everything about life that we know is out there is blended into the pages almost seamlessly as though they were born there."

~Valkyrie Fatality, Rockin' & Reviewing (5 Stars)

~*~

"I would definitely re-read it."

~Victoria Lane, The Romance Reviews

~*~

Also available from The Wild Rose Press, Inc. and written by Jennifer Wenn

~

The Royal Family Series

A FAMILY AFFAIR

NEVER HAD A DREAM COME TRUE

THE BEAUTY OF YOU

AN HEIRESS IN DISGUISE

~

The Barnesville Collection

A FATHER FOR DAISY

ALWAYS YOU

An Heiress in Disguise

by

Jennifer Wenn

The Royal Family, Book Four

This is a work of fiction. Names, characters, places, and incidents are either the product of the author's imagination or are used fictitiously, and any resemblance to actual persons living or dead, business establishments, events, or locales, is entirely coincidental.

An Heiress in Disguise

Contact Information: info@thewildrosepress.com

Cover Art by *RJ Morris*

The Wild Rose Press, Inc.
PO Box 708
Adams Basin, NY 14410-0708
Visit us at www.thewildrosepress.com

Publishing History
First Tea Rose Edition, 2017
Print ISBN 978-1-5092-1529-4
Digital ISBN 978-1-5092-1530-0

The Royal Family, Book Four
Published in the United States of America

Dedication

To my children—
Don't worry… Be happy…

Chapter One

The harbor of Bayonne, June 1813

"Murderer."

Lord James Darling took a deep, staggering breath as he recognized the strained voice behind him. Ignoring a desperate urge to simply walk away and pretend he hadn't heard, Jamie clenched his jaw until it ached before turning to face his accuser.

Raphael Delon looked distinguished and utterly elegant, as always, his expensive clothes more suitable for a ballroom than a small, bedraggled French harbor no one had ever heard of. His well-cut hair, as dark as Jamie's was blond, moved slightly in the warm summer night breeze, softening the harsh outlines of his handsome face.

But nothing could soften the cold hatred pouring from his brown eyes, eyes that only days before had laughed with Jamie, showering him with admiration. Showering him with brotherly love.

"I'm not a murderer," Jamie tried without heat, without belief, knowing in his heart he was fighting a lost cause.

"Liar."

Sighing, Jamie felt worn out, like an old rug walked upon by thousands of merciless feet. "Please leave me alone," he whispered, turning his back to his accuser again, as if the simple gesture could erase all the evil in the past. "It is done, and there isn't anything more I can do about it. God knows I have tried."

The pain when the sword edged through his skin and into the flesh of his arm made him whimper, and he fell forward, down onto the dirty gravel of the dock. In shock he stared down at his arm in the dim light from the flickering streetlamp, watching blood color his dirty shirt red.

"It's only a flesh wound, so don't you fret yet, *mon cher*. Save those tears for when I am done with you, when I know you suffer as much pain as I do."

"Why?" Jamie's hoarse question seemed to amuse his former friend.

Raphael laughed coldly, kneeling and putting the bloody end of the sharp sword against the side of Jamie's neck.

"Such an odd question to come from you, *mon cher*. One would think a devious mind such as yours would be able to not only come up with destructive plans but also understand why the people affected might feel…offended."

"I'm merely an English soldier. My quest is for my king and my king alone. I know of no other plans."

This time he let out a painful roar as the sword penetrated the delicate skin of his shoulder, near his neck, scraping the bone as it was pushed deeper into him.

"My, my, *mon cher,* how you disappoint me. I thought a soldier like you, who is famous for his bravery and courage on the battlefield, would have more stamina. More…perseverance. Instead you don't even defend yourself. You simply lie at my feet like the shivering rat you are, unable to rip your gaze from your executioner." Raphael leaned closer until his lips almost touched Jamie's ear. "Like my sister did when she died because of you."

The pain in Jamie's shoulder and arm was nothing against the soaring agony which ripped through his heart at the mention of Raphael's younger sister.

Aurélie.

The name alone made his whole being sing, and as he closed his eyes, images of her lovely face danced through his memory. Oh, how he had loved her, that beautiful, fickle girl who had mesmerized him with her teasing eyes and secretive smile from the first time he saw her. A vision of beauty, with her thick, black hair and brown eyes over a pert French nose, she'd had him following her around like a jealous, lovelorn fool until that memorable day when she'd finally agreed to what he had known from the start—they were meant for each other.

He would have done anything for her. Anything.

But the horrifying truth was that in the end he had killed her. Without mercy he had put her in front of death and never given her a chance to find a path back to life.

"There was evidence…"

"What evidence?" Raphael snapped, adding more pressure to the sword at the side of Jamie's neck. "How could there be evidence? My sister was an angel, a gift from God. She was an overprotected nineteen-year-old maiden who had never known the darker side of life until the day she died. All the contact she'd ever had with soldiers was in a ballroom or assembly hall. How could there have been evidence that she was a spy?"

"I don't know," Jamie moaned, almost unable to withstand the pain. All he wanted to do was to defend himself, to tear the sword out of his accuser's hand and press hard into the man's heart, but he couldn't. Not to Raphael. Not to Aurélie's brother. "I couldn't believe it myself when I first heard, but by then it was too late. Everyone else was already convinced she was guilty, and there was nothing I could do. Nothing…"

"You could have hidden her! You could have helped her to escape! But no, not Lord James Darling. You chose to bring her to them, taking her right into the hornets' nest. She hadn't a chance against their accusations, and because of you she died. Because of you the night sky has one more star watching over us."

Jamie knew Raphael spoke the truth about Aurélie, that she had been an angel in disguise as a French noblewoman. She had been loyal, loving, and incredibly supportive of him, always there to listen and help him through what he had experienced out in the field, out in the war.

She had been there for him. She had cried for him. She had without restraint given him her virginity out of pure love, and in return he had sent her to her death by presenting her to the men who accused her of betrayal. Of espionage.

"Believe me, killing you, *mon cher,* will hurt me more than you. I thought of you as a brother, as a relative, and I loved you like I have loved no other man. But you betrayed us. You killed her. And now you shall die."

Jamie tried to turn away, but Raphael was too strong. Without mercy, full of hatred, the Frenchman pulled the sword away from Jamie's neck before pushing it right into Jamie's torso. As Jamie collapsed completely to the ground, the last thing he saw before the pain eased and the world turned black was Raphael determinedly walking away without looking back. Without mercy, the Frenchman left his friend alone on the dark dock, slowly bleeding to death, just as Jamie had left his sister alone to face her accusers.

Faint from loss of blood, Jamie closed his eyes. All he could think of was the love of his life, Aurélie. "Soon we will meet, my love," he whispered as running steps and shouting voices closed in. "Soon we will be together again."

Chapter Two

Hampshire, the beginning of September 1814

"I don't want to marry Mother's paramour!"

Harold Aubrey looked up from the letter he'd been reading, intense blue eyes in an otherwise homely face sparkling with laughter.

"Really, Mina? Paramour?"

With as much drama as she could muster, Mina threw her hands out in an overly theatrical act of utter despair. "I wish she simply could marry the bore herself, and give me the chance to meet someone special to *my* heart."

With a defeated sigh, Harold put the letter down on the worn desk in front of him and sank back deeper into his leather chair.

"A sound wish," he mused, crossing his fingers in front of him. "Only your solution has one small problem. Your mother is already married to me."

Mina's strawberry-blonde ringlets bounced against her slender shoulders as she snorted loudly. "I know *that*. You are my father, after all. I simply nurse a desperate wish that mother will cease this annoying nagging about the Honorable Luther Whyte being the perfect husband for me."

"Maybe he is."

She stopped midstride, glaring at the man who

hid…er, sat behind his large desk. "Do *you* think the Honorable Luther Whyte is a good match for me?"

"I won't say he is your perfect match, sweetheart. But you have to admit you have nursed a quite unhealthy grudge against the poor man ever since your mother first introduced him. You have never allowed him a chance against your own prejudice."

"He's a vicar!"

This time it was Harold who snorted. "Please enlighten me as to what possibly can be wrong about him being a vicar? Isn't that a profession respectable enough for you?"

"Father…"

"You started this, sweetheart."

Mina sank down into one of the chairs on the other side of the desk, crossing her legs at the ankles in front of her in a very unladylike manner, one which would have had her mother neighing with frustration if she'd seen it.

"There's nothing wrong with being a vicar, I guess. But the Honorable Luther Whyte is such an awful one. He thinks his profession gives him the right to give his honest opinion on any subject, no matter how personal."

"Now you're exaggerating."

"No, I'm not!" Mina had to stand again, too agitated to stay motionless. Her father always joked about her inability to stay still, telling everybody she'd been this energetic since she was born. His favorite tale was how at birth she hadn't had the patience to wait for being delivered and instead chose to surprise her parents and come into the world on the couch in the salon as they shared a nice cup of tea.

"Yesterday he told me that I slouch. Slouch!"

"He did, did he?"

"Yes! And most patronizingly, I assure you."

"And you became offended because…?"

She took a deep breath, trying to stay calm and serene, an almost impossible mission for her. "*Because I don't slouch!*"

"Well…"

Mina's eyes narrowed as she stared at her father, who couldn't hide his amusement. What was wrong with the man? Didn't he understand how important this was to her? If he didn't help her, she would be Mrs. Honorable Luther Whyte sooner than she would like to think.

Her mother had made up her mind, and nothing was going to stand in her way, especially not an unwilling bride-to-be. That it was her own daughter she would force into an unwanted marriage didn't bother Ophelia Aubrey at all. *She* would be happy enough for both of them.

Mina loved her mother dearly, and in the beginning she truly had tried to like the man her mother had chosen for her. She had forced herself to smile invitingly and encouragingly, flattering him as much as she could in an attempt to make some sort of connection to him.

But he was impossible to like.

The Honorable Luther Whyte was not only too aware of his own importance. He knew he was a handsome man, and he had a knack for sending gazes meant to subdue toward every woman he met. Mina's mother insisted, with a very girlish giggle, that he had smoldering eyes. To Mina they looked more like puppy eyes, all wet and yearning.

All the married ladies of their acquaintance had adored him at first sight and fought for a second of his attention. When they realized he was a very eligible bachelor, the game changed—now they threw their daughters in his path, silently praying for him to choose theirs.

To Mina's horror, he had chosen her.

Ophelia had gloated for days, filling her daughter's delicate ears with tender words about the man she now almost had in her hand. There was only one little obstacle between Ophelia and eternal bliss—getting her daughter to accept his proposal.

"I don't want to marry him," Mina now repeated to her father, determinedly searching for the right words to persuade Harold into seeing things her way. "He doesn't care who he marries, as long as the wife brings money into the nest. He didn't care a bit about me until mother informed him about me being one of the wealthiest heiresses in the country. You should have seen him, Father. The calculating smile he bestowed on me was ugly."

"Unfortunately, you will have to learn to live with men wanting you for your dowry. I happen to be a very wealthy man, and you are my only child. There will always be men who want you for what you bring with you into the marriage. But it doesn't mean you can't bond with such a man. What if he turns out to be the perfect choice for you, if you get to know him better?"

"Father…"

Harold held up a hand, and Mina immediately shut her mouth. She knew better than to force him to listen before he was ready to. If she ever would be able to make him see this from her view, she knew she would have to let him inform her about his thoughts first.

Then she would make him change his mind.

"Mina, sweetheart, you are such a dear child, and you know how much you mean to me."

When he seemed to expect something from her, she nodded in full agreement. Even though he was a bit awkward when it came to showing her his feelings, she knew without a doubt how much he loved her.

"Good, good," he praised her, before continuing. "Your happiness is most important to me, and I want you to rest assured that I will never force you into something you don't want to be a part of."

She nodded to let him know she still listened to him, and he awarded her another appreciative smile.

"That said, I want you to try to understand what your mother and I face when it comes to finding you a suitable husband. There are so many strange men out there, Mina, and we would hate to see you ending up in the hands of a man who doesn't appreciate your sweet person. Mr. Whyte might seem to be a bit too impressed by your hefty dowry, but the truth still remains the same—he *is* better than what you think."

"No, he isn't."

"You would have a good life with him."

"No, I wouldn't."

"The Soberton vicarage is quite a handsome house, with plenty of room for a family."

Mina closed her eyes, a wave of nausea overwhelming her at the mere thought of having a family with *that* man. She could hardly stand being in the same room with him. How would she ever be able to endure everyday life close to him, unable to avoid him? To be unable to shut a door and leave him and his wet puppy eyes on the other side?

She could forgive her father for thinking highly of the Honorable Luther Whyte; he was a man, after all. Men never seemed to see deeper into another man's soul than what carriage he drove or how many horses he had.

But her mother…

That was a completely different story. Ophelia Aubrey wasn't known for her intelligence, but she possessed a good and affectionate heart. Deep down, Mina knew her mother only wanted what was best for her. It wasn't Ophelia's fault that the cur had bewitched her so completely that she couldn't recognize what he really was—a sniveling, conniving scoundrel.

"If you open up your heart to him, you might be surprised what you find when you get to know the real man," her father said, as if he had heard her thoughts and wanted to defend her suitor. "It's not easy to always be nice and likeable when one is only met with suspicion and contempt."

He had a point there; she had to give him that. She had built a wall high enough to hide the Honorable Luther Whyte's church, but still… Somewhere deep inside her she knew he was no good.

She *knew* it.

Unfortunately for her, her parents didn't. Especially not her mother. The Honorable Luther Whyte had done an excellent job with her, wrapping her around his little finger with his fawning and flattering words, and now Ophelia was a puppet in his repelling hands. A puppet who wanted nothing but to marry away her only daughter to him, no matter what it would take.

"I know I haven't been altogether polite toward him," she admitted, ignoring her father's amused eyebrow arching up. "But you don't understand what it's like, having Mother constantly trying to persuade me to accept his proposal. She simply doesn't understand how I can find him unacceptable, and I'm terrified she will come up with some scheme which will put me in a position where I can't deny him."

A frown marred Harold's high forehead as he took in what she'd said. "Are you telling me your mother is threatening to force this marriage?"

Before Mina had a chance to answer, the door burst open, and her mother floated into the room, a vision in pink muslin.

"There you are," she exclaimed dramatically when she saw Mina by her father's desk. "I've been looking all over for you. Mr. Whyte is here for you, and I want you to immediately seek him out in the salon."

"Mother!" In desperation, Mina grabbed her mother's hand, pressing it against her chest. "I don't want to go to him. Please, can't you simply tell him I'm unavailable?"

"Philomena Aubrey," Ophelia gasped dramatically, sounding a bit too much like her daughter, while Mina fidgeted under her father's amused gaze. It was embarrassingly obvious that this apple hadn't fallen too far from the tree. "I have already told him you will grant him his wish to see him. I tell you, he must be on the verge of proposing to you again." A big, happy sigh escaped Ophelia's smiling mouth as she stared, starry-eyed, at her daughter, apparently already envisioning the occasion. "Can you imagine the triumph?" she continued, almost breathlessly. "You, married to the most wanted bachelor of our acquaintance? It would vex Hester Primrose more than anything. The other day she hinted about Mr. Whyte showing an interest in Rosalind, and with quite a patronizing smirk, mind you. Oh, how I would love to be the one telling her about your engagement. Such a victory…"

"Let Rosalind have him," Mina said, trying hard to stifle an almost overwhelming urge to pout. "If she wants him, she can have him. Better her than me, I say, even though it would mean I would have to go to his house when I want to visit her."

"Mr. Aubrey," Ophelia whined to her husband, seeking aid. "You have to talk to your daughter. She is too stubborn for her own good. Here he is, the perfect man, asking for her hand in marriage. A gift any other woman would be ecstatic about But not Mina. No, she is determined to ruin her one chance for happiness. Soon she will be a spinster, unwanted, on the shelf, destined to spend her life either alone or in a loveless marriage with some man who's not too picky about his bride."

Mina closed her eyes, weary of the battle. How would she ever be able to reach through her mother's craziness? Ophelia Aubrey had always been the most wonderful, caring mother, loving her daughter dearly, no matter what. But that all ended when the Honorable Luther Whyte arrived in Soberton, gallantly bowing to all the ladies, collecting hearts.

Somehow he had changed a sane although slightly gossipy woman into a shivering wreck desperate for attention. And not only her mother had been changed. All the ladies of the parish yearned for him. The married ladies threw their daughters after him, and the unmarried ladies without helpful mothers more or less threw themselves in his path. Wherever he went, all women turned into giggling, unintelligent wenches.

"But marrying the Honorable Luther Whyte wouldn't change anything for me," she begged, searching for a way to once and for all convey to her mother how she felt. "I would still be caught in a loveless marriage. Worse, I would be in the hands of a man I despise. Is that what you want for me? Lifelong misery?"

"Of course not." Frustrated, Ophelia sat on a chair, a sad sigh escaping her. "I want what is best for you, and I know, with all my heart, that your happiness lies in the hands of Mr. Whyte."

"A man I can't stand?"

"I truly cannot understand why you are so set against him. He is nothing but perfect. He is tall and handsome, well-mannered and intelligent. Being the youngest son of four to a viscount doesn't leave a large income, but admiringly enough he has found his own way in life as a man of faith. A man of God."

If this hadn't been about her life, her future, Mina would have laughed hysterically over her mother's silly look of utter admiration. The seriousness of the situation removed all joy, and she looked at her father, still resting behind his desk, and searched for any sign he was on her side. But her father had an annoying habit of hiding his true feelings, something she normally wasn't concerned about but now found most unnerving.

"Father, please tell Mother to stop this," she begged, ignoring her mother's outraged gasp behind her. "I want to find my own road to happiness, not walk someone else's."

"What if your mother is right? What if the vicar is the perfect choice for you? You could be making the greatest mistake of your life by not accepting his proposal. Have you considered that your feelings for him might change when you lower the wall you have built against him?"

Mina couldn't hold back an amused snort. Sometimes her father was hilarious. "And why would I want to get to know him more if I can be finally rid of him?"

Blue eyes sparkled mischievously at her. "If Mr. Whyte no longer presented a threat to your marital status, you might relax enough toward him to see the real man and not your unfortunate picture of him. Who knows, you might even find him likeable."

"Impossible."

"You could be destroying your chances with him, if you again refuse him."

"I don't want him."

Ophelia, who apparently sensed her husband's leaning toward agreement with Mina, flew up from the chair and walked briskly over to her daughter. "Mr. Whyte told me he found you most attractive and even mentioned to me that he wouldn't mind walking through life with you. He is a man to worship, a man to adore. Any other woman would be honored to have him ask her to marry him."

"So let him marry any other woman, then. He doesn't want *me*. All he wants is my dowry. I'm only the person who comes with the money."

"Philomena Aubrey! How utterly rude of you to even think that Mr. Whyte only wants the money. He's a man of the cloth. A man who believes in mankind. He doesn't care about personal wealth, not even one as hefty as yours."

"It's the money," Mina stoically told her father. "If you would disinherit me, he would turn his back on me immediately."

"You are a stubborn, ungrateful girl, and I can't believe you are disgracing me like this." Ophelia marched resolutely toward the door, anger and frustration oozing from her every pore. "But mind you, dear child—There are ways to make a marriage happen, and wanting only what is best for you, your father and I might help the affair along."

Mina stared at the now-empty doorway, listening to her mother's angry footsteps receding down the stairs. She couldn't believe one man had the power to change a woman as the Honorable Luther Whyte had her mother. What was his secret? How could a man who was nothing but ordinary make the women of a whole county compete viciously over him? Turn friend against friend and mother against daughter?

"Your mother only wants what's best for you. You know that, don't you?"

"Does she?"

Rising and going to her, Harold put his hands tenderly against her cheeks like he had ever since she was a little girl, kissing her lightly on her freckled nose. "Indeed she does. Quite deeply too, I assure you. You mean the world to her. Always have, always will."

"Then why does she insist I should marry a man I detest, simply because *she* holds him in high esteem? I'm so afraid she will do something stupid against my will, so she'll have the happy ending she wants so much."

A frown marred Harold's high forehead as he took a step back, removing his warm hands from her cheeks. "I must admit her ending monologue did make me a bit uncomfortable. She knows I would never force you to do anything against your will, especially not something as life-altering as marriage."

Mina's spirit lifted. If her father fought with her, on her side, she could endure anything, no matter what devious plans her mother and the Honorable Luther Whyte laid.

Especially the latter.

"I'll make sure to be on my guard," she promised with a light smile, feeling much better and more secure by the minute. "No matter what traps they set for me, I will prevail. Oh, this might be quite fun, now that I think about it."

A strangled chuckle escaped her father as he shook his head at her. "You will be the death of me, for sure. All these pranks you have played over the years… It's a wonder the house still stands."

"Oh, Father, please don't worry. I'm an adult now, and I don't do pranks anymore, not too many, at least."

Harold sighed even more deeply, ignoring her joke. "I have to confess your situation does bother me, the more I think about it. You can't live in constant fear of being trapped into an unwanted marriage. I have to admit, against my will, that your mother seems simply too determined to marry you off to him. I have tried to talk some sense into her. Don't you look at me like that. I *have* tried to talk to her, but every time I say something not so nice about the vicar, steam blows out through her ears and she rushes away most dramatically. It doesn't matter what I say to her, she still insists he is your perfect match."

"I can manage," Mina said with more gumption than she felt.

"The thing is…" Harold sighed. "I'm going away in a couple of weeks and won't be back until January. Urgent business in London and Edinburgh is beckoning me. I won't be here to act as a shield for you. You will be alone with your mother."

"Oh…" Mina felt her shoulders sink under the sudden weight. Alone with a lovesick mother? Heaven forbid!

She watched her father pace in his office, mumbling inaudibly as his intelligent mind worked the problem from every angle. He was such a good man, Harold Aubrey, always making sure his wife and child had everything they needed. He had transformed an already lucrative business into a shipping empire, making his family financially secure should anything happen to him.

"Aha!"

Harold's triumphant voice broke through Mina's thoughts, and happily she clapped her hands together, as she recognized the expression on her father's face.

He had the solution.

Chapter Three

Berkshire, end of September 1814

As the carriage made a turn on the neatly made road, the whole splendor of Chester Park came into view, and Mina laughed, surprised.

"Oh, dear me," she breathed, impressed, as she took in the enormous castle which was to be her home during the next few months. The ancient building seemed to stretch indefinitely as far as her eyes could see. Hundreds upon hundreds of windows looked down at her as the carriage slowly rocked closer toward the grand entrance, where she could see a footman waiting at the top of the stairs.

To her surprise, the footman waved to the driver to continue, and instead of stopping they drove alongside the beautiful limestone building until they reached a gateway. After barely making it through the very narrow archway, they finally stopped at an entrance much less grand but much more inviting.

Enchanted by the picturesque courtyard, Mina didn't wait for the driver to open the door. She climbed out by herself, staring breathlessly at the beauty of her surroundings.

To her left was the short side of the magnificent castle rising four levels above her, and to her right lay the stables, made of huge granite blocks that must have been piled up by giants. Both buildings were joined together by a high wall on each side of the courtyard, making it a perfect hidden oasis.

Both walls had one gateway each, the one behind her she had passed through, and the opposite gateway open to a view of an inviting lake hiding behind hanging willows.

Cobblestones covered the ground, while ivy and rambling roses nearly hid the stone walls of the stable. In the middle of the courtyard an old-fashioned well stood, an obvious meeting place for gossiping servant girls, playful children, and a few haughty-looking geese.

"Miss!"

An old woman stood in the doorway leading into the castle, her hand discreetly urging Mina to come her way. Grabbing her bag from the driver's hand, Mina thanked him profusely for the safe journey before following the woman inside the castle.

They walked down a long corridor, passing more doors than Mina had ever seen in her life. Now and then she heard voices talking and laughing, and she knew without a doubt this was a happy house, filled with content people.

Not a spot of dust was visible anywhere; everything, from the lamps and paintings to the quirky door handles and the wooden floor, shone in clean splendor. Yet this magnificent castle was not like other country houses she had visited; they had felt more like museums than homes. No, this house was made to live in, not wander through in awe. It was a home, not a museum, and she became even more curious about the unknown people she was to share it with for the next couple of months.

After climbing a winding stair and walking through another long corridor, the maid stopped at one of the impressive-looking doors and knocked lightly before opening. For the first time since she left her home, Mina felt a bit nervous.

The bedroom was magnificent, large and light, with grand windows overlooking the lake she had seen when arriving. A huge bed stood by one of the shorter walls, a small group of sofas at the other, embracing a fireplace. In the middle, between the windows, a small desk stood, and the lady who sat by it looked up from the letter she had been writing with a polite smile.

"Philomena, I presume?"

There was no doubt who this woman was. Her natural dignity and overwhelming authority introduced her. "Yes, Your Grace."

"Did you have a safe trip here?"

"Yes, Your Grace."

"Uneventful, I hope?"

"Yes, not much happened at all, I'm afraid," she answered, trying not to sound as disappointed as she felt.

Something flickered in the solemn duchess's eyes, so fast Mina almost missed it. But it had looked like…laughter…

"You sound disappointed."

"Er…not at all."

The duchess didn't pursue the matter. Her intelligent eyes quietly took in Mina's person, as if she were measuring her. It was hard to think that this grand dame once had been a young girl who had made Harold Aubrey fall deeply in love with her. Anna Howard had been one of her father's best friends in his young scoundrel days. They had been part of an inseparable group of friends until the young lady met and married the powerful Hannibal Darling, the Duke of Berkeley.

Amazingly enough, their friendship had stayed strong, although they had only met occasionally, years apart. And when Harold wrote to his friend asking her to help him rescue Mina from a most unwanted suitor, the duchess had responded immediately by sending a carriage, no questions asked.

"I'll come and get you on my way home," Harold had assured her before she left. "Anna will make sure no one finds out you are there, which will give you three months of peace and quiet before I bring you back to your mother."

"Sounds lovely indeed." Peace and quiet weren't really Mina's favorite circumstance, but she still preferred it to being presented as the Honorable Mrs. Luther Whyte.

"I hope you won't feel lonely."

Harold had looked at her over his glasses, and she had brushed his worry aside, as she then hadn't thought much of it. Instead she was almost rejoicing at the fact she would be seeing new places, meeting new people, and having a chance to live life without her mother hovering over her and pushing where she did not want to go. But now, as she stood in front of the duchess, she started to shrink from her choice mentally.

What if the duchess was as smothering as her mother? What if she would expect Mina to always behave correctly? Or worse, be dressed correctly?

If so, this was a failure meant to happen.

Mina was too filled with life to sit still, too

interested in the world and the people in it to stay quiet, and too adventurous not to explore a newfound path.

"Harold wrote you had an unwanted suitor?"

"Yes, Your Grace."

"May I ask why your father, one of the sanest men of my acquaintance, feels he has to hide his daughter away from a suitor, not to mention from her mother?"

Mina squirmed uncomfortably. How honest should she be with the duchess? Her father obviously had told her the truth in his letter, but Mina couldn't help but hesitate. The duchess, in all her noble aristocracy, didn't seem to invite sharing secrets about silly love affairs.

But then again... There *had* been a definite spark of laughter.

"If I may start from the beginning?"

The duchess graciously pointed with her hand toward a door, almost hidden in the wall beside the bed. "Why don't you go and refresh yourself first. My maid will fetch us a tray with tea and scones, and you can tell me all about it while we have our refreshments."

Grateful at being able to take care of some quite urgent business, Mina left the duchess alone. When she came back into the large bedroom, she felt much better, and much less dusty.

The duchess, who had moved to one of the sofas, was gracefully pouring steaming-hot tea into lovely, delicate cups. Careful not to knock anything out of place, Mina sat down on the other side of the small table, and soon her stomach was full of incredibly delicious scones.

"Do you want another scone?"

"Oh, no, thank you, Your Grace," Mina almost

moaned. “I wouldn’t be able to eat even a crumb more. Those scones were divine.”

“Yes, they are. The cook here at Chester Park is very talented and one quite large threat against my waistline.”

This time the sparkle was impossible to miss, and Mina started to relax. Maybe the duchess wasn’t such an unreachable person after all. Her father seemed almost in awe of her, and as he never had fancied people stuffed with their own importance, except the Honorable Luther Whyte, there must be more to Anna Darling than met the eye.

“It all started when the old vicar of Soberton died, and a new one was appointed. The Honorable Luther Whyte is his name, and soon he had all the women of the parish fainting at the mere thought of him.”

“A womanizer?”

“Oh, no, not at all. He thinks himself much too important to throw away his reputation by causing any kind of scandal, not even a mild one. Instead he thrives on lecturing others, pointing out everyone’s faults and dwelling on their mistakes.”

The duchess made a small, disgusted grimace. “He sounds like an awful bore. How can the women be so much in favor of him?”

“Because he looks like a picture of the angel Gabriel painted on a wall inside the Soberton church. It pains me to admit it, but he is sort of handsome, with golden hair and vivid blue eyes.”

“It pains you…?” The duchess pursed her lips slightly, and Mina couldn’t help wonder if it was because of laughter or disgust.

A bit more carefully, she continued, “All the

mesmerized mamas eagerly put their daughters in front of him, hoping he would choose one of them to become his wife, but he never looked at them twice. Not one young lady interested him, until he met my mother and she, in a desperate attempt to attach him, told him about my dowry. You should have seen him, Your Grace. His uninterested eyes started to gleam, and he immediately sought me out, relentlessly telling me about the vision he had about the lucky woman who would become his bride."

"He told you what kind of wife he wanted? That is one odd way of courting someone you want to wed."

Mina shook her head lightly. "Oh, no. He didn't tell me what *he* wanted in a wife. He told me how *I* should act when I became his wife."

"What a monstrous man!"

"Indeed!" Mina squealed, starting to get a bit worked up as the duchess was openly agreeing with her. "I thought him hilarious, if not ludicrous, and when he later asked me to marry him, I most heartily declined. To my surprise, Mother became furious with me. She had already promised him my hand in marriage, and it never crossed her mind I wasn't as partial to him as she was."

"What happened?"

"Mother whined and whined for days, unable to grasp the truth that her daughter didn't want to marry the man of her choice. When the Honorable Luther Whyte started to show interest in the girl with the second largest dowry, she became desperate, and that's when she threatened to do something which would force me to marry him."

"What!" The duchess stared, outraged, at Mina, all

her earlier solemnity washed away. "You are her daughter! How could she even think to force you into an unwanted marriage?"

Mina shrugged lightly. "Because the Honorable Luther Whyte is a sniveling, conniving devil who doesn't think highly of anyone but himself. But all the same, he has managed to enchant all the ladies enough to make them competitive. And when my mother had the victory over all her friends so close to being won, she sort of lost her connection to reality when I took it away from her."

"And that's when Harold wrote to me," the duchess said matter-of-factly. "Well, dear girl, you are very welcome to stay here at Chester Park for as long as you like."

"Thank you."

"How you will stay will be your choice, though," the duchess continued with a definitely mischievous sparkle this time.

"I'm not sure I follow." Mina frowned.

"You can stay here either as a friend of the family under your own name, or as my new lady's maid, completely invisible."

Oh.

"Of course I don't mean that you will have to work as a maid," the duchess continued. "But you will, in the eyes of my family and to the rest of the servants, be merely another servant girl."

Oh!

For some reason the mere thought of disappearing completely and becoming one of the servants in this enormous house was incredibly tempting to her. Not only would it give her a freedom she seldom had had before, but she would also be even harder to find.

The Honorable Luther Whyte was a man *this* close to a fortune almost too large for him to comprehend, and she was no fool; she knew he would do anything to get it. Especially as he knew he had her mother on his side. He would search for her. Or at least force her mother to.

It was not such a long distance between her home in Hampshire and Chester Park in Berkshire. If she chose to stay under her own name, she knew she would soon have the two of them knocking on the door, asking the Darlings to release her. And then she had no chance of denying the stodgy vicar again, especially not as her father was too far away to stop her mother.

But if she stayed as a maid...

"I can see you have made up your mind." The duchess leaned forward again. "May I ask what you chose?"

"Maid," Mina said as quickly as possible, before she could change her mind.

"How interesting," the duchess almost purred. "I must admit I do look forward to this. You, hiding here as a maid for almost four months. Will you be able to not act the lady and answer up to my family in a too-familiar way?"

"I hope so. I will at least try. I can't promise you anything, though, Your Grace. My mouth has a way of speaking before my mind is awake."

The duchess laughed as she stood up and rang the bell for Agatha, her lady's maid, the one who had brought Mina here when she'd arrived. Within minutes the sour-faced maid arrived and was immediately informed about Mina's predicament and her new situation here at Chester Park.

"Are you sure about this, Your Grace?" Agatha asked, almost a bit reluctantly. "Have you even considered what she will have to face when she meets your family? Especially your boys?"

"No, I haven't," the duchess admitted and started to look a bit unsure. "Maybe it's not such a good idea having you hide as a maid. You will have more freedom to roam by yourself, but at the same time you will be a little bit easier to…"

The duchess's voice trailed off, and Mina felt herself frowning. What was it Agatha and the duchess were so worried about? Her sudden freedom? No, it was something else, something which had to do with "her boys."

"Easier to, what?" she finally asked, unable to wait for the duchess to set her thoughts straight.

"Easier to seduce," Agatha answered coldly, before the duchess had a chance to react.

"Agatha!"

"Well, don't you look so upset, Miss Anna. You know as well as I that those boys of yours are a bit too fond of bedding women."

The duchess squirmed uncomfortably, but it was quite clear that, against her will, she agreed with her maid. "They are such sweet boys," the duchess said with a proud yet embarrassed smile to Mina. "But they have a tendency to chase after women a bit too much now and then."

Agatha didn't say a word, but her snort told the more.

"How many sons are there?" Mina asked, with a sinking feeling.

"Four," the duchess whispered, and again Agatha snorted loudly, but a patronizing look from the duchess made her close her mouth again. "We have seven sons, but the three eldest won't be a problem for you. George and Harry are both happily married, and Charles, although a bachelor, has too much to do with being our local vicar to chase after women."

"You have seven sons?" Mina asked, feeling almost faint. Seven sons… Poor woman.

"George, Henry, and Charles were born in the duke's first marriage. His young wife died quite tragically while giving birth to Charles. Then we continued with having two sets of twins, first Edward and William, and then James and Richard."

"You named them after the kings of England?"

"Indeed we did," the duchess said, a pleasant, proud smile effectively wiping away the last of her role as haughty duchess. "Our dear King George found that most hilarious and immediately named us the true royal family, and the nickname sort of stuck."

"So it's the two sets of twins I should worry about?"

"I wouldn't say worry," the duchess cut in with a small grimace. "I would rather say to stay out of their way, especially Richard's. He's infamous for his libertine lifestyle, and I don't want to have to do what you're trying to avoid at home, force you into marriage."

Those sons definitely sounded interesting, Mina mused. Not that she had any intention of being forced into marriage with one of them, but she was sure there were stories hidden here, and stories were something she found very interesting.

"And then there are Henry's sons, Drake and Raleigh. They too are in their early twenties and a bit irresistible in their own ways. Not to forget George's boys, Sinclair and Sebastian. They are as old as their cousins, and so under this roof we have eight unmarried young men in their twenties who all have a tendency to enjoy women too much."

"Especially Rake," Agatha cut in, and was gifted with another irritated look.

"Yes, Richard is a bit…lecherous… But I will find a way to make sure he knows that you are off limits."

A rake named Rake? How appropriate. Mina could hardly wait to meet him. To be truthful, she could hardly wait to meet all of this illustrious family. The more the duchess and Agatha told her about them to warn her off, the more curious she became.

"You will stay here with me. There are two small bedrooms connected to this room, one which Agatha occupies, the other one which will be yours. Besides the three of us, only the duke knows the truth about you, and we will make sure it stays that way. But stay out of the way of the young men, and you will be fine."

Agatha took over, describing how life downstairs worked and what she should think about, but Mina found her thoughts wandering away from the lecture about how to act as a servant. Instead she thought about all the infamous men who lived under this splendid roof.

She knew she shouldn't be so happy about it, but all the same she couldn't hide the truth from herself.

This was going to be a quite interesting time ahead of her.

Chapter Four

"Get away from my horse!"

Mina looked up from the horse she had been caressing and met the silvery eyes of Lord James Darling, the sixth son of the duke and duchess and a member of the last set of twins.

"Oh, don't mind me. I'm merely introducing myself to the horses," she said before she had a chance to stop herself. As his eyes narrowed suspiciously, she knew she had, as always, spoken too fast and too freely.

"Who are you?"

"I'm her grace's new maid," she said as humbly as she could manage, not an easy task for her wild spirit, and then she curtseyed a little awkwardly, suddenly wishing she had listened to Agatha when being advised how to address the family.

Jamie's eyes narrowed even more until they were only light gray slits under dark eyebrows. "I didn't know Mother had employed a new maid."

"Oh?"

"Mother usually tells me everything."

Mina smiled politely while moving on to the next horse, trying hard not to answer him even though her whole being longed to chat with him. In her eyes, he was the most interesting of all the Darlings, he and his cousin Raleigh, as both of them were men of war.

She adored soldiers. They were so handsome in

their red uniforms, and the ones she had met back in Soberton had been the most exquisite dancers, blinding her with their arrogant smiles and horrid tales of what it was like to live on the frontier. Or, to be more truthful, at the headquarters in Brighton.

But where Raleigh was the wounded hero, the hurt soldier who vividly told everyone everything he had gone through, over and over and over again, Jamie was the strong, silent sort of man. No one knew what he had experienced when in France, as he hadn't shared his memories with anyone.

Agatha had told her how worried the duchess was about her son. Coldly, he denied everyone a chance to be any comfort for him, even his twin brother Rake, although they had been inseparable before the war. Before France. Jamie was, by his own choice, turning himself into an introvert, a hermit, unable to interact socially with others.

"He used to be such a dashing scoundrel," Agatha had said, a bit starry-eyed even at her age. "He had the ladies piling themselves up in front of him wherever he went. He has always been a looker, you know, with his silvery coloring, wearing his blond hair unusually long, cascading down his back like a waterfall in the sun. And those eyes… Polished silver. They used to mesmerize the ladies, as if he could cast a spell on them by simply looking at them. But nowadays the warmth in them is gone. I heard someone call them wolf-eyes, and I tend to agree. He sends shivers down my spine when he looks at me with those cold, dead eyes."

But Mina didn't agree with Agatha. As she met Jamie's probing gaze she felt her heart beat faster. Even though he was clad like a farmer who never had heard of fashion, he still was one extremely good-looking chap, and his hidden past made him all the more interesting to her. As always, it was the untold story that captured her attention.

"When did you start your employment?"

She jumped as his voice cut through the thick silence. "A week ago, my lord."

His cold eyes narrowed even more, something she had thought impossible without their closing entirely. He took a few steps closer to her, his hand stroking the horse's shiny coat absentmindedly as he passed.

"What's your name?"

"M-Mina."

"Who was your last employer?"

With one last affectionate pat, Mina moved to the next horse and then the next after that, pretending not to have heard his question. She could feel his eyes on her person as he followed her steps across the stable. He made her nervous, and she felt a desperate need to run as fast as she could from the stable. That was quite an achievement, she had to admit. Not many men—or women, for that matter—had managed to have that effect on her before.

"Why are you ignoring my question, Miss…?"

She glanced over her shoulder as she moved to the last horse in the row, feeling faint as she found he had soundlessly moved until he stood close behind her. "I beg your pardon?" she asked, nervously, tenderly stroking the horse's soft muzzle.

"What's your name?"

"Mina."

He was looking a bit frustrated with her. "Your surname, if you please."

Oh, dear me. She hadn't thought about that, no one had, not even the organized Agatha. Her mind raced as she tried to come up with something quickly, but unfortunately her normally well-functioning brain didn't work.

"Eh…"

One of his dark eyebrows arched up, and for some reason she suspected he was enjoying himself. Immensely. "Your name is Eh?"

"Almost," she breathed, finding her way back to her mind, remembering her mother's maiden name. "Ayle. My name is Mina Ayle."

"Like the brew?"

"With a 'y.' "

He stared at her triumphantly. "So you can read? Not many maids know how to, especially young ones like you."

Sending him her brightest smile, Mina moved backward toward the stable door which led to the courtyard. "I know how to spell my name, that's all."

"So, Miss Ayle, who was your last employer?"

She couldn't help herself; she simply had to send him a teasing smile as she moved through the doorway. Before he had a chance to stop her, she ran across the yard, greeting the scullery maids who sat at the well tossing bread to the squabbling geese as she passed them.

Not until she stood in her bedroom, with the door closed and locked, did she take a staggering breath, mixed with laughter. What an odd conversation to have with a man she didn't know. Was this how all male peers addressed lowly servants? She didn't know, and she most definitely didn't want to find out.

From now on, she had to make sure to stay out of the way of Lord James Darling. It was clear he suspected she wasn't what she looked like. It was a bit unnerving how easily he had caught her game. They had only met this once, and, to be completely honest, it hadn't been the most intelligent conversation.

"Mina, is that you?" a voice called out from next door, and with a happy smile Mina continued into the connecting room, where the duchess sat at her desk.

"Yes, Your Grace."

"I'm so glad to see you. I have hardly had a chance to talk to you at all this last week, with all these parties and outings we have been invited to. How do you like your room? Is the bed as inviting as it looks?"

"Yes, Your Grace. It is very comfortable. I've slept quite soundly in it."

"I'm glad to hear it. So what have you been up to this first week here at Chester Park? Getting to know your surroundings?"

"Indeed I have. I've been all over the park, and walking by the lovely lake, and in the rose terrace and the herbal gardens. I even hesitated at the opening to the maze, but as it seemed a bit formidable, I decided it would probably be better to wait until I had someone with me, to show me the way."

"Ah, the maze. It's quite impressive, I must tell you. People really do get lost in it all too easily. It doesn't look so large, but I must admit, the man who designed it must have had a very sly mind."

"Maybe I could inform you beforehand if I'm entering the maze, and then you would know where to send the search party if I'm still missing at dinnertime."

The duchess laughed heartily, and Mina had to

smile with her. Oh, how she liked this special lady. Knowing her father, she had assumed her new guardian wouldn't be the pompous sort, but the duchess was so much better than she had expected.

Mina had only known Anna Darling for one week, and yet she would without a second thought put her life in those two small hands. The duchess might seem a bit haughty at first, but after a while, when she started to relax, she was the most wonderful, dramatic person.

She loved her family very much and seemed to thrive when interfering with their lives. Especially when they became frustrated with her. The duchess certainly had a thing for vexing her loved ones.

"Well, I can smell you have been visiting the stables." The duchess wrinkled her lovely nose. "Do you want me to order a bath?"

Mina frowned unwillingly. "Do maids have baths ordered to their rooms?"

"This maid does."

"How do other maids take their baths?"

"Hm…" The duchess chewed thoughtfully on her lower lip. "Now, as you mention it, I don't know. I've never thought about how the servants clean themselves. They probably do it somewhere near the kitchen, perhaps in some shared room for baths. Maybe I should call for Agatha; she'll know what to do."

Quickly Mina grasped the cord to the bell, which would have the duchess's personal maid there soon, before suddenly remembering the odd conversation she'd had with the duchess's son.

"Oh, and my name is Mina Ayle, ale with a y."

"It is?"

"Your son asked me what my surname was and in

my scatterbrained confusion it was all I was able to come up with."

"Which son?"

"Jamie."

The duchess froze, her eyes turning unreadable as she stared silently at Mina.

"Your Grace…?"

"James asked what your surname is?" the duchess finally squeaked, and Mina nodded.

"Yes. He seemed quite interested in my person, asking who my former employer was and how long I had been here. He was most disgruntled you hadn't informed him about hiring a new servant."

"I never talk about the servants with James. What an odd remark for him to make."

"He seemed most suspicious of me, almost as if I were a spy or an intruder with an evil agenda."

"How interesting…" the duchess said a bit airily, almost as an afterthought. "I think I do have to speak to my husband about this…unexpected twist. Ah, Agatha, could you please take Mina to where the servants take their baths? She is, as I'm sure you can smell, in desperate need of one."

"As you wish, Your Grace. Anything else I can do for you?"

"No, no. I have to go and see my husband. I have something I must discuss with him. Something odd has happened."

Always the exceptional servant, Agatha curtsied before rushing Mina out through the door and down to the scullery, where Mina was handed a pitcher and a sponge and sent back up to her room.

No soaking in a bathtub for this maid, Mina

thought with a smile. When she went back home again she would make sure her maid had a chance to take a bath at least once a week. A sponge bath was a very poor substitute for a bath, and it certainly didn't make you feel as revived as an hour in the tub did.

Later, as she walked through the gallery to assemble with the other servants for dinner, she thought about how interesting it was to be able to see the other side of life in a country house. She had found herself enjoying dining with the servants in the servants' hall very much. Agatha had hinted it was the best part of the day, and Mina had indeed found it a delightful experience.

The servants had without any doubt accepted her as one of their own, everyone from the bearlike Russian butler Ivanoff down to the flirting stable boys. Sometimes she thought the housekeeper, Mrs. Dingley, suspected something, but as she never said anything and treated Mina as kindly as she did everyone else, Mina didn't care.

Music strayed from the family part of the house, filling the gallery where she walked, and she remembered the duchess mentioning they were having a small soiree for their acquaintances here in Berkshire.

"Oh, I wish you could join us, Mina," the duchess had said with a wicked grin. "It is always such a treat. We sit there, armed to our teeth in our finest evening wear, listening to each other perform. It's family against family, friend against friend."

"Sounds almost like a battlefield."

"It is!" The duchess had laughed. "We smile and praise, but behind our fans we snicker and spread our venom. Ah, they are such wonderful evenings."

Mina had always loved to dance, seeing it as a perfect way to spend an evening. Unfortunately, she hadn't had a chance to dance as much as she had wanted to since being officially introduced into the Soberton and later the Southampton societies. And that was all due to the Honorable Luther Whyte. As quickly as he had been able too, he had cornered her at every outing and soon, quite accidentally, his behavior had created a rumor about her not being as available as she seemed. Many eligible men had therefore chosen to scribble their names on other young ladies' dance cards, the ones who weren't already spoken for, leaving her to the deceitful vicar and the rest of the vultures who wanted nothing more than her dowry in their empty pockets.

It wouldn't have bothered her so much if it hadn't been for the Honorable Luther Whyte's gloating when he noticed the other men abandoning Mina, leaving her much more available.

The music ended rather sharply, and a vague applause was heard before a muffled voice spoke shortly, obviously introducing the next victim…or rather, performer. As the music started, Mina couldn't stand still. Slowly she rocked from side to side, following the music as she walked.

When the music grew bolder, she twirled around, her arms stretched out in front of her, as if she was dancing with an invisible partner. Closing her eyes, she could almost see him, the tall, lean body, the long blond hair, and his for-once-warm gaze caressing her. Faster and faster she twirled, until her strawberry-blonde ringlets flew out around her, and she laughed as the gallery turned into a colorful blur.

It was a small, unnoticed bump in the carpet which ended her spontaneous dancing. With a yelp, she flew across the floor, bracing herself for the hurtful impact she anticipated. But just as she saw the floor closing in, muscular arms grabbed her by the waist and saved her.

As she looked up she met the silvery eyes of Lord James Darling, the last person she had wanted to meet simply because she so desperately wanted to.

"Miss Ayle," he said slowly, his hands twitching slightly where they rested on her hips. He didn't let her go or even ease his hold of her. "Has no one told you twirling can be quite hazardous to practice alone?"

She shook her head numbly. "No."

His eyes glistened, reflecting the light from the chandelier over their heads. "You should never dance alone. Never. A young, inexperienced woman such as yourself needs someone cunning to lead her, someone who tells her what to do and what to say and how to act."

For some reason she didn't think he was speaking of dancing. Instead, he was talking about something else, but she hadn't a clue about what. What she did know was the simple fact that she would love to dance with him. The thought of waltzing through the gallery in his arms, together immersed in the new dance despite its being branded improper, made her heart skip a beat.

She had never been one to sit idly back and not do anything about her spontaneous feelings, and even though she was supposed to be at Chester Park in disguise, she couldn't help but feel she had to grab this opportunity.

He couldn't do more than deny her, could he?

Another applause from downstairs sounded, and as

the music started again, she took a deep breath. It was now or never. "Would you fancy a dance, my lord?"

He stared at her blandly. "What?"

She moved slightly from side to side, doing small dance movements to underline her question. "You. Me. Dance?"

He snorted loudly. "No."

With a teasing smile, she made a larger movement, forcing him to either let her waist go or follow her lead. To her satisfaction he chose to follow her, taking a step to the side, still pressing her to him.

"And yet you are," she teased and was awarded a small smile—which didn't really reach his eyes, but still, it was a smile.

"I am not dancing, I am simply trying to stay ahead of you."

"Ahead of me?"

"You are not what you seem to be, Miss Ayle, and I will not rest until I find out exactly what you are and why you came here to my home."

She couldn't help herself. She smiled slowly at him, as flirtatiously as she could. "So what do you think I am?"

"Definitely not a maid."

This time it was she who snorted loudly.

"You are too brazen," he continued while slowly dancing over the gallery floor, almost subconsciously. "You talk to me like I'm your equal, when you shouldn't be talking to me at all. But what is most telling is the fact that my mother has no need for another maid, yet suddenly she hires you."

"Hasn't it occurred to you that perhaps I am exactly what I say I am? A young woman, working as a maid?"

"Perhaps you are. But for some reason I don't believe you. It is more than clear that you weren't born into a working-class home. You are too sassy and too saucy, yet well-behaved, and sometimes…" He made a theatrical pause, acting like a true son of the duchess. "Sometimes you are even polite enough for me to think you are nothing but a noble woman."

It was a strange sensation to have her hand resting in his larger one while feeling his other hand in the small of her back, pressing her close to him. He made her feel weak and small, almost fragile. As she usually was a quite formidable young lady, who her father with a sigh compared to a mild hurricane, she felt almost awed by how easily this man could turn her into someone else. Someone who suddenly felt all warm and breathless.

"I thank you," she breathed, feeling dizzy as she stared up into his unreadable silvery eyes. "My mother will be most pleased to hear that her endless tries to educate me have you thinking I am better than I am."

"Where does your mother live?"

She opened her mouth to answer, but managed to stop herself in time before she blurted out Soberton. "Far away."

"Not Berkshire, then?"

"No, my lord."

"Oxfordshire?"

She laughed, amused at how stubbornly he sought information. "You think Oxfordshire is far away? One would think a soldier such as yourself would know that the world is a bit larger than your own courtyard."

The transformation was immediate. Abruptly he

stopped and let go of her, taking a step backward, away from her. Unprepared for his fast release of her person, she stumbled back in a most unladylike way, and she felt her cheeks grow warm in embarrassment as she took in his sudden return to being a hermit, wolf-eyes and all.

"So where is far away to you?" His voice was clipped and icy. "France, perhaps?"

"N-no," she stuttered, unsure how to react to this man made of ice. Seconds ago he had been, if not warm, at least on the edge to lukewarm. But now…

"You are lying to me," he accused.

She shook her head. "No, I'm not."

"You stutter."

"Yes. I tend to do that when I'm nervous."

"So I make you nervous?"

This was starting to become a bit awkward. She felt cornered by him, even though they were standing in the middle of the quite airy gallery.

"I have to go." She took a step toward the backstairs, but his hand shot out, effectively stopping her as he grabbed her arm.

"Stay."

It was an order, not a request. She closed her eyes in an effort to find the strength to force him to leave her, but a voice interrupted the situation before she had a chance to act.

"Chasing servant girls now, Jamie? I would have thought that was beneath you."

Jamie's twin brother Rake strolled toward them, an amused smile on his handsome face as he took in the picture of the two standing there like statues, facing each other.

"Rake, this is not the time..." Jamie began harshly, but his twin ignored him as he was too busy looking at Mina.

"Well, and what do we have here? An unknown dove?"

His words were beyond ridiculous, but somehow his flirting went straight to her heart, making it flutter in response. She remembered what Agatha had said about him being the most lecherous one of the boys and now, as she faced him, she knew the old maid hadn't lied. The man was simply adorable.

"Leave her alone. She's not for you."

Jamie's voice was cold and hard as stone, and Rake's smile changed, from amused to wicked.

"How would you know whom she's for? Is she yours?"

"No!" both Jamie and Mina said quickly, unanimously, and Rake took a step back, holding his hand up as a shield in front of him.

"Stand back. Please. I was only making a joke. You two need to relax a bit. Perhaps take a little nap?"

The last word came with the most lecherous smile she had ever received. It practically spilled over with hot promises, and if she hadn't known any better she would probably have been running as fast as she could the other way in a desperate attempt to stop herself from following him.

But what Jamie didn't know and Mina did, thanks to the kitchen gossip, was that Rake didn't mean anything by it, since the gorgeous, flirting man who stood at her side, trying to entice her with his wicked smile, had already given his heart to another young lady. It was highly enlightening to spend time with the servants. She had learnt a lot about the Darling family, much more than she thought any of them ever would like anyone else to know. But that was the thing with servants—they were all over the house and rarely noticed by their employer.

What the servants didn't know wasn't worth knowing. And when it came to Rake, she knew he had already lost his heart to the young house guest, Lady Penelope de Vere.

She felt Jamie tense beside her, and a devil took over her as she noticed his discomfort. Why not tease him a bit? She had nothing to lose, as he already seemed to think the worst of her. Biting back a giddy giggle, she took one step toward Rake, giving him her best smile, the one she knew no one could withstand.

"Is that an invitation?"

To her amused pleasure, Rake moved backward slightly, apparently not expecting her to be this agreeable.

"Why…eh…yes. My bedroom door is always open for any young lady, should she suffer from a need to relax a bit. I must admit, though, I can't promise you will get any sleep."

"Sounds absolutely perfect."

She winked at him, when she noticed Jamie was too busy glaring at his brother, and Rake's eyes started to twinkle. The awkwardness disappeared, and instead the wicked libertine returned in full force.

But this time she was ready for it.

Holding out his arm for her to take, Rake turned toward the eastern entrance of the gallery. "Shall we?"

"No, you shall not."

Jamie's cold voice cut through the air, and Rake

turned slowly, as if he had only just noticed his brother standing there.

"Why not?"

"What would Penny say?"

Rake frowned, as if pondering his brother's input. "Oh, I don't know. But I know Penny wants me to be happy, and as I am convinced this little one can make me one *very* happy man…"

The sigh which left Jamie was deep and dejected. Without a word he shook his head and left them there staring after him as he disappeared in the opposite direction.

"You worry about him," Mina said softly, noticing Rake's sudden sadness, and he turned his head to meet her eyes. At first she didn't think he would answer her, a lowly maid, but in the end he surprised her, as he sighed as deeply as his twin had.

"I do."

"It must be hard to stand idle and watch him suffer as he does."

"If I only knew what it is he has lived through, I know I could help him, but he is too stubborn about not telling us."

"Maybe he doesn't know how to say it?"

Rake's eyebrow arched up as he released her hand and faced her. "Why on earth wouldn't he know how? We are his family, the one thing in his life which always will remain the same and will always, *always* be here to care for him. He has lived through a war, been on site during battles. He has seen what the rest of us have only read about in the paper. He is more likely to want to withhold what he has experienced rather than not knowing how or what to tell us."

Growing up in a household containing a man who constantly scoffed at her and was amused when her thoughts and ideas didn't match his own had taught her to never stress any matter when it came to men. Let them dwell a bit on whatever it was, and then they would emerge calling her idea theirs.

"Of course he is," she agreed sweetly.

Rake's eyes started to laugh at her. "Are you patronizing me?"

"No, not at all," she said lightly, trying to look as innocent as possible, but his amused smile told her she'd failed.

"Of course you aren't."

"As if I ever would, a lowly maid such as I."

They shared a smile, two kindred spirits who had just found each other.

"So you are Mother's new maid?"

"Yes, my lord."

"Ah, back to politeness, I hear."

"Indeed so, my lord."

"I think I like you."

"Of course you do." She laughed. "Most people do. It is quite annoying sometimes, I tell you. Everyone needs to have at least one person who can't stand them."

Throwing his head back, Rake laughed straight out, and she couldn't stop herself from laughing with him. He had such contagious laughter, Lord Richard Darling. It could have melted an iceberg if it had encountered one.

"Can I escort you somewhere?"

"No need, my lord. I was heading down to the servants' hall. Dinner time, you know."

"Ah, yes. You are lucky indeed, that you get to sit down and eat. The rest of us have to endure at least another hour of that wailing until we finally can fill our howling stomachs."

She couldn't stop herself from snorting, he sounded a bit too self-assured.

With a wicked grin, he took hold of her hand and put it in the crook of his arm. "Come, my dear. Why don't I take you there? It will give me a reason to stay away a few more minutes, and perhaps I'll be lucky enough to snatch a piece of Cook's wonderful pie."

"You don't have to attend the soiree," she said as they walked down the stairs, heading toward the back of the house where the servants' quarters lay. "There is always a choice."

"Oh, no, my dear. In this case there isn't. My mother has these utterly bizarre ideas about the whole family attending social functions together. And you must have learnt by now that no one tells Mother no. No one. Not even Father dares to go against her will, and he is not known for being weak-willed."

"In my family, it's quite the opposite," Mina admitted as they walked through the corridor. "My mother seems to be in charge, her voice constantly heard ordering everyone about. But when it comes down to things, my father needs only to look at her to make her change her mind in his direction."

Rake frowned slightly. "Is your father a violent man?"

"Oh, Lord, no." Mina's amused laughter eased her company's worries immediately. "My father is the sweetest, most caring man and would never hurt anyone, especially not his loved ones. But he told me once how he early in their marriage had learnt to choose his fights. 'You can't win them all,' he said, 'so chose wisely, and you will be the victor in the ones most important to you.' "

Rake lifted one impressed eyebrow. "That sounds like a man I would want to have on my side in war."

"I wouldn't." Mina smiled. "He would be too engaged with writing lists about everything to even notice there was a war surrounding him."

Rake halted in front of the door which led to the servants' quarters, his hand on the doorknob as he grinned at her. "You are a delightful young woman, and I don't believe for a second that you are a maid."

Mina opened her mouth to again rush to her own defense, but he held up a finger, effectively quieting her.

"No, don't even bother to come up with some lie. I can tell you are of noble birth, and I'm sure no one would even think twice if you were to join us at the soiree downstairs. You have some reason for hiding as a maid, and knowing my mother, who obviously is a part of this, it must be a good one. I will tell you this, though: I won't pressure you for the truth if you promise me that you will come to me if you ever need help, or if the reason for you being here comes back to haunt you. Agreed?"

She looked up at him, this handsome man who had a reputation for being *the* libertine of his time, but all she could see was a thoughtful man looking down at her like a concerned older brother. So instead of trying to explain herself out of the situation she simply nodded and was immediately awarded a grin.

"Good girl. Now go and fetch me some pie, will

you, before you join the others. I'm starving here, and I can't listen to one more vocalist bent on destroying my ears without at least one delicious piece."

Cook was very obliging when Mina told her who needed something to nibble on. The basket she handed over to the very grateful peer was filled to its rim with delicious foods and snacks and topped with a casket of wine.

When she had finished her own meal, she bid the kind servants good night and slowly made her way toward her small chamber. It had been one odd day.

A day to remember.

Memories of Jamie's warm hands touching her waist, her back, and her hands made her blush with excitement. She had never felt anything like this for any man before.

Was this love?

Somehow she didn't think so. Jamie made her excited, both in mind and body, but to go from there to love felt too much. She hardly knew the man, had only met him a couple of times during this day and…and to be completely honest, those meetings hadn't been romantic at all.

The dancing had been nice, though. At least until he got spooked by something she said and started to interrogate her. Then he had been almost frightening, the look in his silvery eyes so cold she had shivered in response.

But then again…

What did she have to lose by trying to get to know him a little? He made her tingle. Why not explore that a bit more? Who knew, perhaps she had met her perfect match?

The man she was going to marry…

If the attraction she felt for him was a start to something deeper, something much grander, then why not use this unusual situation she was in and get to know the man? He had an obvious interest in her person, so getting him to talk to her wouldn't be too hard, now, would it?

So maybe they had different ways into this, but why couldn't the going out be on the same level? Perhaps she would find him a bore and highly unattractive when she got to know him more closely, but she highly doubted that. He was such a gorgeous man, tall and lean and deceivingly strong. His long, white-blond hair might be far from the fashionable windswept hairdos such as the one the Honorable Luther Whyte strutted around with, but to her it was beyond merely becoming.

To her it was captivating.

Everything about him was captivating. His dark eyebrows, such a complete contrast to his hair, were utterly enchanting to her. Even his silvery eyes, that became narrow slits when he stared at her suspiciously, made her heart flutter.

He was simply too gorgeous for her to resist.

If only *he* weren't so bent on resisting *her*. If only he had shown her an ounce of the interest the Honorable Luther Whyte had shown for her, or rather for her dowry, she would be beyond happy. Instead Jamie seemed against her, even accused her of being from France.

As she lay down on her bed, she couldn't help but frown. It was almost as if the man thought of her as some sort of vicious spy. But why on earth would she be a spy? And furthermore, why would even a spy be interested in a noble family residing in the English countryside?

In Berkshire, of all places.

Nothing could be further from interesting for a French spy. No, there was a mystery here, and if there was something Mina loved to solve, it was mysteries.

As she closed her eyes for the night, a content and quite smug smile crept over her face. Tomorrow she would start her new quest. Tomorrow she would begin to solve the mystery called Lord James Darling, and if everything went her way she would soon be able to get to know the real man. The real Jamie.

Now, how hard could that be?

Chapter Five

It started out quite nicely.

She made sure to bump into him in the stables the next morning, catching him as he came back from his morning ride. Ivanoff, the enormous, black-bearded butler, had proven to be a perfect source when it came to the Darling family's daily schedule, and she had learnt everything there was to know about Jamie, including when and where she could find him.

When he noticed her standing there in the stable, trying to look as if she weren't waiting for him, his eyes narrowed deliciously in suspicion, and she had to struggle to keep herself from bouncing around out of pure excitement.

"Miss Ayle," he greeted her coldly, and she made sure to curtsy as humbly as she could muster.

"My lord."

"If you are searching for my brother, you will probably have to go back to where you came from. If I know him correctly, he is still in bed."

She wanted to roll her eyes over his rudeness but managed to keep her eyeballs still as she recognized the jealousy oozing from him. So instead she shrugged lightly, hiding her excitement. "I wouldn't know, my lord, I haven't seen him since we parted in the gallery last night."

He didn't answer that, but as he dismounted she

thought he looked a bit less rigid.

"Did my mother send you for me?"

She almost groaned. Why hadn't she thought of that? It would have been a much better and much more valid excuse for seeking him out, rather than mumbling something airy about how she had happened to bump into him while visiting the horses. Had she been a bit better on planning ahead, thinking one step further, she could gladly have told him that his mother wanted to see him, because that would have meant walking with him through the castle.

But unfortunately she hadn't thought so far. To be completely truthful, she hadn't thought much about it at all, as she had been too excited to see him again after her nightly conclusions. So she simply made another curtsy and shook her head as solemnly as she could muster. "No, my lord."

He didn't say anything in response, only handed the horse's reins to the stable boy and watched the beautiful animal disappear deeper into the large stable, while she grabbed the sudden opportunity to gawk at him.

He was the picture of a country gentleman, beyond splendid even if he was clad in a scruffy brown riding outfit which had seen better days a decade or two ago. But the rich brown color of the worn cloth made his blond hair shine and his light gray eyes glisten. He was such a handsome man! The more she took in his appearance, the more certain she became about him being the one for her.

Lord James Darling had none of what she considered the less attractive qualities the Honorable Luther Whyte possessed and rejoiced in showing off.

Instead he was a wallflower by choice, always on the edge of whatever company wherein he found himself. His body was in one place, but his mind, his heart, and his soul were elsewhere. He had an air of loneliness, but instead of seeking the company of others he preferred to keep everyone at as many arms' lengths as he could.

Especially when it came to his family.

Looking at him, she couldn't help but think she had to save him. She had to bring him back to life. Back to his family. Something dark bothered him—it was obvious to anyone who took a good look at him, and she had to admit she was desperate to find out what it could be.

Jamie was a mystery, and for better or for worse, she couldn't walk away from the riddle he presented.

When he noticed her staring at him, he frowned, unimpressed. "Was there something else, Miss Ayle?"

"No. my lord."

"Are you *curtsying* to me?"

He seemed aghast, as if something with her bobbing her knees bothered him. Of course she had to do it again, to tease him, and received yet another frown.

"We both know you are anything but a maid, so please stop the knee bending."

"Yes, my lord."

"And stop calling me that."

"Yes, my lord."

"I said stop it."

She kept quiet for a second more before lowering her gaze so he couldn't see the twinkle in her eyes. "Of course, my lord."

He surprised her by being quite resourceful,

grabbing her chin with his strong fingers and forcing her to look him in the eye. “I said stop it.”

“Yes, my lord.”

“I mean it.”

“Of course, my lord.”

“Stop it before I do something we both will regret,” he said, lowering his head until their noses almost met.

Feeling his breath against her lips stirred something inside her, and she couldn’t hold back a shiver of delight. Mesmerized, she stared into his eyes, watching them as they turned warmer, burning into her.

“Whatever you say, my lord.”

His gaze turned darker, hotter, and before she could think one straight thought he lowered his head until their lips almost touched. “What would you say if I do the unthinkable and kiss you?”

“Thank you?”

He stared at her for a second, as if in shock over her honest and direct approach. His normal coldness disappeared as he reluctantly smiled down at her. Slowly, he lifted his other hand and put it around her neck, stroking the sensitive skin of her neck with his thumb.

“Remember that you asked for it,” he whispered.

“I did.” Her voice was only a whisper away from audible, but he still caught the meaning of what she’d said to him, and before either of them had a chance to stop this insanity, he lowered his head until his lips pressed against hers determinedly.

The groan which slipped out from him as their lips met made her knees weak, and a moan ripped itself out from her chest in response to his pleasure and the divine feeling of his full lips against hers. He planted small, delicious kisses on both her lips before returning to her upper lip and the corner of her mouth, as if he couldn't decide which part of her mouth he liked best. Tenderly, he nibbled on her lower lip, sending waves of pleasure through her. Just as she thought this couldn't get any better, his tongue forced its way into her mouth, and she died a thousand divine deaths.

It was pure heaven.

Grabbing his shoulders hard so she could make sure she remained standing as he deepened the kiss, she shuddered as her surroundings disappeared into a mist and all she could think about was him and the way he made her feel.

She didn't know for how long they stood there in the stable, kissing, but to her it felt like a mere second before it was over. As Jamie lifted his head, ending the wonderful kiss, he looked down at her with a strange mix of astonishment and suspicion on his handsome face.

"Who are you?" His whisper was hoarse, strained, and for a moment she wanted to cry out the truth to him, tell him all about who she was and why she was there.

But something stopped her, and that something was none other than Jamie's mother and her own special guardian angel. When Mina had arrived at Chester Park, she had promised the duchess not to tell anyone in the Darling family the truth, and now she had to lie to Jamie. Over and over again.

Of course, she might possibly ask the duchess about permission to tell Jamie, to end this drama. But that would mean she had to tell the duchess *why* she wanted to tell Jamie, and that was a situation she didn't want to experience. The duchess, no matter how kind and generous, was still Jamie's mother, and quite an interfering one, too. Mina knew how the duchess's heart ached when it came to Jamie, and how frustrated she was about his elusiveness.

If the duchess learnt about the kiss and Jamie's obvious struggle when it came to the odd Miss Ayle, then Mina, who knew that she was special to the duchess because of her father, soon would find herself married into the Darling family.

If she were honest with herself, she wouldn't have much against that ending. But marrying a Jamie who wanted to marry her sounded so much better than being forced into marrying a Jamie who thought all sorts of dark things about her.

And that wouldn't do. She had already decided that he was highly interesting as a potential future husband, but she knew she would and could never marry for anything but love. Lord James Darling might find her most kissable, but he didn't love her. At least not yet.

So instead of trying to soothe him, she shrugged lightly and kept her voice calm and indifferent. "I am merely Mina Ayle, my lord. Her Grace's new maid."

"No, you are not."

She sighed as deeply as she could, giving him her most frustrated look. He didn't budge, though. Instead he put his hands against her cheeks, rubbing his thumbs gently against her jaw.

"Why are you here?"

She hesitated for a moment before giving him a smile. "To kiss you, my lord."

The man obviously didn't have a sense of humor. He frowned down at her, not a bit impressed by her joke. "I'm serious."

"So am I."

"Are you telling me the true reason you came to Chester Park was solely so you could kiss me?"

She most definitely didn't like the patronizing look he gave her, and she couldn't stop an edge in her voice. "Of course, my lord."

"You are angry."

She took a step back, feeling oddly cold and alone as he let go of her. "No, I am not, my lord."

He threw his head back and laughed. Hard. Annoyingly hard. She felt herself becoming more and more upset with him.

Upset over him laughing at her.

Upset over him quizzing her.

But most upset because he had stopped kissing her.

"You, my dear Miss Ayle, are the worst liar I ever have encountered, and I have met my share."

"I never lie," Mina snapped. "I am the most honest person there is!"

"Oh, is that so?"

He had her there. Of course he didn't believe her, and she certainly couldn't blame him. She was, after all, living a lie this very moment, pretending to be someone she wasn't.

"I don't usually lie, only when I'm forced to." Her honest reply didn't impress him, though.

"No one *has* to lie."

"I do."

"Why?"

"It's complicated…"

"I have time."

Of course he did. He was as stubborn as the geese

occupying the courtyard, persistently trying to chase everyone away from the well, and he would probably continue to probe until he got all the answers he sought. But the thing was, she would tell him all in due time. Only not now. For the moment, she needed to stay hidden so her mother and the Honorable Luther Whyte didn't find her and destroy her chances to have a future of her own heart.

"I have to go back," she mumbled, humbly, curtsying again. "Her Grace needs me."

"No she doesn't."

No, not a goose. Not even a goat. Goats were nice animals. Greedy, yes, but still nice. No, Lord James Darling was as stubborn as a bloody mule. "Yes, she does. She most specifically told me to arrange her hair in the latest coiffure which is *the* highest fashion in London."

"Aha!"

He looked so pleased with himself, she almost didn't ask him the origin of this sudden smugness, wanting to vex him. But then again, she was too curious not to. "Excuse me?"

"You are not a bad liar. I give you that. You are simply the worst actress I have ever met."

She stared at him, openmouthed, unable to force out even one word, at first, as the impact of his words hit her with every humiliating syllable. The worst actress he'd ever met? How dared he!

"I am *not* a bad actress."

He leaned toward her, until their noses almost touched again. "Yes, you are."

She gasped, outraged. "*I am not*. I was the constant leading lady in our dramatics group in my hometown.

The crowd cried when I was on stage. Cried!"

"Out of boredom?"

"Aaargggghhh," she screamed at him, too angry to find the right words to shut his mouth and erase that smug, patronizing smile from his handsome face.

Lord James Darling was the most horrid man ever to set foot on the good Lord's earth, Mina thought as she stomped through the stable, ignoring his laughter, which followed her as she left. Really, the man was a brute, a bore—and most of all, he was as stubborn as a mule.

What had possessed her to even consider him as a future husband? She must have had a weak day, an hour when her mind had been broken and unreliable. That man was definitely *not* husband material. Not even the most unwanted of wallflowers would settle for him as a husband.

How could she ever have wanted to find out more about him, to see if he happened to be her perfect match? The man was impossible and improper and had, with his outrageous behavior, managed to erase all her curiosity regarding him as possible husband and instead made her draw one very, very fat cross over his name on her mental list.

Why, she would rather marry the Honorable Luther Whyte than him, and if *that* didn't tell how completely she had discarded Jamie from her mental list, she didn't know what could.

The rest of the day she spent wandering through the great house, muttering about men in general and about self-satisfied hermits who should go back to avoiding her instead of displaying their low intelligence simply by opening their mouths. In the end, it was

Ivanoff who interrupted her stewing.

"We miss your sunny smile, Miss Mina. Why don't you let what it is that bothers you rest for a while and instead do something more useful with your time?"

Mina's cheeks grew warm. "Oh, I'm so sorry. I didn't know I was bothering you. And please, stop calling me Miss Mina. I'm simply Mina, you know."

"You don't bother me at all, child," Ivanoff said, as always ignoring her last request, a faint smile touching his proud Russian face beneath the bushy black beard. "But Kitty, the little scullery maid, confessed becoming a bit upset when you told her she was as deranged as an old lopsided carriage wheel. And not to forget, you scared Cook half to death with your muttering echoing down the hallway to the kitchen, transforming your mumbling voice into a choir chanting what she swore sounded like an evil curse. She was so upset she refused to go back into the kitchen, claiming the room was haunted by ghouls of death trying to take her with them."

The picture the butler painted for her was quite vivid and hilarious. Unable to stop a giggle, she pressed her palm against her mouth. "Oh, dear me, I am so sorry," she whimpered when she managed to calm herself down enough that she could talk without laughing like a madwoman. "I didn't mean to offend Kitty and scare poor Cook. I was a wee bit upset with…someone. I simply had to express my dismay before it gnawed its way out from inside me."

"I know you didn't mean to, Miss Mina, and so does Kitty. She admitted as much to me earlier. Not only had you and she never engaged enough for you to have such deep feelings about her, but also, she was on her knees, cleaning the stove in the duchess's salon, and she confessed you could have missed her being present." Ivanoff's pepper-black eyes glistened at her under his thick black eyebrows. "Cook, on the other hand, is a completely different matter. It took us an hour to persuade her from her chamber, and not until we had her listen to your ranting as you were moving through the ballroom did she believe the truth. But a small advice, Miss Mina—stay out of the kitchen for a couple of days. Cook is not too fond of you for the moment, and I honestly think she would rather welcome the ghouls than you."

"I will." Mina smiled, and was rewarded by another beardy smile.

"May I ask what had you so upset, Miss Mina?"

"Please, Ivanoff, I'm Mina, no 'Miss' at all," she stressed, avoiding his question about her earlier show of bad temper.

"Yes, Miss Mina."

"I am serious about this, Ivanoff."

"I am too, Miss Mina."

She sighed deeply, dejected. "Am I correct to assume you will not cease calling me 'Miss,' no matter how much I ask this of you?"

"I might…" The Russian gloated, sensing his victory. He crossed his tree trunks of arms over his broad chest, looking more like an ancient Asian war hero than the butler of one of England's most prominent families.

"You might?" Mina chirped, her irritation growing again.

"I might."

"If…?"

Ivanoff leaned forward, his bushy beard almost touching her chin. “If you tell me the truth, I might stop.”

She gave him her most innocent look. “The truth about what?”

He frowned down at her without answering, looking at her as if she were a small child instead of the grownup woman of eighteen that she really was. But then again, she hadn’t been acting her age today. To be completely truthful, she had behaved more like a spoiled child, splattering her anger everywhere.

She finally gave in. “I was angry with someone.”

“We noticed.”

“But it is fine now, really. Nothing to worry about. I’m all over it now.”

“May I ask with whom you were angry?”

“No.”

Ivanoff didn’t miss one breath. “Was it one of the other servants?”

She shook her head, casting a longing eye toward the door behind the butler, wondering if she could make it the whole way to it before he caught her.

“So it was one of our peers?”

“Eh…No. It was …someone else. No one important.”

“A stranger?”

“What? No!” She sighed, frustrated. “It’s nothing, I promise you. Someone, one very unimportant person, said something to me, a comment which upset me a bit for a while.”

Ivanoff bowed slightly, his posture a bit more relaxed, as if her answer had eased his worries. “Her Grace will be relieved to hear this.”

The duchess had sent Ivanoff after her? Mina stared openmouthed as the butler gave her another bow before leaving her alone in the room. She sat down on one of the plush chairs, her hands unknowingly twisting the sturdy fabric of her servant's dress.

Suddenly Ivanoff's uncommon stubbornness made sense, if it was his mistress who had sent him after Mina to press her for answers. In fact, she realized with a grateful exhalation, she had managed to escape quite unblemished. If it had been the duchess interrogating her, Mina would never have been let off this easily. But Ivanoff was a man and not as prone to details as Anna Darling. No, he was satisfied knowing Mina had calmed down and had stopped the tantrum.

All in all, this could only mean one thing. She had to stay as far away from the duchess as possible and for as long as she possibly could manage.

"Ah, Mina, there you are."

She hadn't even been given a chance to hide, Mina thought as she stood to greet the duchess, who came floating into the room, holding something which looked like a big pile of pink fluff.

"You have to help me with my gown for the masquerade ball. I bought it quite some time ago and haven't had a chance to wear it until now."

"A masquerade ball?" Mina couldn't hide her excitement, and the duchess patted her cheek happily, her satisfaction with the upcoming event evident.

"Indeed. Oh, I must confess, I do look forward to it. Beside the August Festival and the soirées with our friends and neighbors, we never have any grand parties here, which is quite sad when you consider that the man who built this large mausoleum loved assemblies and made sure the house could fit hundreds of guests."

"So what made the duke change his mind?"

"Penny is getting engaged, and he agreed with me when I told him that I think we need an extravagant setting for the announcement, especially considering how much pain the poor girl has suffered during these last months."

Mina didn't know the whole story about the pretty young house guest, Lady Penelope de Vere, only that something awful had happened to her and now she couldn't go back to live with her own family. The duchess loved her young friend very much, and Mina knew nothing would mean more to her than Penelope marrying her youngest son, Rake.

"Oh, I'm so happy for them," Mina squealed and saved the brightly colored dress from the duchess's arms. "I know how much you love Lady Penelope, and you must be so relieved that your son finally came through. Oh, this must mean so much for you, your Grace. It's like having a dream come true!"

"If only," the duchess sighed, sinking onto one of the elegant sofas in the salon, her ever-restless hands still moving, patting a pillow, straightening the wrinkles out of the skirt of her dress. "Penny is not marrying Richard, but Thomas Bedford. I tried to make her change her mind, but the girl is too stubborn for her own good."

"But why throw a ball for them if you don't want them to marry?"

The duchess smiled slyly. "Well, my dear Mina, planning a ball takes time, and we have already set the date for one month from now, which means I have one month to prod Richard into taking matters into his own hands. The boy loves Penny; he only needs to admit it to himself. And if he doesn't, I will be there pushing him. A little."

Poor Lord Richard Darling. It didn't matter that he was *the* libertine of his time and a most elegant and attractive man of the world; he still lived life under the interfering but loving thumb of his mother.

"The wedding will be held at Christmas," the duchess continued. "But I know Penny and her loyal heart. She will never break off an engagement after it has been announced, so I only have one month until it's too late for Richard to come to his senses. Which, given whom we are talking about, is a bit too little time. The boy is too stubborn, like his brothers. I don't know how I could give life to such men, ones so hard to push in the right direction."

"A masquerade ball," Mina said dreamingly, ignoring the duchess's frustration with her offspring. She swayed the pink dress slightly in front of her. "How utterly delightful it must be to attend one. To be able to dress up as someone else, hiding your true identity behind a mask while flirting outrageously with all the men… Why, it must be the most amazing event."

The duchess nodded, in full agreement, unable to stop herself from touching the pink fabric. "And that is why you are going there, dressed in a costume which will have no one recognizing you."

Joy filled Mina's heart when she heard the duchess's kind offer, but her brain kept interfering, dragging her down toward earth again. "I can't go to a masquerade, Your Grace. What would your family say if they found out? And what would the other guests think if they knew a lowly maid was amongst them?"

"First, Mina, you are not a lowly maid. You are not only the daughter of one of my oldest friends but one of the wealthiest heiresses in the country. I assure you, our guests wouldn't dismiss you. Instead they would welcome you with open arms. They would probably shove their sons and any other male relatives they could find your way, praying you and your dowry would end up in their family. And besides, when there are masquerades held in London, you should know there are scandalous men who prefer to leave their wives at home and bring other, more…colorful ladies with them."

"They do?" Mina breathed, her eyes almost popping out of her head.

"Indeed they do. And that is why a masquerade is a perfect assembly for you to have some fun and get a chance to meet others than my obnoxious family and the servants of this house. No one will know, Mina. No one will recognize you. I promise I will make sure you will not be found out."

What the duchess said made sense, Mina had to admit, but still…it felt wrong. Perhaps because she knew Jamie would be there. And maybe, because she would be hiding anonymously in a costume, she might do something wrong, like seek him out. Perhaps even dance with him. Or worse…she might flirt with him.

That wouldn't do.

"You are so kind, your Grace, but I simply couldn't. I must admit going to a masquerade ball is something I've looked forward to for as long as I can remember. Indeed, I've hardly been able to wait for adulthood so I can attend one. But it's too much. What if someone recognizes me? What if I bump into someone I know?"

"You *are* going to the ball, and we will make sure you will go in a costume no one will recognize you in. I need you there to help me keep an eye on Penny and Rake. I can't push them together by myself. I need you to be there too, Mina. You have to be there for me, aiding me in this."

Well…if she put it like that. "For your sake I will attend the ball."

The duchess laughed straight out. "For my sake? Oh, my dear child. You are such an amusing young woman."

Satisfied with the outcome of their chat, Mina held up the duchess's dress in front of her again. "So, what will my dress be like? Something this grand?"

"Oh, no, my dear. You will not attend in something as spectacular as this dress. No, you are going as a shepherdess, as it is the most common costume, and therefore you will blend in perfectly. No one will recognize you, I assure you."

As Mina followed the duchess out of the salon and up to her bedroom, carrying the fancy dress, she couldn't help being excited. A masquerade ball! Imagine that. And that before she even had a chance to debut in the *ton* next spring.

"Oh, by the way…" The duchess hesitated as they climbed the magnificent stairwell from the foyer. "I need you to do something for me tomorrow which might not be socially correct. Richard is taking Penny to Sandhurst, to order a masquerade ball dress for her, and I need you to go along as their chaperone."

"B-but I can't be a chaperone."

"No, Philomena Aubrey can't. But Mina the maid

can. You will be fine, I assure you. But I need to get the two of them away from this house and away from everyone else's interference. Richard and Penny need to talk to each other, and this is too good a situation for me not to use. And I can't send anyone else. No other maid would have the decency to stay as far away as possible and furthermore not gossip about what is said or done."

Mina nodded curtly, unable to tell her benefactress no. After all, how bad could it be? Traveling with an unmarried man in a closed carriage wasn't heard of, but Lady Penelope would be there. Neither of her traveling companions would be interested in her person, and instead she would have plenty of time to shop around and explore the small rural town of which she had heard so much from the other servants.

"Thank you," the duchess sighed, relieved. "This means so much to me. With any luck, those two will find their way to each other and will finally live happily ever after, as they deserve. And besides, you will be able to look for what you want in your dress while in Mrs. Frazer's shop."

With that last inducement, the duchess left the subject and concentrated on her own dress, mumbling about adding pearls and lighter fabric. But Mina didn't listen to her mistress's ramblings. Instead, she left the duchess in her bedroom and went over to her own modest chamber, where she lay down on the bed with her arms crossed beneath her head.

Tomorrow would be a wonderful day. Not only would she see the town of Sandhurst, but she would also, most secretly, order her very first masquerade ball gown. She could hardly wait for tomorrow to begin.

Chapter Six

"You have to make sure they have enough space to interact without feeling followed by you," the duchess lectured as they briskly walked through the castle, in the early morning hour, toward the courtyard entrance. "But they can never, ever end up in a situation which leaves no option but marriage. Penny has been quite clear about not wanting Richard to be forced into marriage, which is a bit unfortunate, but still, there are other options."

Oh, she was such an interfering mother, Mina thought with an impressed smile as she half ran to keep up with the duchess. To the outside world, Anna Darling seemed to be a most serene and mature matriarch, always well behaved and elegant, her petite body always dressed in demure yet highly fashionable gowns.

But the truth was quite the opposite.

She was constantly voicing her opinions, especially regarding matters of the heart. And if words weren't enough, she used drama to have them all see her point of view. Or rather to make them give up and let her have her way, because it was not possible to win when she smelled victory.

She loved her husband and sons immensely, always interfering with their lives and completely lacking a bad conscience about it. They were her family, and therefore, in her mind, they were hers to rule.

As with the approaching trip to Sandhurst.

If Rake and Lady Penelope had known how much the duchess had conspired about the outing, they would run and hide, never to be seen again.

Comparing Anna Darling to Ophelia Aubrey was like comparing night to day. Her own mother did love Mina with all of her heart and wanted nothing but the best for her. The thing was that Ophelia always forgot to ask what Mina's wish was. To her, it was more important to be the most shining mother and the leading lady in their county. What others thought mattered the most, and therefore her choices were mostly spun from what the other ladies would think, especially Hester Primrose, her best friend and worst enemy.

Anna Darling was sneakier. Everyone thought the world of her, but she was the devil in disguise. She too loved her family, but where Ophelia rushed forward, ignoring Mina's wishes, the duchess interfered as much as she liked to, or found need for. But she would never go against anyone's true wishes.

Lady Penelope was a perfect example there. The beautiful young woman was daughter to one of their neighbors and a close friend to the duchess's only granddaughter, Francesca. She had loved Rake with all her heart since she was a small girl with pigtails, but he had never thought about her as a woman until very recently. Unfortunately, his awakening happened just as the young lady gave up on him and instead accepted another man's wish to court her. If Mina wasn't completely wrong, Rake would be more than happy if Lady Penelope agreed to marry him. But somehow they had never got around all their obstacles and accepted the love between the two of them. Instead they sparred with words and sultry looks.

Lady Penelope was now engaged to the other man, and this trip was all about picking a dress for her engagement masquerade ball, yet still Mina and the duchess found her on the top of the stairs, staring starry-eyed at Rake, who was putting small lingering kisses on the top of her fingers in full view for anyone who liked to watch.

But Mina hardly noticed the indecent behavior of the couple because of the man who stood beside them, his irritated gaze showing his opinion. She felt faint as she saw him there in the warm morning sun. Tall and handsome, he was for once wearing suitable clothes under his dark greatcoat. His long blond hair was neatly combed and held together at the base of his neck by a thin leather strap.

When he noticed his mother, he removed his hat and bowed courteously, his blond hair glistening in the sun. He was too handsome for Mina's fickle heart to handle. Everything else surrounding them faded out as she took in his person, every last stunning part of him.

"I thought you had left already," the duchess said curtly, discreetly urging Mina closer with a small movement of her hand as they watched the embarrassed couple jump apart. "And that you had forgotten the promise you made me yesterday."

As Mina took a step forward, closer to the duchess, the threesome in front of them looked at her. Jamie's wolf-eyes narrowed into slits as he frowned at her, obviously not too happy to see her, whereas Lady Penelope tried to hide a smile, for some reason highly amused by Mina's presence.

"Great." Rake grinned wickedly. "She will fit perfectly in the other carriage."

"What other carriage?" The duchess frowned at her son and was rewarded with an innocent look in return.

"Oh, did I forget to mention I was taking my new phaeton for a drive? Testing it, you know. And as you are well aware, a phaeton holds only two people. So I had the town coach ordered forward for the maid to travel in."

The duchess snorted, unimpressed. "The town coach? For one person? A bit much, don't you think?"

Mina could have laughed out loud. Oh, they were so smug, both mother and son. Apparently both had laid careful plans for this trip, and it was so amusing to see how both seemed more than happy with the outcome. Of course the duchess didn't mind Rake and Lady Penelope traveling alone. To her it was the best solution, as it would mean they would have time to talk and maybe…maybe they would be able to work through their problems and end up as they should—together.

And Rake… Considering the foreplay they had walked in upon only moments ago, he most definitely wanted time alone with the lady of his heart.

"I'm going, too," Jamie interjected sternly. "I have some errands to do in town, and this arrangement suits me fine. The maid can share my carriage, and I will make sure the phaeton stays close and in sight the whole way."

Oh, lord, no.

Again the world became a blur, and the only thing staying sharp was Jamie, who stood silent, staring at his mother with that ridiculous lock which only a son to Anna Darling could muster, as she sputtered objections about Rake and Penny traveling by themselves. And, with more urgency, some quite vague reasons as to why Mina couldn't travel alone with him in the town coach.

"Are you out of your mind?" Jamie finally cut in as his mother kept on. "Why on earth would there be highwaymen hiding on the way to Sandhurst? There is absolutely not one place on the road where they can hide so you can't see them as you approach. And besides, she is a *maid*. Why would they want to kidnap her?"

In the end, the duchess had to give up her most admirable effort to convince her eye-rolling sons that they all should go in the town coach as she ran out of even mildly sensible reasons. It all came down to either breaking her promise and confessing about why Mina couldn't go alone with Jamie or praying that nothing would happen and sending the two carriages on their way.

And as the duchess was a woman of her word, she sighed ruefully and gave Mina a nudge toward the town coach. "You better behave," she whispered quite outrageously in Mina's ear, as she herself was completely innocent in creating this unheard-of situation.

With a heart that beat tremendously fast, Mina begged the duchess to try another round of saving her. This was worse than the worst. Trapped in a closed carriage with Jamie? This was absolutely not good.

How far was it to Sandhurst? Hopefully not more than half an hour, she thought, desperate. The mere thought of being caught alone inside a carriage with

Jamie for more than a minute or two seemed like hell on earth to her. Or, to be completely honest, it seemed too much like heaven for her to become deeply afraid. How would she ever be able to save herself from herself? Too soon Jamie urged her to climb into the carriage and followed her closely. She sat as far away from him as she possibly could before turning her back to him, silently staring out through the small window in the carriage door. The phaeton raced away, not too surprisingly, leaving them to slowly roll down the road, following the cloud of dust.

To her surprise, Jamie didn't say a word.

Silence as thick as London fog filled the carriage until Mina couldn't stand it anymore. She had never been one to turn her back to anything, and now was not the time to start.

He sat on the opposite bench, staring out through the other window with unseeing eyes, slowly fingering his hat, which rested in his lap, a distinct aura of sadness surrounding him. This was not the man she had met so far. This was not the angry and suspicious man who had interrogated her harshly and kissed her until she would have died happy in his arms.

No, this man was sad and lonely.

Immediately her heart went out to him, and she wanted nothing but to grab his hands and hold them warmly until he lost his sadness. But she was supposed to be a maid, and maids most definitely didn't hold hands with lords. Not even Miss Philomena Aubrey could do that without breaking every social rule there was.

As if he felt her gaze, Jamie turned his head and looked straight at her. The sadness disappeared, and instead the cold determination returned in full force. But this time she didn't feel as overwhelmed, because she had seen his vulnerable moment, and it had made him more human, more reachable.

More adorable.

She smiled compassionately toward him and immediately he scowled fiercely back at her, obviously finding her more and more suspicious by the second.

"What?" he snapped, clearly irritated.

"Oh, nothing," she said lightly, smiling invitingly, which had him scowling even more darkly at her.

"What is your game now? I thought you were angry with me for calling you a bad actress."

She forced herself to ignore his overbearing half-smile and instead shook her head, trying to look like a humble servant. "No, my lord."

He leaned back, his arms crossed over his chest. "You are up to something."

"No, my lord."

"Oh, yes, you are. I can see that, clear as day. I thought I told you that you are a bad actress."

It took all her mental strength, but she managed to stay calm. "No, my lord."

He snorted, not fooled for a minute. "Now you're angry again."

"No, my lord, I'm not angry with you."

"So what are you then? Asking me for forgiveness for being a liar *and* a humbug?"

"No, my lord. I'm only trying to be polite. You should try it sometime. It can be quite uplifting."

"Being polite would mean telling the truth, like what your real name is, where you're from, and most importantly, what it is you want with me."

She couldn't hold back a surprised laugh. "You? You think I'm at Chester Park because of you? Oh, dear me, you are such a foolish, self-centered narcissist. Why on earth would I be here for you? I didn't know about your existence before I arrived here and your mother warned me about you." And almost as an afterthought, as condescending as she could muster, she continued: "My lord."

"My mother warned you about me?" He seemed befuddled, like all the Darling men did when the duchess was involved.

"Not you in particular. She merely told me her sons were a bit on the promiscuous side and asked me to stay away from the lot of you."

"Yet you kissed me."

Her cheeks grew as hot as the look he gave her, and suddenly the whole conversation had made another unexpected turn.

"I didn't kiss you. You kissed me." She tried to move farther away from him, though she was already to the edge by the window.

He didn't seem to mind, though. Instead he followed her and moved over to her bench, sitting down so close to her that she found herself caught between him and the carriage wall.

"You most definitely asked me to kiss you."

He had a point there, and she nodded breathlessly as his mouth came closer to hers.

"Well, then," he said slowly as he put his hands on her arms, slowly caressing them before sliding them behind her back. "Maybe this time it is *I* who should ask *you* to kiss *me*?"

Looking up into his handsome face, she knew she

could never deny him something she wanted to do probably more than he did. Instead of pushing him away as she should do, she lifted her arms and put them around his neck, gently dragging his head closer to hers.

"Please do," she whispered softly.

His smile was incredible, warm and tender, and she felt an odd urge to cry out of sheer happiness.

And then he kissed her.

All her thoughts disappeared as his arms pressed her body closer to him until there were no way to tell where he ended and she began. His tongue played with hers with highly arousing movements, and she moaned out of surprised pleasure. Her hands found their way down his neck and in under his cravat, and she felt his shoulders shiver under her light, innocent touch.

He grabbed her hips and moved backward, dragging her with him in one swift motion and laying her down on the bench. His mouth traveled down her jaw to her ear, and she groaned when he nibbled on her earlobe. She could hardly believe the sensations he created inside of her, and she had to groan as his tongue made a wet path down her modest neckline and found the top of her breasts. He shifted his weight slightly, so his hands became free, and he started to unbutton the bodice of her dress.

Dimly, she looked up into his face, noticing the frenzy in his hot eyes and his staggering breath, and she lifted her head up, pressing her lips against his. This time it was he who groaned as if in pain, and she felt his hands leave the buttons. Instead, one of them traveled down her leg and pulled the hem of her skirt upward. Cold air caressed her bare skin, and she started to shiver, both with delight and fear.

This was not right.

She most definitely shouldn't be in this position with Jamie. She shouldn't be in this position with any man. Awkwardly, she tried to push him away from her, but he didn't notice, instead deepening the kiss, taking her to heights of pleasure she hadn't known existed.

Again she got lost in the storm of emotions he woke in her, and not until she felt his hands against her legs did she wake up again, but this time she didn't hesitate. Pushing him as hard as she could, she caught him by surprise, and he tumbled backward, landing with a thud on the floor of the carriage.

She sat up, her hands immediately dragging the unbuttoned cloth of her bodice together as she stared down at his confused face. For a moment she wished she could forget who she was, but she couldn't. She could never dishonor her family by casting away every caution and her own future for a moment of passion with Jamie, no matter how much she wanted to.

"I'm sorry," she whispered softly as he stood up in the rocking carriage, harshly pulling his pants up again, pants she hadn't even noticed he had loosened. "I'm so sorry, but I can't…"

Her voice trailed away as he sat down on the opposite bench again, looking at her with more contempt than she had ever met in all her life.

"You whore," he spat. "You know exactly how to play a man, don't you? I can't believe I let you fool me into believing you are something more, something special, when my first impression obviously was the correct one."

She blinked. Then she blinked again.

Whore? Really?

She tried to hold back the laughter, but as soon as she managed to button her bodice again, she lost the fight. That man, surly and self-righteously staring at her, was beyond hilarious.

He was…daft.

She laughed until she cried and had to find her handkerchief in one of the pockets of her coat. Jamie didn't say a word, but she could tell he wasn't as amused as she was. His full lips became tighter and tighter until they were just one irritated stretch.

"Oh, dear me," she snuffled when she finally found her voice again. "I haven't laughed this much for quite some time. Thank you."

"You think this is funny?" His voice shook with anger. "You think *I* am this laughable? You should take a good look at yourself, Miss Ayle, before making fun of others. Your dress is unbuttoned and wrinkly, and that red hair of yours is all tousled. Mother would fire you this instant if she could see you."

Immediately her hands flew up to her hair, and she sighed ruefully when she felt the curly ringlets unfastened from the once almost tidy bun. It had taken her nearly ten minutes to make herself presentable enough this morning, and now it was all ruined.

"My hair is not red," she said as she tried to redo the bun. "It's blonde."

"No, it's definitely not blonde," he snorted before cursing behind his teeth. "Oh, stop that. Let me do it. You're only making it worse."

He moved over to her side again and turned her with her back to him. With one swift motion of his hands, he collected all the unruly ringlets, and she could see in the wavery window of the carriage door how he made a perfect bun, much tidier than the one she had made this morning.

"It *is* blonde, you know," she persisted when he'd finished and had moved back to his side of the carriage. "It merely looks different in certain lights."

He had no objection to rolling his eyes, she noticed. Like his mother, he did it exceedingly well.

"You are such a strange young woman," he sighed, looking a little less aggravated than before but still distant and clearly suspicious. "You don't take anything seriously, do you? You laugh and you dance. It's impossible to talk to you because you never stay on the subject. You look like you are as innocent as Mary, but you behave like Mary Magdalene."

"Maybe it's you who take things too seriously, my lord," Mina replied icily, feeling a bit offended at his honest words, mostly because there was more truth in them than she liked to admit.

But she couldn't help who she was. Her mother was always telling her to calm down, to stop fidgeting, and to behave more properly. More like Rosalind Primrose, the reigning beauty of Soberton, the girl Ophelia Aubrey found perfect and envied of her mother. It wasn't that Ophelia didn't love Mina, she simply wanted her to be more easy to love.

Her father had asked her to try to calm down for her mother's sake and try to behave, if not as perfectly as Rosalind, at least less than Philomena. And Mina had, till her teeth ached from calming down.

No one was perfect, not even Rosalind, but sometimes Mina wished she would meet someone who didn't expect something else from her or want her to change for him. She had thought Jamie was different, that when he stopped being so suspicious of her he would accept her for being the person she was. But hearing him dissect her like this told her more than anything that he never would.

He was unfortunately like the Honorable Luther Whyte, too caught up in himself to be able to understand that she was different. And that maybe…maybe different was good. Maybe different was…perfect.

"If you had seen what I have seen in France and Spain, you would never again say that I am too serious," he snapped, his anger returning in full. "Good men killed for a cause which is not their own. They have families waiting for them, lives to live. But instead they lie in the ground in a small village they could never pronounce the name of, in a faraway country, their bodies torn beyond recognition. I don't even know how many dying men I have held in my arms while the generals and the commanders sit and plan the next big hit, the next deathtrap into which they will send us. They don't care about the innocent lives that are destroyed as they strive for power. Innocent girls are sent to prison because powerful men won't listen to the truth. No one survives those prisons, Mina, especially not sweet, inexperienced young girls."

She could see tears in his eyes as he turned his back to her, staring out through the window, ignoring her. Her heart pounded as she looked at his broad, dismissive back, trying to make sense of what he had shouted to her.

There had been a girl.

A sweet, innocent girl, who had been sent to prison

and died there, unprotected. A young woman Jamie obviously had loved with all his heart, and still did.

She must have fallen in love with him already, unbeknownst, because the pain in Mina's heart as she finally understood the truth was overwhelming. No wonder Jamie hurt as much as he did. No wonder he couldn't see through her façade and like her anyway; she had lost him before she'd even had a chance to woo him.

The duchess had told her he had come back home a wreck, both in body and mind, and now Mina knew why. In the midst of the awful war, Jamie had found something pure and in the most horrid act lost it all.

"What was her name?" she whispered softly, and just as she thought he wouldn't answer her, she heard his hoarse voice.

"Aurélie."

He pronounced it so softly, so gently, and tears filled her eyes. Of course the young woman had to have a beautiful name, all perfect women seemed to.

Aurélie.

Rosalind.

No perfect women were ever named Philomena.

When the carriage stopped, Mina couldn't get out of it fast enough. She needed space from Jamie so she could think through what he had told her. Sitting next to him made her feel weepy and, strangely enough, a bit abandoned.

He had never promised her anything. No matter what he said, in his eyes she was still a maid, and lords like him never married maids. Bedded them, yes, but married? Never.

But still…

There was some connection between them, some string of unwanted emotions (unwanted on his side) which tied them together and made it impossible for him to ignore her completely.

She knew he wanted her. She wasn't too innocent to realize what would have happened in the carriage if she hadn't come to her senses. And if it had happened, she would have had to tell the duchess about it, there was no way around it, which would have meant that Jamie would have been forced to marry her against his will.

She most definitely wouldn't have put up a fight. Not in a million years. In light of the new love she felt for him, marriage to Jamie would only mean her very own fairytale ending. But it wouldn't have been his. If he'd had the choice, he would have been married to a perfect young French woman, not to Mina.

And that was not the sort of fairytale ending Mina wanted. Marriage to Jamie would have been the perfect end, but she would rather marry a man who had feelings for her and wanted to be married to her, not someone who always would remember the girl he had lost.

And she couldn't fight a ghost.

"There you are," Rake called out, as he and Penny came strolling down the street from where they had hitched his shiny phaeton. "I was hoping we had managed to lose you completely."

Jamie didn't answer up to the joke; instead he scowled darkly at his brother. "Why don't we meet at the inn in a couple of hours? I have errands to do and don't have time to stand here chitchatting about nothing with you."

Without looking at Mina, Jamie turned his back, and soon he had disappeared into the crowd.

"There is something bothering him, something which consumes him from inside out. But he won't tell me," Rake said sadly to Lady Penelope as he too watched the spot where Jamie had last been seen.

"Maybe he doesn't know how to."

Rake clearly didn't agree, sending the lovely lady on his arm a dark look. "I'm his twin. He can tell me anything."

"But maybe he has seen or done something which he feels is so horrendous that he doesn't know how to tell anyone, even you," Lady Penelope persisted. "You know what your cousin Raleigh told us when he came back from the frontier—it was worse than hell on earth."

"But I'm his twin," Rake repeated stubbornly, clearly not able to stop worrying long enough to listen to reason.

Mina had to agree with the lady, especially after the conversation she'd had with Jamie in the carriage. As she followed the chatting couple through the town toward the seamstress shop, in her head she went over what he had told her. Jamie was suffering from more wounds than one, but it seemed that the one to the heart was the wound which had left the deepest scar. Jamie was a proud man, and telling anyone about his heartache wasn't easy. He had spat it out to her in the heat of the moment, but then again, she wasn't someone he cared about. He didn't know that the lowly maid he found strange, suspicious, and kissable was in love with him. And if Mina got it her way, he never would.

Suddenly January felt too far away. She

desperately wanted her father to come now, even though it was just the end of September and she had only been at Chester Park a couple of weeks. A part of her wished she'd never left Soberton. She should have stayed put and faced her fears instead of fleeing.

What had sounded like a perfect plan then had turned out to be the dumbest thing she'd ever done, and she had done her fair share.

It took quite some time at the seamstress's shop, as Rake and Lady Penelope couldn't stop their mating game. He flirted and she was jealous, then she flirted and he was jealous. Mina wanted to shake her head patronizingly over their waste of time. She could understand the duchess's frustration. Why wouldn't those two stop their fidgeting and get it over and done with? How hard could it be to say "I love you" to someone? She wouldn't have had any problem telling Jamie those words, at least not before he had told her about Aurélie.

Now the situation had changed, slightly.

In the commotion surrounding Rake and Lady Penelope, Mina managed to hand Mrs. Frazer the note from the duchess without anyone noticing. The dressmaker read it and then discreetly took Mina's measurements before promising to have the dress ready and delivered in good time before the ball.

Ah, the ball.

Mina wanted to dance around out of pure joy. She could hardly believe she was going to her very first ball, and not just any ball. A masquerade! She could hardly contain her happiness, and she noticed both Rake and Lady Penelope looked at her with odd smiles, but she didn't care.

She was going to a ball!

When they arrived at the inn, Jamie was already standing outside, awaiting them, his face dark and gloomy. As they reached him, Mina stepped on a rock and lost her balance. If Rake hadn't reached out and caught her close to him she would have, in a most unladylike manner, fallen down into the street, where a horse quite recently had left a gift.

"Thank you," she whispered to him, grabbing his arm to find her balance again, and he grinned back, amused.

"Well, what kind of gentleman would I be if I let a damsel in distress fall into the gutter?"

"There you are," Jamie snapped. "Finally."

She could feel Rake's arm tense under her hands, but he had no chance to react as Jamie ushered them quite rudely through the door, almost knocking Mina to the ground. Again.

Rake, faster than seemed possible, grabbed her arm and saved her. Again.

"Bloody hell, Jamie, what's your problem?" Rake said, irritated, as they sat down at an empty table in the crowded inn.

"Nothing," his twin replied, equally as irritated. "I merely want my tea. You!"

Mina jumped as Jamie waved at her, staring at her condescendingly. "You can go and make sure there will be some tea and sandwiches brought here as soon as possible."

He was unbelievable. For some reason he was beyond furious with her. For some reason he thought it all right to openly stare menacingly at her in front of his brother and Lady Penelope. But she didn't mind the easy escape. Instead she was grateful for the moment of respite.

Leaving the problem of Jamie for Rake to solve, she scurried away between the tables, taking in the colorful picture surrounding her. Dashing gentlemen and beautiful ladies were scattered throughout the room, creating small colorful islands amongst the much more soberly dressed merchants and farmers. She liked this, the natural mix of different classes. In Soberton, it was different. Either you were one of the peers or you weren't.

The innkeeper flirted wildly with her while taking her order, promptly declaring her the next Mrs. Innkeeper. Something the present Mrs. Innkeeper laughed at.

"You can have the old dog, dear," she said, giving her husband a pat on the behind. "He's not much to have around the honeypot nowadays anyway."

The other guests surrounding them howled with laughter, and Mina blushed, not really sure what the woman meant but very much sure that it wasn't the least decent.

As she returned to the table where Rake and the others sat, dragging her feet as much as she could without standing still, she found to her relief the atmosphere had become much lighter. Jamie was almost smiling, if one could call that stretching of the lips a smile, but she wasn't picky. She sat down in the empty chair behind Lady Penelope, as far away from Jamie as she could, and this time there was a definite sparkle in his eyes as he watched her.

The rest of their stay in Sandhurst was uneventful. Starry-eyed, she stared at the stylish men and women, impressed by their gracious ways. Lady Penelope, bless her warm heart, kept slipping her sandwiches when no one noticed, and they tasted wonderful. Her company at the table kept a light conversation throughout the rest of their stay, all three making an effort to keep their time there smooth and friendly.

As they walked out of the inn, Mina reluctantly waved back to the infatuated innkeeper, and the sun warmed them as they approached their carriages. Jamie opened the carriage door and looked back at his brother.

"Penelope can go with us in my carriage," he said gently, but Rake only shook his head with a wicked gleam in his eyes.

"She's with me."

They hardly had time to blink before the couple had climbed up into the phaeton and it was racing down the street, leaving their chaperones as quickly as possible. Jamie shook his head, smiling softly before turning around. He opened the carriage door and with a courteous bow with his head he beckoned Mina to enter.

"My maid."

Laughing softly, she curtsied. "My lord."

"Take your time," Jamie called out to the driver before following Mina into the carriage.

"We are supposed to stay as close as possible to them," Mina said as the carriage started to roll down the street.

"I know."

"Your mother will be most upset."

"No, she won't."

He had her there.

"If anything, she will thank us profoundly if this

works out and Penny and Rake end up getting married." He made a small, funny grimace which made her giggle in response.

They sat silent for a while as their carriage followed the runaways. She looked out through the window, enjoying the beautiful countryside changing its coloring to vivid autumn dress. She felt Jamie's eyes on her person, probing, but she didn't mind. She knew there was a lot on his mind, especially considering how he had lashed out at her only a few hours ago.

Jamie must have thought the same. "I'm sorry for my behavior earlier. I-I let my emotions cloud my judgment, and I was not the gentleman I'm brought up to be."

"Think nothing of it, my lord," Mina said softly, and his eyes narrowed slightly.

"I called you a whore."

"Yes, you did, my lord."

"You're not supposed to think nothing about being called a whore."

She turned and met his serious gaze. He was trying hard to soften his stare, to look kind, and she felt an overwhelming urge to laugh again. But considering how badly her last burst of laughter had ended, she held her stance.

"I mind being called a whore, my lord, but since you seemed a bit confused at the time, I'm letting it pass. No one will ever know, and we will forget it ever happened."

Seeming suddenly insecure, he looked down at his hands, resting on his lap. "You won't tell anyone about what happened?"

"No."

"What about what I said…about Aurélie?"

He looked so sad, and this time she didn't hesitate. She fell down on her knees in front of him and grabbed his hands in hers. "I will not tell anyone about her, but I ask you to please confide in someone. You need to talk about this. Your family cares too much about you, and when you hurt, they hurt."

"I told *you*."

"It doesn't count, my lord. I'm only a humble servant—and stop that eye rolling. I *am* a humble servant and not someone for a man of your standing to confide in. You need to tell someone else, someone like your twin brother."

He snorted softly. "One could almost think Rake put you up to this."

"He might have, unknowingly. I've seen how much he hurts from being cast aside, from being left outside your confidence, when you've always before been so close. He desperately needs to be there for you, but you don't let him."

"I know."

He released his hands from her grip, instead grabbing her waist to haul her up beside him. With his arm around her shoulders, he pulled her closer, and she laid her head on his shoulder with a contented sigh.

"You sound like you enjoy this." He grinned and put his cheek against the top of her head.

"I must admit I do, my lord. You are made to cuddle with."

"You are one strange maid, Miss Ayle."

"You told me as much, earlier."

"I'm sorry about that too. I went too far."

She sat up and gave him her best glare. "Yes, you

did, my lord. Calling my hair red! I must confess I'm having a hard time forgiving you for that, but I want you to know I am struggling with it."

His laughter filled the carriage as it started to decrease its speed until it pulled to a stop beside the phaeton standing still on the quiet countryside road.

"Rake, you bastard," Jamie shouted through the carriage door. "Don't you ever try such a prank again. Mother trusted me to keep your hands off Penny, and the first thing you do is get a little…"

Mina leaned forward to see what it was that had silenced Jamie, and what met her curious eyes was an angry Rake and a teary-eyed Penny, sitting silently side by side.

For once Jamie seemed to use his common sense. "Why don't we take the lead home," he suggested softly.

Rake nodded curtly, and Jamie called out to the driver. As he sat down again, leaving the phaeton to follow them, the frown was back. Mina wanted to sigh loudly, but she didn't dare. This was not her cuddly Jamie. This was the Jamie who called her a whore and insisted that her hair was red.

He didn't say a word the rest of the trip, and when they halted at Chester Park he immediately jumped out of the carriage. Mina watched him walk up to the phaeton as Rake left it, giving all his compassion to the abandoned Lady Penelope. Watching them from afar, they looked more like husband and wife than neighbors and friends, and suddenly she felt like an outsider, someone always looking in, never participating.

Quietly she left the carriage and went into the castle, feeling more bewildered than ever. Torn between a need to stay hidden and an overwhelming urge to tell Jamie the truth, she didn't know what to do. She simply didn't know where to go from here.

And even if she did tell him who she was—Miss Philomena Aubrey, one of the wealthiest heiresses in the country—and thus receive full access to socializing with him, she couldn't help but think she would lose him. He was a distrustful sort of man and was already suspecting she was lying through her teeth. Slapping him in the face with her lie wouldn't exactly help her cause. And besides, if she became his equal, she didn't think she would meet the cuddly version of Jamie much. He sort of saved that for Mina the maid. Which in its way was a bit disheartening. But all the same, she couldn't give up the maid yet. She might be on the verge of giving Jamie up, but she couldn't stand having him do the same to her.

No, she had to see this through. She had to make sure to stay out of his way as much as possible and treat him with the respect she should. And maybe, just maybe, she could fool him into dancing with her at the ball. For now, that was all she asked for. It was all she *could* ask for.

Determined, with a cause of her own, she raced up the stairs to the duchess's bedroom, to give her report about what had happened with Rake and Lady Penelope. And she would make sure she didn't even hint at anything which had happened between her and Jamie.

Now, how hard could that be?

Chapter Seven

"You look lovely, dear."

The duchess's voice sounded from somewhere behind her, but Mina had no intention of finding the source as she stared at her reflection in the mirror, in full agreement. She looked utterly divine.

"Are you sighing because you agree, or because you think you look a disaster?" The duchess laughed, and Mina had to sigh again.

"The dress is beautiful. Thank you so much."

"My pleasure. But please, be aware you will not be the only shepherdess there. Your sort tends to overwhelm these functions."

"Oh, I don't mind. Not at all. The more shepherdesses, the more easily I will melt in amongst the crowd. And besides, not one of them will have a dress as beautiful as mine."

"She is a bit full of herself, isn't she?" Agatha said as she put more powder on Mina's hair. "There, now no one will recognize you by the hair, at least."

With one lingering look at her reflection, Mina turned to face the lady's maid. "Whatever do you mean? Are no other blonde women attending the assembly? Lady Penelope is as blonde as I am, and she is coming, isn't she? It's her engagement ball, after all."

"Child, you have to stop this foolishness about the color of your hair," Agatha began, but the duchess silenced her with one very pointed look.

"It's the curls, dear, but rest assured, no one will be able to recognize you now."

Something about what the duchess said didn't add up, but Mina shrugged it off. This was her time. This was her ball. Or, to be honest it was Lady Penelope's ball, but all the same… This was Mina's time to actually have fun and dance without the Honorable Luther Whyte standing in a corner, staring at her possessively.

She simply had to twirl a little across the duchess's bedroom, enjoying the sensation of her skirt's airy movement against her legs.

"Oh, this dress is absolutely gorgeous," she exhaled before dancing over to where the duchess stood laughing. She hugged the grand lady fiercely. "Thank you so much, Your Grace."

"Oh, no," Agatha shrieked from behind her. "Mind the dress, won't you, you crazy child!"

But Mina didn't care, and neither did the duchess. Instead she hugged her back, placing a soft kiss on her cheek.

"You are most welcome, my dear. I must admit I regret placing you as a maid. It would have been so much fun being able to shower you with gorgeous dresses and having parties you could attend. You would have been the center of every one of them, I assure you."

"Yes, she would." Agatha huffed and ended the embrace by dragging Mina backward. "By not acting as she should and destroying the dress I've spent the whole day straightening out."

"And what a good job you did, Agatha." The

duchess beamed and went to Mina's new favorite spot in front of the large mirror. "I look absolutely divine too."

"Indeed you do, Your Grace, indeed you do." Agatha nodded a bit too much, and Mina bit back a smile.

The duchess did look a bit too divine. Her dress was layer upon layer of pink fabric, with small glistening stones sewn all over it. She claimed to be a sunset, but Mina could have sworn she was one of those strange, rather large pink birds, with long, scrawny legs, she had seen illustrated in a book in her father's office. But as she cared for the older woman, she followed Agatha's lead and nodded as if she did agree in full.

It was a very satisfied duchess who told Mina to wait a while before joining the party. "No one will notice you in a full ballroom, but if you are the first guest to arrive, the whole family will take a look at you, and someone might recognize you."

Someone like Jamie.

As the duchess and Agatha left the bedroom, Mina walked up to the mirror again, but this time she didn't feel as excited. A month had passed since the trip to Sandhurst. One month with absolutely no contact with Jamie other than a greeting or two.

At first she had kept her promise to herself, to avoid him as much as possible. It had turned out to be a much easier task than she'd thought it would be. She never ran into him, and not even when she had made sure to avoid him in places where he usually spent time. Then it dawned on her: Jamie must be avoiding her too.

After a week of not seeing him even from afar, she felt compelled to seek him out. Resourcefully she talked to Ivanoff and had, with his help, succeeded in bumping into Jamie at the stables as he arrived from a ride. But although she had feigned surprise before flashing him her most radiant smile, he had only bowed his head slightly before turning his back to her.

She had sulked for two days before she decided to try again, and this time she made sure to trap him alone in the salon. But he didn't falter. Instead he walked right past her, as if she didn't exist.

Stubbornly she had refused to give up on him. So she had done the unthinkable and waited for him outside his bedroom a whole evening, because she knew he had to come there sooner or later. Unfortunately, staying there all night made her miss the fact that he and most of the Darling family had left earlier for London, as his niece Francesca needed aid in getting her elusive husband back.

Three weeks he had been gone. Three long, lonely weeks during which she had been more miserable than she'd thought possible. All she wanted was Jamie back here where he belonged, by her side.

Or at least under the same roof.

When the family had finally returned yesterday, she had been ecstatic and rushed down to see if she could find Jamie alone so she could throw herself into his probably not-so-waiting arms. But he had been busy with his parents.

A lowly maid was clearly not on his must-see list.

It was not the first time she'd found herself wishing she had chosen to stay as herself and thus had a chance to interact with him in a more acceptable way. He might not have opened up as much to Philomena Aubrey, but the spark would still have been there. At least she hoped so.

"You can go down now, child," Agatha interrupted her sad thoughts as she returned, and Mina took a deep breath, strengthening herself so she would be able to stay away from Jamie and not seek him out the first thing. It would have ruined the duchess's plan of her joining the party without being noticed.

"Thank you, Agatha."

"He's already there, you know, bored to his teeth."

Mina looked back at the surly maid, trying to look as innocent as possible. "Who is there?"

Agatha snorted disdainfully. "Master Jamie, of course. Don't you think you can hide anything from me, child. I know exactly what you two have been up to."

"You do?"

"Dancing in the gallery. Kissing in the stables. Not to mention an entanglement in the carriage that would have had you walking down the aisle with the man, if anyone had caught you."

"H-how d-did you kn-now?" Mina stuttered, more embarrassed than she'd ever been before in her life.

Agatha snorted, disdainful. "I thought spending time as a servant would have taught you that there is always someone who sees you, even if you don't see them. We are all over the place, and you can thank your lucky stars that the servants of this family are loyal to their employer. Otherwise there would be no end to the gossip."

The maid walked up to her and started to straighten her appearance harshly. "Now, I love Miss Anna and would never do anything that could make her unhappy, and therefore I have not mentioned this to her."

The maid's words stung harder than Mina would have thought possible. "You think me marrying Jamie would make her unhappy?"

"Goodness, no." Agatha snorted again. "Miss Anna would be more than happy to welcome you into the family. No, I think your unhappiness with him would make her suffer, and that wouldn't do. Now off you go and have fun with the other shepherdesses."

Before Mina knew how it happened, Agatha had pushed her out of the room and closed the door firmly behind her, leaving Mina standing alone in the corridor. Beautiful music mixed with laughing voices was heard from downstairs, and slowly she followed the sounds until she stood at one of the large doors to the ballroom, staring openmouthed at the scene in front of her.

It was like a dream come true.

She had been awed by her own dress, her bonnet, the flimsy mask, and her shepherdess staff. But her outfit was nothing compared to the ones before her, and she forced her mouth closed as she slowly walked along the wall, taking in the view.

Soldiers from all over the world mingled with every famous historical person she could think of. There were flowers, animals, and to her relief, quite a lot of shepherdesses. Behind a most spectacular sunset, a whole crowd of men in black evening clothes, their faces covered by black masks, stood looking uncomfortable.

She had no problem picking out Jamie, as his long blond hair gave him away. It fell down his back in one white cascade, and he looked more like a Viking trying to pass as a gentleman than a lord amongst his peers. Quickly she sat down in one of the chairs pushed up against the walls. From there she could watch Jamie without being noticed.

She had missed him, she realized, more than she liked to admit, especially since he so easily had dismissed her from his life.

She had dreamed about this night for over a month, ever since they had been to Sandhurst. But now she couldn't make herself go over to him and force him to dance with her. So much had happened, so much time had passed, and she was too afraid he would reject her. Again.

Ruefully she sighed, deeply, and caught the attention of the shepherdess sitting next to her, who followed her gaze to the hosts.

"They are absolutely divine, aren't they?" The other shepherdess sighed as ruefully.

"Excuse me?" Mina blushed, grateful for the mask covering most of her face after being caught staring at the men.

"The Darling men. I noticed you admiring them. I do too, you know. Admire them. They are such handsome men, and I would not say no if any of them asked me to dance."

"Which one is your favorite?" Mina asked, curious against her will. But this was a masquerade, and she was hidden in an outfit, so why not go ahead and talk to another worshipping shepherdess?

"Oh, Rake, of course. He's such a flirt, that one. I don't know how many times he has made my heart flutter with that wicked grin of his. But…I can't see him amongst his kin, so I guess he's not here yet. Or, heaven forbid, he's out there dancing with someone else. Well, well."

The shepherdess sighed again, and Mina couldn't help but feel for her. Fancying Rake was a dead end, not only because of Lady Penelope but because the man was known as a most comfortable bachelor.

"How about you? Which one is your favorite?"

Mina harrumphed. "Eh, Jamie."

"Ah, the twin. Yes, he is almost as divine as his brother. I don't like his hair, though. Too long for a modern man, I'd say. I think it makes him look more like a heathen than a fashionable gentleman of his class."

Mina gasped, outraged.

The other shepherdess didn't know it, but she was quite close to being boxed on the nose by a very upset Mina. Fortunately for her sake, a very bright red rose called her over, and she left Mina without finding out.

Calling her Jamie a heathen! The nerve…

Mina sent another glare in the direction of the other shepherdess before she turned her gaze back to the Darlings and looked straight into Jamie's furious eyes.

She didn't know how, but somehow he had recognized her amongst all the other guests and shepherdesses, and when he noticed her noticing him, he immediately started toward her. With a yelp she stood up, quickly moving in the opposite direction.

She had fantasized about dancing with him, but in that fantasy he had never known who she was. He was supposed to think she was a stranger, and therefore she would be able to enjoy the closeness to him so much more, especially as the duchess most brazenly had introduced that new dance, the waltz, to the ball.

She didn't make it across the dance floor before he grabbed her hand and hauled her closer, pressing her body against his. It took her a moment before she realized they were dancing, which made her feel more panic. She tried to rip her hand loose from his, but he held on tightly, not once easing his fast grip.

In the end, she gave up and let him dance her through the crowd until they reached the other side, and the doors leading out to the terrace. As soon as they were outside, he pulled her into the shadows and pushed her against the wall as he took off her mask.

"I knew it," he hissed angrily, and she shivered in response. "I thought there was something familiar about you as soon as I spotted you, but when you looked ready to kill that other shepherdess, I was certain. No one glares like you do."

"Jamie, please."

He ignored her plea, ripping his own mask off before tossing it aside onto the terrace floor. "I wanted so much to believe in you. For the first time in my life I found myself wishing I was wrong when I accused you of being a spy. But this…" He waved his hand over her body. "You, sneaking into a ball like this, are proof enough I wasn't wrong, that I only let you fool me into believing you were something else. Oh, lord, I must have been such an easy target."

She really didn't know whether to roll her eyes wildly or slap his handsome face. The man was beyond ridiculous. He was more simpleminded than the angry geese in the courtyard.

So she was a spy again? She must have missed the part when she did something too French or something only a spy did, because she simply couldn't understand where he got that crazy idea.

Or perhaps she did.

His sweet, perfect Aurélie had been sent to prison. Young, innocent women weren't sent to prison without cause, and considering Jamie's obsession with spies, spying must have been what she had been accused of.

"I'm not Aurélie," she said softly, catching his immediate attention.

"I know you aren't," he snapped. "No one would mistake you for her. You are much more brazen and forward. Aurélie was sweet and pure. She w-was…"

"Perfect," Mina sighed, and he nodded.

"Yes, indeed. She was perfect."

"I'm not perfect."

He laughed patronizingly. "Oh, I know you aren't. I've told you as much a few times since we first met."

"You have remarked about both my inability to lie and my…bad…acting," she admitted, much against her own will, but getting through to him was more important than her pride.

"I have."

"So maybe it's not me you should accuse of spying. Perhaps it's your perfect Aurélie who was the one guilty of betraying her country?"

She braced herself for his response, but to her surprise he didn't lash out at her for trying to diminish his feelings for Aurélie. Instead he looked as if in pain.

"I did," he finally said, so softly she almost missed it. "I accused her of betrayal and forced her to stand up in court. They didn't believe one word she said and sent her to her death. It's my fault she died in vain. My fault she had to stand in front of those men, begging them for her life."

"Oh, Jamie," Mina breathed. "Don't hate yourself for something beyond your control. It's not your fault she died. Had she been innocent, she should have been able to prove it."

She must have hit an open wound. Jamie staggered backward, staring at her. "How could you say that? How can you suggest she was anything but innocent? I never believed the rumors. Not for a minute. That's why I brought her to court, because I was so sure they would free her. But they didn't. They got all worked up over something she couldn't explain, and that was it. I lost everything that was dear to me. I sent to death the woman I was going to marry, and with her my child in her womb."

Oh, dear Lord. Mina's eyes filled with tears as she watched his agony, heard his broken confession. No wonder he was only a shadow of the man everyone told her he had been.

He had killed his own child.

"Oh, Jamie," she cried and threw her arms around him, forcing him closer to her. At first he struggled to get loose, but not for long. Soon his arms embraced her as he cried into her hair, wetting her powdered hair with his tears.

She didn't know for how long they stood there in the shadows, or who might have watched them, but when he finally calmed down they were still alone on the terrace.

Slowly he backed away from her, releasing himself from her embrace. His face was wet from all the tears, and powder from her hair was all over it as well, making him seem more fatigued than normal.

"I'm sorry," he whispered hoarsely. "I didn't mean to tell you this. Please forgive my honesty."

"I don't mind," Mina said compassionately, and he

gave her something which she guessed was supposed to be a smile but looked more like a painful grimace.

"Of course you don't. The information I just gave you in my moment of pain is just the kind people like you look for."

"Oh, lord, save me from simpletons." Mina sighed as she started to walk away from him, leaving him to face his misery by himself instead of accusing her as he had Aurélie.

"Where are you going?" Jamie asked, giving her that look in which his eyes narrowed suspiciously.

"To my room," she clipped out, feeling more than annoyed with him. "If that is all right with you? Or would you prefer to walk with me, to make sure I go where I'm supposed to?"

"You think I'm making some sort of joke with you, but I'm not." He loosened his cravat and used it to dry his face and clean it of her powder. "I am going to find the evidence I need to tell the world who you really are, Mina Ayle-with-a-y. I will follow you closely, because I know that one day you won't be able to keep your act together, and then I will be there."

She knew she should be annoyed with him for thinking all these low thoughts about her, but the mere thought of him following her around, always looking at her, made her sort of…happy. Maybe he did feel something more for her, and in some odd, backward way he was trying to save his heart from more pain by doing the same thing all over again.

Or maybe he merely wanted to save his black soul by making amends for his sins. One real spy for a fake one. Or a very-much-not spy for one accused and lost.

"So, shall we?" she couldn't stop herself from

teasing, and he immediately glared at her.

"Shall we what?"

"Go to my bedroom?"

"You are impossible!"

She watched him barge through the dancers, not once stopping to excuse his rude pushing. Well, this stay was becoming even more interesting. From having to spend one month without him, it now seemed she would spend the next one plastered to him.

With a contented sigh, she left the terrace and walked through the crowd much more discreetly than Jamie had, her head filled with plans for the next couple of days.

She was going to become a spy.

Chapter Eight

Mina yawned as big as she could before stretching the sleep out of her body. The sunshine filled her small chamber with its soft autumn light, and as she remembered what had happened at the ball yesterday, she smiled happily.

She was going to spend the day with Jamie.

What a marvelous treat to be gifted, after spending a whole month feeling miserable without him. Determinedly she ignored the little voice inside her reminding her that the only reason he was going to follow her around was because he believed her to be French spy.

After washing up, she put on her sober servant dress and tangled with her hair for a while, trying to force the obnoxious ringlets into something which was supposed to be a bun but looked anything but.

She missed her own maid. Lizzie's deft fingers created magic when it came to her mistress's unruly hair.

Whistling a happy little tune, she skipped out into the hallway, almost stumbling over Jamie, who sat beside her door, a book in his hand. He closed it carefully before reaching for his pocket watch.

"Nine o'clock? Really, Mina. Don't you think a maid should have been up and about for at least four hours by now?"

He stood up, a bit stiffly, and it dawned on her that he had been sitting there for as many hours, in the firm belief that servants were early risers. Well, this servant wasn't, which he had learnt the hard-floored way.

"Did you happen to notice if your mother has left her room already?" Mina asked cheerfully as she started briskly down the corridor, her empty stomach growling in anticipation of a morning meal.

"Mother left for breakfast half an hour ago," he replied, walking beside her, imitating her speed.

"She must have been surprised to find you outside her door." Mina had to tease him, and to her satisfaction his ears turned a darker shade of red.

"She was."

It took its toll, but she managed not to laugh out loud. "It must have been awkward, my lord."

He gave her a menacing glare, looking more than ever like a Viking, with his blond hair falling free down his broad back. "It was."

Oh, how she would have loved watching them have that conversation. It must have been hilarious. She would ask Agatha about it later; the older maid usually knew everything about everyone.

As she reached the servants' staircase, Jamie reached out and grabbed her hand, effectively stopping her from running down the steps to join the rest of the staff for breakfast. Or those few who still remained at this ridiculously late hour.

"Am I correct if I assume you are going to have breakfast?"

"I am, my lord."

His stomach growled loudly in response, and she bit back another smile. Poor Jamie. He probably hadn't had a chance to grab something to eat before making sure he wouldn't miss her, and he was now famishing. Well, she wasn't going to make it easy for him. He was the one insisting she was a spy and had made a solemn vow to expose her as such. She had tried to convince him otherwise, but the man was too stubborn for his own good.

If he wanted something to eat, he had to make a choice—follow her into the servants' quarters, which was unheard of, or take a chance and leave her for a quick meal and hope she was still around when he came back. Or remain hungry.

"Stay here until I've had my meal," he demanded, and she curtsied without answering before she escaped through the door and down to the kitchen, where Cook was preparing luncheon.

"Well, well, if it isn't the ghost of yesteryear who has come back to haunt us," Cook snorted when Mina arrived. "Here to scare a poor, innocent woman into an early grave?"

Mina, who had learnt Cook was more smoke than fire, went to the chubby woman and put a kiss on the glossy cheek. "I'm too hungry to scare anyone to death right now. I'm desperate for something to nibble on. Perhaps a pie? Or two?"

Cook rolled her eyes as a true Darling servant before filling a basket as full as the one she'd had Mina give Rake the day she had danced with Jamie in the gallery. "Now, off you go, and try not to scare anyone else, you silly child."

With a merry wave, Mina walked down to the courtyard, where she carefully made sure Jamie was nowhere to be seen before skipping out through the gate leading to the lake. She ran over the well-mown lawn and didn't stop until she reached the water and could hide under the hanging branches of the willows gracing the shore.

Cook had packed enough food for an army, and on top of it she had folded a tablecloth, which Mina spread out under an especially thick branched tree and promptly sat down. The food was delicious, and soon she had filled her stomach. She fingered the casket of wine Cook kindly had enclosed.

Her mother was against women drinking anything which would affect their behavior and have them act anything but ladylike. But her mother wasn't there right now, and Mina was curious, so she opened the casket. She wrinkled her nose as she smelled the contents, but she felt courageous and poured some into the mug.

The first sip was awful, the second sip much better, now that she knew what to expect. By her tenth sip, she was a firm believer that wine was the best thing that had ever happened to mankind.

Stretching out on the tablecloth, she dozed off and missed the quiet steps approaching. Not until Jamie sat down beside her did she realize she wasn't alone anymore, and dizzily she looked up at his angry face.

"You were supposed to stay in the kitchen."

"I was hungry," she said, taking in his gorgeous, handsome, magnificent face. Such nice silvery eyes. Like polished…silver. Even when he rolled them, like he did just then, they were beyond comparison.

"You are beautiful," she told him, and he lifted the now not-so-full casket.

"And you are drunk."

"I am not," she said, profoundly upset. She

struggled to sit up, but when she finally managed to stay erect, she was too dizzy to remember why she was angry with him, so she let it go and went back to her favorite subject.

"You are, you know. Very beautiful."

"Mina, men aren't beautiful."

"You are."

"Mina…"

She stared at his irritated, pursed lips and knew she just had to kiss them. Why else would they be so kissable?

When she pressed her lips against his, he became stiff as the hard, wooden floor he had spent the morning sitting on, but when she pressed her tongue against his lips, she felt him shudder as he opened his mouth for her.

She crawled up into his lap, embracing him as firmly as she could. He slowly caressed her back, and he deepened the kiss until both of them were panting with passion.

"We shouldn't do this," he mumbled against the back of her ear. "We really shouldn't."

"Then don't," she sighed as his mouth traveled down toward her neckline as it had the last time they had kissed.

"I really shouldn't," he said as he loosened the ribbon holding her bodice closed. His sigh, when he finally could cup her breasts with his hands, mixed with her gasp of pure sensation.

"W-what are you doing?" she whispered, not knowing whether to scream or to moan.

He lifted his head and gave her a teasing smile. "I am investigating you, my dear Miss Ayle. I'm trying to find out if you are a spy."

Her befuddled mind didn't understand his words, but her heart recognized the comfort of his smile, and she relaxed against him. "All right."

He arched his dark eyebrows, amused. "All right?"

"Investigate me, my lord."

His laughter echoed over the surface of the lake as he leaned closer to her again, and she opened her mouth in expectation. But he only gave her a peck on her nose. And then he gave her a peck on her chin, before leaning down and letting his tongue travel over one of her breasts until he reached its small knob. Slowly he started to suckle on it, and Mina almost fell off his lap. It was such a strange, odd sensation, and she held his head, which rested against her, dragging her fingers through his long, silky hair.

It was the sound of the gardeners' laughter from the lawn above which broke the bubble of their concentration on each other, and reluctantly Jamie lifted his head. The effect of the wine was starting to wear off for Mina, but she wasn't ready to face what she had just done. What she had let Jamie do.

Quietly he knotted the silk ribbon again to hold her bodice together, placing one last lingering kiss on the top of her soft breast before gently pushing her away from his lap. He lay down on his side, resting his head in one of his hands while grabbing the wine jug with his other, an amused smile on his face.

"Can you spare me some wine, or would you rather keep it all for yourself?"

"I'd better not, my lord." She laughed and helped him fill the mug with wine. "We have already experienced why it is better that I stay sober."

"I like you drunk."

She blushed under his hot gaze.

"Me too," she confessed. "A bit too much. Now that I know what wine tastes like, I should not taste it again."

"You have never tasted wine before? Why not? Most young women of your age have at least had one or two glasses."

"Mother thinks wine takes the lady out of a woman, and therefore alcohol is strictly forbidden in our house. Father revolts by keeping a secret cabinet in his office in which he has a bottle of port."

"Your mother sounds very English." He grinned mischievously, and she laughed with him.

"Indeed she does. All her life centers on how others judge her. What the neighbors think of our family is much more important than our own wishes. I'm quite the opposite, to my mother's maternal horror."

"I can imagine you are quite the handful for a small-minded mother."

"Oh, she's not small-minded. She's just too insecure to believe in her own worth. She desperately seeks confirmation through the eyes of others. If her friends become envious, she knows she has succeeded."

"Does your mother work?"

He almost had her there. With great expertise, he had lured her into a state of relaxed trust in which she, as the interrogated victim, would answer honestly on a direct question. What he didn't know was that her mother, the very one he was asking her about, used the same tactics to get the truth out of her daughter.

"Sort of. She keeps the house for a local

businessman, making sure everything runs smoothly, as he travels a lot."

"And your father?"

"He's a businessman too, only a less fortunate one, I'm afraid. That's why mother and I have to do our share, she as a housekeeper and I as a lady's maid."

He tried to hide his interest, but she could see right through him, and it was easy to tell he wanted to ask her more, to follow up the easy questions with much harder ones, but something held him back. Perhaps he was unsure how she would react if he pushed a bit more. He probably thought he'd almost reeled her in and was afraid any wrong movement would make him lose her.

"Why not become a governess? That would be a more suitable placement for a gently bred young woman such as you. Many daughters of gentlemen without income have served as governesses without losing their place in society."

"Oh, lord, no." She laughed. "Can you see me handling children with authority? No, that simply wouldn't do. I would only end up playing with them instead of teaching, and that is not what a good governess would do."

"I think you would excel as a governess."

His faith in her was endearing.

"You are too kind, my lord, but the truth is uncomfortable but simple. I will one day become one very softhearted mother, but I will never be able to handle anyone strongly enough to be a good governess."

"I must admit I disagree with you. Anyone who can handle my mother as well as you do would make an excellent governess. But rest assured, I will not persuade you into changing your mind, Miss Ayle."

He turned to lie on his back, his head resting atop his crossed arms comfortably. She watched him close his eyes as the sunbeams found their way through the thinning foliage, warming his face. He looked relaxed, almost asleep, and she picked up a piece of pie to nibble on as she tried to etch his picture in her memory.

Looking more than ever like a Viking, with his tall, broad-shouldered frame and long white-blond hair, she thought him the most handsome man she'd ever encountered. So maybe he wasn't the most fashionable gentleman, or the best-behaved for that matter, but in her mind he was perfect.

The only fault with him was Aurélie.

The mere thought of the perfect French girl made Mina want to grind something more than just her teeth. Preferably Jamie's memory of her.

She wondered what Aurélie had looked like. Probably exquisitely feminine, with long, shining hair framing a petite face. Jamie seemed overly protective about Aurélie, which had Mina guessing the young lady hadn't been someone for him to rely on but rather someone to take care of.

Was that the key to Jamie's heart?

Could her independent personality work against her finding the way to his guarded heart? Perhaps she should do what her mother had been telling her since she was born—start acting more like a lady instead of insisting on being able to handle herself.

"Was Aurélie a governess?" she asked before she had a chance to stop herself.

He was quiet for so long she thought he must have

fallen asleep. When he finally answered, his voice was sad and hoarse. “No, she lived with her brother, a highborn gentleman who was my friend.”

“An English officer with a Frenchman as a friend?”

“His mother was English by birth, and so their family never chose sides during the war; they chose to stay as neutral as they could.”

“Must have been a hard situation for them, being part English on French soil. I can imagine life wasn’t too easy for them.”

“Their home was in the south of France, near Bayonne, almost at the Spanish border. It was not until Wellington attacked from the south that Aurélie and her brother came in touch with the war. Some of us officers were sent to Bayonne to secure passage to England if needed, and that’s when I met Raphael at a local assembly. We became friends from the start. We were like two peas in a pod, merrily agreeing about everything, from politics to horses.”

“And one day you met his sister.”

“Yes. Unfortunately for her.”

Oh, he was such a martyr when it came to the lady of his heart, and Mina felt like hitting him on the head with the basket. “Jamie, if she loved you half as much as you still love her, I’m certain she thought it quite fortunate.”

“Are you angry with me again?” He squinted at her with an amused grin, for once resembling his brother Rake, the libertine, and suddenly it wasn’t so hard for her to see what he once had been before he went to France and met his perfect girl. “You know, it’s easy to tell. That’s the only time you call me by my name and not ‘my lord.’ ”

"No, I am not, *my lord*. I'm only making a point here."

"You *are* angry."

"No, I'm not," she practically growled. When he laughed at her she had to laugh too, realizing what a hypocrite she was. "Maybe I am a *wee* bit angry with you, my lord. I just think it is so sad that someone throws his life away because the woman he loves died."

If looks could kill, she would probably have been a pile of dust at that point. "You are out of line, Miss Ayle," Jamie said as he sat up, the relaxed, gorgeous gentleman all gone.

"Am I?"

He sent her another chilling look, the one which turned his eyes into wolf-like slits, clearly not very pleased with her blasé response to his outrage. "You don't understand…"

"My sentiment exactly," she cut off, rudely. "I don't understand how estranging yourself from your family honors Aurélie's memory. Losing someone you love should make you appreciate what you have left, the people who are still there for you and who love you, but not you… No, the mighty and wounded Lord James Darling ignores everyone who tries to be there for him and snarls at them if they try to help him."

"I do not snarl!"

"No, of course you don't." She patted his knee as patronizingly as she could, and to her satisfaction, his ears turned red. "But some people might find your ice-cold stare and habit of turning your back to them a bit off-putting."

He pinched the bridge of his nose before shaking his head with a reluctant smile. "You will be the death of me, Mina Ayle."

Funny that he too should mention her being responsible for someone's death. She was starting to feel like a plague. "You can't help yourself, my lord," she continued, now that she finally had his full attention. "Distrust is your point of view nowadays, and therefore you push people as far away from you as possible. If you would talk to your twin brother the way you talk to me, a mere servant girl, he would be beyond happy."

"It's easy to talk to you, Mina, too easy. I-I know I shouldn't act like this with a maid, but there is something about you I can't…resist."

Smiling softly toward him, Mina felt like crying out of pure joy. It was a fragile moment, but for once they weren't fighting each other. Somehow she had managed to reach through his walls without angering him, at least not too much.

"You know what?" he whispered, lifting his hand and resting it against her soft cheek. "I believe you, Mina. Truly I do. I'm so sorry for accusing you of being a spy. But after…after what I had to go through in France, I couldn't trust anyone about anything. Not even myself. And especially not my own judgment. You have been nothing but kind and open toward me, and it's I who have been pushing you farther and farther away from me. Please forgive me."

Oh, dear me.

"Jamie," she started, but he put a finger against her lips, effectively silencing her.

"You don't have to say anything, Mina. Let me learn to trust you by myself. You were right when you said I've been turning my back toward everyone, and I feel so ashamed over my selfishness."

"You were mourning."

"But I didn't let anyone know. Instead I chose, just as you have said more than once, to keep that part to myself and not invite my parents and my brothers, or anyone else for that matter, to mourn with me."

She just had to kiss him. His open seriousness was simply too endearing, and he chuckled into her mouth as she forced him to open his mouth with her tongue. It was a delicious kiss, one she didn't want to end, but the gardeners were closing in on them, and she most definitely didn't need a scandal at this tender moment.

"Ah, Mina," he sighed when she let him go and stood up. "You do know how to make a man burn for you."

Something about his comment didn't feel right, but she was too breathless, looking into his smoldering eyes that were not at all wolf-like for the moment, to care.

"You go first," Jamie said softly as he stood up beside her, all the evidence of their meeting packed into the basket Mina held. "I'll take a stroll around the lake before following you."

"Weren't you going to follow me closely all day?" she teased and was rewarded with a slow peck on her forehead.

"I'm over that now, Mina. From now on, you and I will start anew. The rest of the day I'll spend with my family. I think both they and I need that. But later tonight, when everyone has gone to sleep, you will come to my room, and I will show you exactly how much I trust you." With a wicked smile he leaned forward again, this time he nibbled lightly on her earlobe. "I hope you know where my room is located?"

She couldn't find her voice, but he seemed satisfied with a hesitant nod in reply.

"Well, then." He patted her behind dismissively. "You go and do whatever a maid does during the day, and tonight, after dinner, we are going to get to know each other *really* well."

Numbly she started to walk back toward the castle, her thoughts fluttering around in her head. Even she, an inexperienced and innocent young lady, or almost, understood what he meant. Jamie, most accordingly, had just told her to come to his room so he could have his manly way with her, and as he obviously thought she was much more experienced than she was, he thought she wouldn't object.

This was going too far.

Joining Jamie in his bedroom was out of the question, but how on earth would she ever be able to tell him that without hurting his feelings? Of course there were maids as innocent as she, but she knew there were quite as many of the other kind, too, the ones who didn't mind going to a nobleman's bedroom.

This time she really had outdone herself and gotten into the one situation she couldn't get out of without telling Jamie the truth. She wanted to cry, because he finally had decided to believe in her innocence, and the first thing she had to do was to destroy all his trust.

Dragging herself up the stairs to the duchess's bedroom, Mina knew there no longer was a way around it. She had to confess her sins about Jamie to the duchess and then hope she still would have at least one or two limbs still left.

With a deep sigh, she lifted her hand and knocked on the dragon's lair.

Chapter Nine

November came, cold and with more snow than Mina had seen for years. She knew she was lucky, as her small chamber was warm and cozy thanks to being beside the large chimney which began in the kitchen and worked its way up through the house. For such a large house, Chester Park remained comfortably warm all over, which was unusual in large country houses or so Mina had been told by the other servants.

Overall, life was comfortable at the Berkeley estate, and she had become quite close with most of the servants, some more than others, and knew she would miss her new friends when she left Chester Park. She would most definitely miss the duchess, who had proven to be her twin in mind and soul.

But most she would miss Jamie.

Not that she had seen much of him since their little picnic by the lake. She had not gone to his room that night, of course, and so much had happened during the last month, things which didn't affect their situation but had changed everything else.

She had been so worried about telling the duchess about Jamie that it had been quite a relief when she found the duchess was too busy to give her a minute of her time that day.

"Tomorrow I have all the time in the world," the duchess had said, stressed about collecting things to take to a family on the estate who had just lost their home in a fire.

Mina had wandered about nervously all evening, trying to come up with something clever to tell Jamie. She was too much in love with him to want to jeopardize a possible relationship, which still didn't mean she would jeopardize her own future by giving him what he craved, no matter how much her stomach fluttered at the mere thought of continuing what they'd started.

But in the end neither choice was necessary, because later that night Jamie, together with his brothers, left Chester Park for London. The sweet Lady Penelope had been abducted by her evil stepfather and taken to London, which had a furious Rake following him, together with Jamie and the other set of Darling twins, Andrew and Edward.

And then, the very same evening, Jamie's nephew Sinclair was found in bed with Lady Penelope's sister, Lady Charmaine de Vere, and had been forced to marry her within a week.

The duchess had been out of her mind with worry about her loved ones, and so Mina had backed off, especially as her grace had completely forgotten her protégé's wish to speak with her.

When Jamie came back from London three weeks later, he was a changed man. Again. Gone was the cold hermit, and the duchess was ecstatic—she finally had her own son back, not a shadow of the man, as he had been for the last year. He joined the family at all meals and all social occasions, and even went to assemblies and spent time with their acquaintances.

Agatha told Mina he had boldly charmed the

unmarried young ladies, seeming interested in something more than just a flirtation, and now the duchess was practically planning a wedding before knowing who the bride would be.

It wouldn't be Mina, though.

After one week back, Jamie hadn't even looked at her, much less sought her company. They had met on the grand staircase one day, completely alone, and he hadn't seemed to notice her presence at all. Sometime during the last month he had reduced her in his mind to a normal servant, someone to ignore.

Her broken heart made her consider many different scenarios to catch his attention, some perfectly harmless, others not so much, but in the end she knew she couldn't do that to her parents. They loved her so much and saw many great things in her future, like the Honorable Luther Whyte, and so she couldn't bring herself to go and knock on Jamie's door, no matter how much she wanted to.

She wanted to go home.

She could almost see herself marrying the Honorable Luther Whyte, as long as she didn't have to stay here anymore, at Chester Park, where she was lonely and miserable. She had mentioned to the duchess that she missed her mother and would consider going home early, but the duchess had refused to send her away.

"What kind of friend would I be if I were to go completely against your father's wishes and send you back to your mother? Not a very good one, I assure you."

So Mina stayed.

She spent her days in her chamber, reading books

from the glorious library at Chester Park, which was a treasure chest for a girl who liked to read. She tried to avoid Jamie as much as possible, but sometimes when there was a dinner or a soirée at the house, she would hide somewhere and watch him without being noticed.

It didn't make her feel less abandoned, but it gave her a chance to memorize for the future the sight of him interacting with friends and neighbors. Her deceptive heart rejoiced that he had not fallen for any of the young women yet. To others he probably seemed more than interested, but she could tell it was just an act. His heart wasn't in it.

Knowing he hadn't fallen in love with any of the beautiful and spirited ladies he'd met made it easier for her to watch, but still…

As December arrived, something changed, and it was definitely for the better. One exceptionally cold night, Mina went to bed early, even though the duchess had a dinner party downstairs and Jamie probably was surrounded by eager young ladies, all dying to become his wife. But she had caught a fever, and the duchess had almost cancelled her party out of worry for Mina. So Mina promised to stay in bed, which wasn't hard, as she didn't have the strength to get up anyway.

Falling in and out of sleep the whole evening, her feverish mind lured her into one horrendous nightmare after the other, until she almost didn't dare to fall asleep again.

After one especially awful one, in which she was chased down the Chester Park maze by the Honorable Luther Whyte and a priest chanting a wedding prayer, a noise broke through her dream, rescuing her as she woke up.

It was someone outside the door, knocking softly, and she decided to stay quiet so the person would go away. But the knocking didn't cease. Instead, louder knocks were heard, and just as she was sure the door would fall off its hinges, she crawled out from under the warm bedspread and made it to the door.

As soon as she unlocked it, the door flew open and Jamie stood in front of her, frowning down at her.

"Didn't you hear me knock? I've been standing here banging on your door for ages. If Ivanoff hadn't assured me that you were in your room, I would probably have thought it empty."

She grabbed the doorframe to stop herself from crumpling to the floor. "I was asleep."

"No one sleeps that hard. You didn't want to open the door and talk to me, right?"

"I was asleep, my lord," she repeated, summoning up strength enough to endure this trying man until he gave in and left her alone to wallow in her misery.

He didn't answer her. Instead he stood silent, staring at her intensely as if trying to read her mind. He was dressed in his finest evening clothes, looking the dashing gentleman from head to toe. Normally she would have rejoiced over how splendid he looked, with his long white-blond hair strapped at the back of his neck and his beautiful body poured into his tight-fitting clothes. But this time she was just too tired, too feverish to care. All she wanted to do was to close the door, hopefully in his face, and pray she would make it back to the bed.

When he didn't continue the conversation, she started to close the door, too tired to care that she would be sending him away when he had finally acknowledged her existence. "Good night."

"Don't you close the door just yet, Miss Ayle," he murmured as he grabbed the door and forced her to open it wider. "Why were you not downstairs tonight?"

She stared at him in astonishment, unsure about what he really meant. "I go to sleep at night, my lord. Being a mere maid means I must sleep whenever I can."

"Liar."

She must be sicker than she'd realized, as she thought he smiled at her tenderly.

"Excuse me?"

"You are always there, at the parties. I know you are. I've seen you every last time, except this one. It made me…worried."

He had seen her? He had noticed her every time and yet hadn't seemed to look at her at all?

Anger like none other rose in her, yet she was faint and in desperate need of lying down. But she would rather marry the Honorable Luther Whyte than admit her weakness to Jamie. Suddenly she felt an overwhelming urge to hurt him as much as he had hurt her ever since the picnic that had begun so splendidly and ended so poorly.

"I have not attended any parties, my lord," she insisted, refusing to agree with him even though she had to tell such an obvious lie. But right now it didn't matter if her tongue would blacken and fall out, as long as she didn't have to give him the upper hand of being the one who was right. "You must confuse me with someone else."

"I didn't say you attended, Mina. I said that I did see you at them. You are very good at hiding, I have to give you that. But I found you every time, even though sometimes it took me quite some time, as you never sit in the same spot. But this time was different. I could feel you weren't there."

Ignoring her heart's fluttering answer to his admission, she gave him her most irritated look. "Please, my lord. The hour is late, and my morning is early. I need my sleep. What do you want?"

He leaned his shoulder at the doorframe, grinning, amused. "My dear Miss Ayle, I know by experience exactly how early your mornings are, and to be honest, I would rather call them midday."

She wished she had the strength to give him some icy reprimand, but the fever was taking its toll. With a whimper she fell, nearly fainting, and just as he had done before, he reached out and caught her.

"By God, Mina, you are burning up. You shouldn't be standing around like this—you should be in bed." Lifting her, he carried her to the bed and laid her down gently before going back to the door.

With a grateful sigh, she scooted in under the bedspread again, shivering with cold. Somewhere from afar she heard the door close behind him, and she closed her eyes, too tired to care about him for the moment. But soon she opened them again as she felt another body lying down beside her, and she looked straight into Jamie's concerned face.

"What are you doing?" she gasped, outraged. "You shouldn't be in here! If your mother finds you here, there will be no end to the scandal."

"You are sick. I can't leave you, knowing you're lying here all alone without someone taking care of you."

Of all the stupid things… "Someone *is* already taking care of me. Agatha has been checking up on me all evening. She just left to get some much-needed sleep before the duchess returns for the night. You must get out of here before she comes back."

"No. I will not leave you again."

And she didn't want him to leave. She felt sick and miserable, and his compassion had her feeling a little better. To be honest, having him there with her made her feel *much* better.

"Fine," she sighed, unable to go against her own wishes. She wanted him there, and the worst that could happen would be a forced marriage, which she wasn't completely against anyway. She would prefer that he would want to marry her, but after missing him so much over the last month, she wasn't as set in her decision as she had been before. "You can stay for a little while, as long as you promise to leave as soon as I ask you to."

"I promise," he whispered, tenderly stroking a loose ringlet aside before taking up her braid, which lay on her pillow between their heads. "I like your hair when you have it braided. You have so much hair it's almost as thick as my wrist. It looks like a stout red rope."

"It's blonde," she whispered, automatically.

"What do you have against red hair?" He grinned. "It's beautiful. Your hair has so many different shades it seems almost striped when you braid it like this."

"I don't mind red hair on others."

"Why don't you like yours?"

"Because my hair isn't red."

"You are so strange, Mina Ayle."

It was so nice, bickering with him like this. She knew he had it in his blood. The whole Darling family thrived when they could argue about something which in reality meant absolutely nothing. It didn't matter what it was, as long as they could choose a side no one else had taken and then use every illogical argument available.

This last month, though, as she had been hiding and watching, she had noticed the cleft still remained between him and his family. It was sad to see, even though he now did his best to build a bridge. But what saddened her most was that he had managed to create it all by himself by being elusive and secretive.

She knew she would completely destroy the comfortable atmosphere between them, but she had to ask. "Have you told your brother about Aurélie?"

He withdrew slightly. "No."

"Why not?" she pushed.

"Rake hasn't been around here for a while, if you haven't noticed. Since rescuing Penny from Lord Bolton, he has been spending all his time getting knocked out at Gentleman Jackson's."

"Why?"

"Who knows? Penny says he is angry with her and needs to get it out of his system. But he's been at it for a month now, and although I've tried everything, he's completely unreachable."

"Did you knock him out?"

"No." He grinned. "Maybe I should have. That would have caught his attention, for sure."

"That it would." She coughed weakly, and he frowned in response and put his hand against her forehead.

"Mina, you are burning up. Are Mother and Agatha doing everything they possibly can to make you better?"

"Of course they are." Sighing deeply, she did what she usually tried to keep herself from doing and rolled her eyes thoroughly. "It's just a cold with a fever. It has wandered amongst the staff for a couple of weeks, and now it's my turn. I will be better in a day or two."

He chuckled in response. "Am I being a bit overbearing?"

"Yes." She nodded.

"Sorry."

"No problem. You simply can't help yourself, I guess, being the overbearing sort and all."

He pecked a kiss on her lips, the most delicious kiss she'd ever tasted, and it immediately made her yearn for more.

"You should rest." He sighed. "Unfortunately, that means I have to leave you, because otherwise I can't stop myself from disturbing you now and then."

The fever was starting to take over her body, and it became harder to keep her eyes open. "Please, disturb me."

"I can't. You need to rest."

Despite her efforts, her eyelids grew heavier and heavier, and soon she drifted away, the world turning dizzier and softer. She slept better than she had for days, and when Agatha woke her up a bit later, it felt like she had slept for a whole week instead of a couple of hours.

"You have to tell me what to do," the older maid whispered urgently, more distressed than Mina had ever seen her. Agatha was usually as emotional as a stone.

"Has something happened to the duchess?" Mina cried out and tried to sit up, only to realize that the reason she felt so warm and cozy was…Jamie.

Beside her, on the small bed, Lord James Darling lay with his face against her hair, an arm around her waist and one leg covering hers, sound asleep.

"Oh, my God," Mina gasped, and Agatha nodded gravely in response, and quite pointedly.

"My sentiment exactly, Miss Mina." She snorted softly so she wouldn't disturb the sleeping gentleman. "I don't know what to do. If Miss Anna finds him here, you won't have time to take a breath before you end up married to the boy. But…"

Her voice trailed off, but Mina had no problem following her thought. Agatha wanted to know what Mina wanted. If the maid cried for the duchess, Jamie would not be able to save his bachelor lifestyle. He would have to marry Mina and pretend to be happy about it. But did she want that? She had thought about this before, and every time she had come to the same conclusion—no, most definitely not.

Oh, she wanted him, more than she'd ever thought she would want someone, even in her most romantic of daydreams. He was everything she could want in a man, and if he only stopped being so elusive and opened up a bit more, he would be her perfect man.

But the tragic truth was…she wanted him to want her too.

Maybe she was silly. Maybe she was downright stupid. She didn't know. But no matter what arguments her practical mind came up with, her foolish heart still remained stubbornly certain.

He had to ask *her*.

"Leave," she urged Agatha, before she had a chance to change her mind, and the maid's eyebrows raised so high they almost joined her hairline.

"Are you sure? Because if you are, you better get him out of here now. The duchess is coming up the stairs, and I know she will be coming in here first, bless her kind heart."

Mina nodded, and with one last snort the older maid quietly left the room again, soundlessly closing the door behind her.

"My lord…" Mina nudged Jamie, but he just mumbled something unintelligible before pulling her closer without waking up.

All it took was one hard pinch on his thigh.

"What are you doing?" he barked as he woke up with a start, glaring at her.

"You have to go," she whispered, making sure to sound as distressed as she could, which was not so hard for an accomplished actress such as herself, no matter what Jamie had to say about her acting skills. "The duchess just returned to her bedroom."

It took him two blinks before he realized what she was talking about, and then he paled. Without saying a word, he got up from her bed and, just as the duchess's voice was heard closing in, snuck out through the door to the hallway.

"Ah, you look much better!" the duchess exclaimed as soon as she had floated in through the door with an agitated Agatha close behind her. "All you needed was a little sleep. Yes, even your forehead feels a lot cooler now, although your face is looking a bit flushed."

The older maid's relief when she found no young

gentleman there was quite obvious, and Mina had to bite her lip hard to stop herself from giggling. The duchess didn't notice, though, and seemed absolutely vibrantly happy.

"Oh, I'm so happy you are feeling better, my dear Mina. Especially as we have just received the most glorious news from Hereford. Fanny has given birth to not one but three little girls! Can you believe it? Triplets! Oh, I'm so happy I can hardly stand still."

"Oh, congratulations, Great-Grandmother!" Mina scrambled to her feet. "I wish I dared to hug you, but if you are going to meet the little girls, you must stay away from my sickness. Everything went well, I presume?"

"Great-Grandmother…" The duchess sighed, looking beyond amazed. "I can hardly believe it myself. It seems like I gave birth to my boys only the other day, and now I'm a great-grandmother. Time does pass quickly when one is happy."

"Are you going there to see the babies?" Mina clapped her hands excitedly, but the duchess shook her head.

"Not this time. The duke and I will stay here and let the rest of the family leave for Pendragon tomorrow morning. All but James, that is. I will send him to London to see if he can't get his badly behaving twin to stop boxing and join the rest of his family in Herefordshire. It is, after all, Richard's best friend and his favorite niece who just had their first babies. Normally he would have left already."

So Jamie was leaving Chester Park?

For a shivering moment, Mina couldn't help but wish she hadn't chased him away. If he had stayed, and the duchess had found him here… Perhaps Mina then could have gone with Jamie to London, and then to Herefordshire, as his new bride.

But now it was too late. She had already sent him away, and he had been quite relieved about it too, the cad. Not that he thought he would have had to marry her if he had been found with Mina in her bed. In his mind it would have been an awkward, embarrassing moment, but still just that—a moment. He didn't know Mina was an heiress in disguise and that he would have been forced to marry her.

The duchess, who was too excited to stand still, disappeared back into her bedroom with Agatha close behind her, while Mina lay back on her bed, all her giddiness gone.

Now, after a horrible month of feeling both lonely and abandoned, she was going to lose him again? And that before she'd had any chance to talk to him thoroughly and find out why he had been so cold to her. So dissociated.

She didn't get much more sleep that night, her head filled with erratic thoughts. Unable to sort them correctly, she kept tossing and turning in her bed, until the bedspread was as wrinkled and damp as her lost soul. When the morning came and the house woke up to a frenzy of running servants and packing, Mina dressed and walked down to the stables. Jamie's horse was still there, which meant he hadn't left yet, and so she sat down on a stack of hay and waited.

It didn't take long before she heard firm steps coming her way, and then he stood in front of her, looking down at her. Lord James Darling. He had a heavy brown coat on, trimmed with thick fur, as was his hat. It was freezing outside, and he had made sure to dress for warmth. But even in the unshapely traveling clothes he still looked absolutely stunning, his long white-blond hair loosely hanging down his back.

"Mina!" He frowned as he noticed her sitting there. "What are you doing here in the cold stables? You are sick. You should be in bed."

Wishing he could have shown at least a little bit of joy over seeing her there, she stood.

"I just wanted to say goodbye," she admitted quietly, even though there were no stable boys around at the moment. "Your mother told me you were leaving for London."

He nodded curtly as he went to his horse, which had already been saddled. "I am. Mother wants me to inform Rake about Fanny's babies and take him with me to Pendragon."

She didn't say anything as he tied a small bag behind the saddle and gave the horse a friendly pat before turning around. His silvery eyes were serious as he looked at her, all the sudden warmth from last evening long gone. She didn't know what to say or do. He seemed too distant for her to dare make even the friendliest advance.

In the end, it was he who broke the awkward silence. "Well, I have to go."

She nodded solemnly in response, too afraid she would start crying if she breathed even one syllable. He hesitated slightly, as if he wanted to say something more but didn't know what. With one last bow, he grabbed the saddle to mount the horse. But instead of heaving himself up, he just stood there, holding the saddle.

Too afraid to even breathe for fear of destroying the shivering moment of hope, Mina watched him sigh deeply and close his eyes, as if in pain. He was struggling with something, she could tell, and in the end he gave up.

Dazed, she watched him let go of the saddle, come to her, and take her cheeks gently in his warm hands.

"Forgive me," he whispered, his breath caressing her face as he looked down at her, his gaze warm and tender.

"For what, my lord?" she whispered back, caught in the intensity of the moment.

"For leaving again."

"It's not your fault, my lord."

He chuckled softly. "I know, but still… I should have sought you out to say goodbye."

She was probably breaking every rule there was between men and women, but she had to ask, "Why didn't you?"

His thumbs stroked her chin and moved up to her lips as he opened his mouth to answer her. But no words came out, instead he leaned forward and softly pressed his lips against hers. With a sigh she slipped her arms around his neck, opening her mouth to let him in as she tangled her fingers in his soft hair.

It was not a kiss to arouse.

It was a kiss to remember.

When he finally lifted his head, breaking the kiss, tears ran down her cheeks as she met his glistening eyes.

"I will miss you, my lord," she admitted, hoarsely, as she let her hands leave his shoulders and travel down his arms until they found his hands against her cheeks.

"I will miss you too, Miss Ayle."

He lifted one of her hands gracefully to his mouth, kissing her knuckles lightly. His eyes never left hers for a moment. Instead they were filled with unspoken promises as he lifted his head again. She shivered as he let go of her and mounted his horse. With one last lingering look, he rode out from the stable, joining a group of grooms outside.

She followed to the stable doors and watched him ride down the snow-clad road until he disappeared into the gloomy light of the overcast morning. Once again he was leaving her. Once again he had left her behind.

But this time was different.

This time he had left her with a silent promise to return to Chester Park. Return to her.

With a shimmering light in her heart, she walked back to the castle, knowing that when he came back she would be here waiting for him.

Waiting for love.

Chapter Ten

"Dear, dear child, how I have missed you."

Mina looked up from the book she was reading and squealed with joy when she saw the homely man walking into the duchess's private salon.

"Father!"

Tears streaming down her cheeks, she ran across the floor and threw herself into his waiting arms so hard he staggered backward.

"You haven't changed a bit, have you, Mina." He chuckled as he hugged her close. "If you knew how much I have longed to see your sweet face. I have never been away from you for this long, but then again, I guess I will have to get used to it. Soon some eligible bachelor will come and steal you away from me."

"Harold!" The duchess laughed from behind him as she and the duke entered the room. "You make it sound like it would be horrible if Mina met someone she could give her heart to. Most fathers want their children married and preferably happily so."

"I don't know..." Harold pretended to muse. "I think I would rather have Mina unhappy at home than me miserable without her."

"No, you wouldn't, you softhearted old man." The duchess smiled fondly toward him as he kissed the hand she offered him in greeting. "If you did, you wouldn't have sent her to me when you thought she would end up miserable in an unwanted marriage."

"True, true." Harold chuckled before turning to the duke. "Berkeley."

"Mr. Aubrey, nice to meet you again. It has been quite a while since we had the pleasure of your company." The duke beamed, ushering his guest to sit down on one of the sofas before calling out to the hovering Ivanoff for tea.

Mina sat down beside her father, holding his arm tightly. With an affectionate smile, he patted her fingers lightly, and tears filled her eyes. She had missed both him and her mother so much more than she had thought possible. It had been a good lesson to learn, how much she really loved and cherished her parents. It was easy to forget in daily monotonous life how much they really meant to her, and she was grateful for this unexpected glimpse into her own heart.

"Thank you for taking such good care of my daughter. I can tell by the smug look on her face that she has had a wonderful time here with you. I wonder about the outfit though…" Harold pinched the fabric of Mina's skirt with a frown. "This is not what a young lady normally wears."

"Mina has been staying here as a maid."

Harold stared at his friend openmouthed. "A-a maid?"

"You said in your letter Mina had to stay hidden, and as we are quite a number living in this house and we do like to throw a party now and then…"

"Now and then…" The duke let out a rumbling laughter. "You throw parties almost every bloody night. Most of the time it is impossible to find a quiet spot here in this house. Not to mention that everyone is required to attend the bloody things, too."

The duchess pursed her lips tightly, giving her husband a good I-will-kill-you-later look, not turning toward her guests until he had shriveled deeper into his chair, properly humbled.

"As I was saying," she continued with a radiant smile to her guests, who tried but failed to hide their amusement. "We do have lots of guests in this house, and I knew there was a possibility that Mina sooner or later would run into someone she knows, so I gave her the choice to stay as a one of my lady's maids instead."

"And you accepted that?" Harold stared with amazement at his only daughter. "I thought young ladies like you thrived at parties and dinners."

Mina shrugged lightly. "Mother has been dragging me to every last assembly, soirée, and picnic the past year. I thought it a good idea at the time to take a break from it all and instead enjoy the freedom of a servant."

"She has been staying in a room in my suite, next to my maid, and we have watched her closely all the time, not giving her more freedom than under supervision."

It was amazing, really, how the duchess could sit so calmly and tell such a bad lie. If it had been Mina, she would have been all flustered and blushed fiercely. But not Anna Darling, the duchess of Berkeley. She sat there with her straight back, flashing her most deceitful smile straight into Harold's face.

He, of course, fell for it. "Thank you so much for caring for my daughter," he repeated, looking thoroughly impressed by his hostess. "You saved me, and her, in a situation which could have become unbearable."

The duchess bowed graciously. “It is I who should thank you. It has been a blessing to have her here with us. She is such a sweet girl and has become very dear to us over these last three months. We will miss her immensely when she leaves us.”

Leave?

Harold answered the duchess fondly, but Mina didn’t hear a word he uttered. Frantically she forgot to breathe as the truth hit her—she was to leave Chester Park. She had known all along that she was only supposed to stay to January, when her father returned from his business trip, but it had seemed so far away, before. To be truthful, she hadn’t even considered going home again, as she’d had such grand plans for herself and Jamie when he returned again.

The problem was that he hadn’t returned yet.

The weather had been quite bad over Christmas, one snowstorm after another making the roads almost impossible for travel, and so the rest of the Darling family had prolonged their trip to Pendragon. Three, almost four weeks they had been gone by now, and Mina had practically been climbing the walls of Chester Park, waiting anxiously for Jamie’s return.

If she closed her eyes, she could still see his eyes, so full of promises when he said goodbye to her in the stables as he was leaving for London. She had spent every waking hour daydreaming about what would happen when he returned.

It had been a myriad of endings, but not one of them had been her father coming back to claim her before Jamie had a chance to return to Chester Park. Return to her.

“Mina, my dear girl.” The duchess broke through

her confusion. “Why don’t you go and change into something more suitable for our dining room, and then you and your father can join us for luncheon. I will have Ivanoff prepare a guest room for you, Harold, so you can spend the night.”

“I’m so sorry, Your Grace,” Harold said with an apologetic smile, effectively stopping the duchess just as she was about to pull the cord. “We must leave as soon as possible. My wife misses her daughter very much and has made me promise to have Mina back home immediately. After keeping them apart for such a long time, I can’t go against her wishes now.”

“Of course you can’t,” the duchess said hesitantly. “But are you sure it is safe to go today? I’ve heard there is another winter storm descending.”

What storm? Mina looked out through the large windows, at the clear blue sky and the unmoving trees. There was definitely not a storm approaching, and a lump grew in her throat as she realized that the duchess was only trying to stall.

This time her father didn’t fall for the obvious lie. Instead he looked up at Ivanoff, who had just come in with a full tray. “Oh, but I wouldn’t mind a good cup of tea while Mina packs her things. Those sandwiches look delicious.”

The duchess looked caught, as if she wanted to say something more but couldn’t. Harold was, after all, Mina’s father and had the right to do however it pleased him. Even if the duchess wanted them to stay longer she couldn’t, as a mother, deny him his quest of soothing his probably quite vexed wife.

“I’ll go with you, Mina,” the duchess said instead. “Why don’t you gentlemen enjoy your tea, and we will be down as soon as we've finished."

"Uff 'orse," Harold mumbled, his mouth full of cake, and the duchess swept from the room. Mina curtsied quickly before she could stop herself, and with her father's laughter trailing behind her, she followed her hostess up the stairs to the small chamber which had been her room for the last couple of months.

Awkwardly, she put the few belongings she had brought with her on the bed before hesitating slightly at the shepherdess dress which hung in the back of the wardrobe. It had been such an amazing occasion, when she had been able to attend the masquerade ball and spend some time with Jamie, even though it hadn't been the dancing and flirting she had imagined. Instead it had become something better, as he opened up to her, telling her the truth about himself and Aurélie.

Looking at the duchess, who was carefully putting Mina's few belongings into her bag, with a very disapproving Agatha behind her, she couldn't help but feel a bit aggravated over how coldheartedly Jamie had kept his parents at arm's length when it came to the truth about what had happened in France.

They knew it was something. One didn't come back and behave as he had without having experienced something beyond horrendous. But they thought it had to do with the war itself. They had never heard about a perfect girl named Aurélie who had carried Jamie's unborn child and had died after being accused as a spy and brought to court by him.

For a second she pondered the possibility of telling the duchess the truth, but she knew she could never betray Jamie's trust. He had opened up his tormented heart to her, to her alone, and she could never repay his honesty by spilling the truth to his parents.

"You were lovely in this." The duchess came up beside her, touching the shepherdess dress lightly. "You should take it with you, in case you are going to another masquerade ball soon. They are not so common during the Season, but who knows what can happen when you return home this summer?"

"I couldn't…" Mina started, but the duchess shut her up with a hard stare.

"Of course you can. It is, after all, your dress, specially made for you. Besides, you can see it as a memory from the time you spent here with us."

She cried when she hugged the duchess, grateful for both the gift and for all the love bestowed upon her while staying at Chester Park.

"Oh, stop it," the duchess pleaded, seeking out a handkerchief in a hidden pocket and dabbing it at her eyes. "Look, now you have me crying too. Dear, dear Mina. How I wish there could have been a way to keep you here. I have enjoyed your company so much. You are such a sweet, funny girl, and you make all of us smile at the mere thought of you. Even Cook likes you, now that she has almost forgiven you for scaring her to an early grave."

They laughed together, still teary-eyed but at least not blubbering anymore. Arm in arm they walked through the house, down toward the salon where the duke and Harold awaited. As they descended the stairwell, Mina found most of the servants standing in the foyer, waiting for them, ready to say goodbye to her.

At first Mina felt almost embarrassed over how she had deceived them all, but as none of them were the least surprised, she realized most of them had known all along about who she really was. Agatha's words about how servants always knew came to her as she hugged her friends. Even the sour-faced Cook and the big, brawny Russian, Ivanoff, found themselves embraced by her before her father joined them, patting himself, quite pleased, on his bloated belly.

"It was nice seeing you again, Harold, even though it was such a short visit," the duchess said, mildly reprimanding him. "But I do understand your wife's feelings, being a mother too, and so I will not be too overbearing."

"Perhaps we will meet in London?" Harold asked as he helped Mina into the carriage. "We are going, you know, Mina's first season and all."

"The duke and I will not attend the Season, but the rest of our family will, and they would be very pleased if you were to contact them."

"We will keep that in mind," Harold said politely, obviously not too keen on contacting people he didn't know personally.

As the carriage drove away, Mina stared silently out through the window at the large castle slowly disappearing behind them. So much had happened during the last months, and she had met many new friends.

And she had met Jamie.

She saw the picture of him in her mind's eye, his tall, broad-shouldered frame, and under the dark eyebrows his wolf-like eyes that turned to slits when he grew suspicious of her. His warm hands which so gently caressed her as his mouth claimed hers.

She hoped he would attend the Season in London.

It was her only hope, now, to ever become what she wanted the most—his wife.

She knew most of the Darlings did join the rest of the *ton* in London, but she wasn't sure Jamie would. He wasn't really the sort of man who enjoyed parties and socializing. Not like his twin brother Rake did.

But if he came…

She daydreamed about that meeting all the way home, hardly talking to her father as they stopped for the night on their way. Not until she found herself caught in her mother's warm embrace, listening to her lecturing her father's ears off, did she wake up from her fantasies.

"It hurt quite badly, you know," Ophelia said later that evening as she brushed Mina's newly washed hair. "That you two would think so lowly of me."

"But Mama!" Mina grinned. "Have you forgotten how you told both me and Father, in his office, how you would force a marriage? You were quite specific, you know."

Ophelia's cheeks turned a shade or two redder. "I know. I'm so sorry about that. I don't know what came over me. I would never force you into anything. I hope you know that, Mina. It was just… I was just…"

"Too in love with the Honorable Luther Whyte."

"Mina, I was not in love with Mr. Whyte. I-I only thought he would make a good husband for you."

"I don't want him as a husband."

"I know."

Mina turned and looked hard at her mother. "Do you, really? So you will not force me into preferring him over others anymore?"

Ophelia sighed, dejected. "I promise you I won't.

These last months have had me thinking more than you can imagine. You are so much more important to me than finding you the right husband. But I still think Mr. Whyte would make you an excellent husband."

"Mother!"

"He would, Mina." Ophelia sighed again. "I do wish you could leave that prejudice of yours behind and instead see him for what he really is—a warm, caring man who thinks highly of you."

"And my dowry."

"Philomena Aubrey!"

Mina laughed as she stood and walked over to her bed. "If you admit to me that he is a fortune hunter, I promise you I will try to be nice to him and see beyond my own prejudice."

Ophelia sat down beside Mina on the bed, her slim hands playing with a ribbon on her skirt.

"I know it was your dowry that had him choose you as a possible wife at first, but you should know it is not for himself he wants the money. If you had taken the time to listen to him, you would know how he longs to help the poor by building cottages for them and giving the children an education, and you would understand that the dowry is for others, not for him personally."

"I don't believe…"

"Mina," Ophelia interjected rudely. "If you promise me to listen to Mr. Whyte without letting your negativism paint black what he says, I promise you to stop nagging about him being the perfect husband. Do you agree?"

What did she have to lose? Being able to socialize without the Honorable Luther Whyte breathing down her neck would make her official debut into society a much nicer affair. And it would also mean she would be able to engage with other men, like a certain blond gentleman, without her mother getting aggravated over her disinterest in the vicar.

It was only two short months until they were leaving for London, so why not keep her mother as happy as possible and try to like the Honorable Luther Whyte a little? They were going to spend the time ordering a new wardrobe for Mina's first season, and for her that was indeed a means to the end.

She wanted to dazzle Jamie.

But to do that, she needed him there, in London, waiting for her.

What if he didn't come?

Suddenly she groaned as if in pain. By God, she was stupid. When her father came to Chester Park to get her, everything had happened so quickly she hadn't had a chance to think things over. She hadn't been alone for a minute or been given space enough to make a plan.

When Jamie came back from Herefordshire, he would find her gone without a trace. The duchess wouldn't tell him of her whereabouts, of that Mina was certain, which meant Jamie might search for a young maid named Mina, when Miss Philomena Aubrey awaited him in London.

Determined, she grabbed a piece of paper and scribbled a quick note, which she gave a maid with strict orders to see it delivered to Jamie at Chester Park. As she stood by the window, watching the maid hurry down to leave the letter with the postmaster, she couldn't help but wonder how Jamie would react when he found out who she really was.

Not a maid but an heiress.

He despised lies, and she had done nothing but lie to him since they first met. But the situation had been difficult, and she had not had a choice but to be dishonest to him.

She could only hope he cared enough about her to forgive her, because if he didn't, she had lost him. The only thing she could do was pray he would be able to see a reason for her deceit and let his heart guide him.

Not that he ever had done that before. The man was, after all, notorious for following his head and his assumptions instead of his heart and his emotions.

With a sigh, she closed her eyes and leaned her forehead against the cold window. She had to have faith. She had to trust that love would conquer and that, in the end, her lies would be as insignificant to him as they were to her.

All she wanted was to live life happily ever after together with him. And all she could do now was to hope and pray that he would feel the same. That her disappearance wouldn't change anything between them. Or at least nothing between Mina, the maid, and Jamie. What he didn't know was that he soon was to meet Philomena, the heiress. The most wanted debutante this season due to the enormous passel of money she brought with her.

Her lie wasn't completely white, rather a bit grayish in the edges. But if she only could get a chance to explain herself and her actions to him, she knew she would come out the victor in this. She had to. There simply wasn't any other outcome she could bear.

She couldn't imagine a future without him. There

was no life without Jamie. He was everything she needed to become happy. He and his smile, which one appreciated so much more as it was so seldom bestowed.

With one last silent prayer, she left the window and climbed up into her bed. And as her mind drifted away into sleep, the one thought that remained was—what would she do if he didn't want Philomena Aubrey?

Chapter Eleven

There was something soothing about coming home, Jamie thought, as he dismounted on the snow-clad courtyard outside Chester Park. Looking up at the still dark building in the early morning hour, he stretched some of the soreness away. He had been riding all day and all night and was so tired he practically staggered as he gave the yawning groom the reins.

He had left Pendragon together with the rest of the family the other day, but the closer they got to Chester Park the keener he had become. The rest of the traveling Darlings had stopped at an inn earlier last night, to get some food and a good night's sleep before continuing their trip the next day.

But he just couldn't wait.

It had been a wonderful couple of weeks in Herefordshire, enjoying his niece's company and admiring the newest three members of the now quite vast Darling family. Such precious little girls. Like the rest of the family, he had been in awe of the babies, but at the same time they made him remember too clearly what he would have had if his choices had been different.

Perhaps he too would have been able to stand there with his beloved wife, proudly showing off their child. But it was too late for that. He had crushed that reality when he dragged Aurélie to the court, ignoring her distressed protests. He had been so sure she would be found innocent and hadn't listened to her when she tried to make him change his mind.

And now she was dead.

As he walked through the dark castle, steps were heard as the servants started to wake up. A maid scurried past him, and something warm built inside him as he thought of another maid, one probably still sound asleep in her bed.

She was an oddity, the strange Miss Ayle, but he had always been rather fond of oddities. After all, he loved his family, didn't he? And they were without doubt the oddest persons he'd ever met.

But Mina wasn't too far behind.

From their very first meeting in the stable she had mesmerized him. Her rippling laughter was irresistible to him, and he'd found it too hard to stay serious when she flashed her radiant smile and called him stupid. Her beautiful blue eyes had always a mischievous gleam, especially when she was up to something, which was most of the time. One never knew how she would respond to anything, which added a freshness to life, since he'd been forced to socialize with people who all acted according to the same measuring stick.

And then it was the matter of her hair.

He laughed out loud, startling another maid lighting a fire as he passed. What was it with her and her hair? It was as red as ripening strawberries, and yet she insisted it was blonde.

Shaking his head with an amused grin, he dove into his bedroom, peeling the dirty clothes from his worn body. When he walked into his dressing room, a bath was already there, waiting for him, and he sent a warm thought to Ivanoff, who had to be behind this. That butler had a sixth sense when it came to the Darlings' needs.

Soaking in the hot water did wonders for his sore body, and he let himself doze off, not waking until the water was almost cold. Feeling more refreshed than he should have, considering how uncomfortable it was sleeping in a tub, he quickly dressed without help, as his valet was still out on the road, traveling.

The house lay quiet and undisturbed except by silent servants as he briskly walked down the hallway to join his parents at breakfast. He hesitated slightly as he passed his parents' suite, his eyes lingering at the small door next to his mother's. It had been almost four weeks since he and Mina had kissed goodbye in the stables, and for a moment he could still feel the gentle pressure of her soft lips against his.

He knew she was a mere servant and that their relationship would never lead anywhere but to a bed, but he didn't care. She alone had awakened him from his self-inflicted estrangement from his family, showing him he was not whole without the rest of them, and for that he would be forever grateful.

He still felt miserable about Aurélie and the baby, something no one could take away from him. But Mina had led him to the light, forcing him to realize that he had to go on with his life, if not for his own sake then for his parents'. They loved him much more than he deserved, especially considering his introverted suffering for the last year and a half, ever since he'd come back from France.

And then there was Rake.

His twin brother, from whom he'd almost never

been separated until he left for France, was suffering too, but Jamie had been too caught in his own misery to be there for him. They had been so close, the two of them, and this alienation between them pained him more than he had thought possible. Perhaps because Rake had always been there for him, and he for Rake.

But that he could still work on. As soon as Rake got home from Scotland with his new bride, Penny, Jamie would make amends in any way he could. He wouldn't give up, even if it meant he had to knock Rake out again. He rather hoped it would come to that; it had been a surprisingly liberating feeling to see his brother, who had made him crazy with his teasing all his life, lying at his feet.

"James!" his mother squealed with delight as he walked into the breakfast room. "I didn't know you had returned already. Are the rest of the family with you too?"

He put a chaste peck on the top of his mother's head before squeezing his father's shoulder, where he sat next to his wife at the large table. Hannibal Darling was a formidable man whom Jamie adored and admired more than he could express, just as he did his mother. They were his loving—although a bit too interfering—parents, and he wouldn't change them for the world.

"No, they chose to stay the night at an inn on the way, as they were traveling by carriage. They will probably be arriving in time for dinner tonight."

"Oh, James. What marvelous news you bring. Ivanoff, tell Cook to prepare a feast for tonight. We are going to celebrate our dear family's return."

"It is good to see you, son," the duke said over his brimming cup of tea. "I hope you will stay for a while now, since it feels you have been nothing but away for the last couple of years."

Jamie met his father's serious gaze, well aware of the gentle reprimand. If Anna Darling was blunt and horrendously outspoken, yet impossible to understand, Hannibal Darling didn't need more than a few words to make his opinion known. Jamie knew his father had worried much more than he had shown while Jamie was in France, simply because the duke knew what *could* happen. He had seen with his own two eyes what war could do to a man, and knowing his beloved son was out there, possibly wounded beyond recognition, would have pained Hannibal Darling more than he'd let his dramatic little wife know. When talking to her about the war, the conversation mostly centered on uniforms and the handsome men wearing them. Anna Darling might be one clever woman, but she was a lady of her time, completely unaware of the ghastliness of war. If it didn't happen in a ballroom, it didn't happen.

"We must throw a ball now when you all are back!" The duchess clapped her hand in excitement.

"No!" the men chimed in unison, their feelings about balls less favorable than the duchess's.

She, of course, didn't acknowledge their pained faces, her head already filled with plans for the upcoming party. "What a splendid idea. We will dance and laugh and just have a wonderful time. And perhaps there will be a young lady who might catch your eye."

Ignoring his mother's winking, in his mind's eye he could clearly see a young woman, with strawberry-red curly hair, laughing in his arms as he twirled with her across the dance floor. They had danced before, twice. Once in the gallery, just after they first met, and the second time at the masquerade, when she had been dressed as the most gorgeous shepherdess he'd ever seen.

Both times he had destroyed the moment by his obstinate but unfounded accusations.

What had possessed him to think of her as a spy? She had not once behaved in a way that would lead a normally intelligent man to think of her as a French intruder, yet he had persisted.

He felt his ears grow warm when he thought about what he had said and done, and he knew he would have to apologize to her profoundly for it when he met her later. Why, even if it meant he would have to kiss her the rest of the day until she begged him for mercy, he would endure it. A gentleman never backed down from a challenge.

And Mina Ayle surely was a challenge.

He knew she had lied to him about who she really was, but then again, she had admitted to him that she was indeed lying, so that sort of took the lie away. His mother, who never would have made Mina her lady's maid without knowing her story, seemed quite fond of the young woman. At least he had gotten that impression from watching them interact.

But what had finally turned him over when it came to Mina was how respectfully the other servants treated her. They even called her *Miss* Mina, which he had found hilarious until he had overheard Ivanoff say it too. Then he didn't dare to even drag a corner of his mouth upward, because you never laughed at the big Russian butler. Never.

He had to do something about her.

He wanted so much more from her, preferably in

his bed, but he didn't think his mother would like it if he turned her sweet young maid into his mistress under this very roof. No, he would have to find somewhere he could install her, so he could visit her daily to enjoy her. Maybe he could spend a night or two there, when everyone else was in London, playing house with her for a while.

As he looked at his parents, who sat closely together on the other side of the breakfast table, heatedly discussing if there was going to be a ball or not, he knew he wanted this too. To be able to sit down with Mina, to read the newspaper together with her and discuss what it contained. If he knew Mina correctly, she would probably always be against him, no matter the subject, and use the most absurd arguments to make her point.

Sometimes he couldn't believe she wasn't a member of his family, as she did seem to be cut from the same branch. She would certainly have made an impact at the table where he sat now. His brothers and the rest of the family were infamous for their constant bickering and their illogical logic, which could drive guests crazy when they had to listen to it.

But Mina would probably have fitted in quite perfectly. She would not only have enjoyed the brawl every other family called a meal, but would probably have led the arguments, fighting Rake for his self-appointed place as leader.

For a second he couldn't help but wish he could indeed make her a part of his family. Just the thought of marrying Mina and spending the rest of his life with her made him feel warm. He had to do something about their situation, because he couldn't throw away what they had. He had lost Aurélie. But he wouldn't lose Mina. Not if he had something to say about it.

She might not be partial to becoming his mistress and not an honorable woman. But then again, who knew? Perhaps they would grow tired of each other after a while and prefer to spend the rest of their lives apart. So maybe she wouldn't be on the top of the most-eligible-wife list after living in sin with him, but then again… If she could stop herself from being too picky, she might find some man who didn't mind her not being a virginal bride.

The mere thought of another man touching Mina made him feel uneasy, and resolutely he pushed the thought of her aside, instead focusing on his still-bickering parents.

"Why can't we just celebrate quietly?" Hannibal sighed, dragging his hand through his bushy white hair. "I have heard that it can be done. If other families can, shouldn't we at least try?"

His wife snorted, disrespectfully. "Have you forgotten who your family is? They will never stay quiet even if their life depends on it. Better to fill the house with guests and let them have fun, dancing."

"They don't think dancing is fun."

"Of course they do." The duchess stared at her husband. "Everyone likes to dance. But if you think they will be too tired for dancing, perhaps we could arrange a soirée."

"Dancing will be fine," the duke barked, and his wife smiled victoriously.

"There. See. It wasn't so hard, now, was it?"

"But, Mother…" Jamie tried to help his father. "Have you forgotten all the work it takes to have a ball?

Perhaps a somewhat lesser assembly would be easier to come up with at this late hour."

The duke looked at him gratefully as the duchess frowned thoughtfully, pondering the truth of his words.

"You are right, my dear James. There is too little time. Not only would Agatha and I have too much to do with overseeing all the preparations, but we would have to write all the invitations as quickly as possible so the guests would have at least an hour or more to get ready and come here."

Jamie couldn't stop himself now, as the duchess served him such a great opportunity to mention Mina and find out more about her whereabouts. "Maybe your other maid could help writing the invitations? She seems like a capable young woman."

The duchess looked at him in confusion. "What? Who? You mean Mina? Oh, she has left us, but I agree, she would have been a great help."

Left?

Jamie froze in his seat, staring at his mother, who continued to mouth her thoughts on whether to pursue the matter of the ball.

"B-but…" he stuttered, hoarsely. "W-where has she gone? I thought she was here to stay."

The duchess looked up at him, still frowning. "James, please. Why are you obsessing about Mina? We have much more important things to discuss than the whereabouts of my former maid. Now…if we move the ball to tomorrow instead, then we would have plenty of time to notify the guests and make sure to prepare properly. Why, the servants might even have time to dust off the chandeliers."

"Why can't we just have a quiet dinner, family

only?" The duke sighed as he stood up, folding the newspaper he had not been able to read. "After traveling from Herefordshire in the middle of winter, I think our family would rather rest for a couple of days, perhaps a week, before engaging with our acquaintances. I'll be in my office if you need me."

The duchess glared at her husband's retiring back but didn't say anything. After almost thirty years of marriage to that man, she knew when to back off and lie in wait to persuade him at a better time.

Unable to stop himself, now that he had his mother to himself, Jamie leaned forward. "Mother, please. Why did Mina leave? I-I thought she was to take over as your lady's maid, now that Agatha is getting old."

The duchess looked up at him, her head filled with preparations for the ball they seemed to still be having despite the duke's hefty resistance. "What? Mina? No, she was never to become my new lady's maid. And don't you go around saying that so Agatha hears it. She would be devastated if she thought I would get rid of her due to her age."

"But…"

"Just stop it, James." The duchess held up her hand, effectively silencing her son. "I can never tell you how absolutely delighted and relieved I am that you have returned to us in full. That is something both your father and I have been thanking our good Lord for these last couple of months. But you have to cease this odd infatuation with a maid. No, don't you deny it. Anyone could see how she affected you, not always to the better, mind you. You are a gentleman, James, and as such you can't go around chasing maids."

"I wasn't chasing her!" Jamie puffed, aghast. "I

wasn't… She was…"

The duchess patted his hand across the table, patronizingly. "Of course you weren't, dear. I know, I asked Mina about it. She told me you almost behaved like a gentleman."

He had to ask. "Almost?"

"You did kiss her. And yes, she told me about that too. Now close your mouth, dear. You look like one of the fishes your father insists upon catching."

Jamie didn't know what to do, a normal feeling when it came to his mother. Either he could strangle her to death and live the rest of his life in perfect, normal peace, or he could succumb to the fact that other than confusing him with a tidbit here and there, she would never give him the whole truth. With a sigh, he stood, bowed politely to his mother, and left the breakfast room.

"Now, that's a good boy," his mother called out from behind him, but he didn't have the strength to turn back and face her again.

So Mina had left.

He sat down on the bottom step of the grand staircase, for once alone in the imposing foyer. He pinched the bridge of his nose, feeling exhausted and unable to think one straight thought.

Why had she left?

She hadn't said a word about leaving when he left for Herefordshire; she had seemed to look forward to his return. At least that was how he had interpreted that magical moment in the stables when they had said goodbye. Somehow it felt as if they had made promises to each other, almost like wedding vows.

At least he had.

He closed his eyes, in agony. How would he ever find her again? Finding a lowly maid in England was like finding a needle in a haystack—impossible. No one knew who the servants were in a house, and therefore there was nowhere he could go to ask about one special redheaded one.

Footsteps broke through his agonized thoughts, and he looked up to find a footman rushing through the foyer, not noticing the lord sitting quietly on the stairs. As the young man took a stand inside the grand door, Jamie stood up with a determined look in his silvery eyes. He knew how gossipy servants were and how his mother got loads of information from Agatha which the maid had heard in the servants' quarters.

"Excuse me," he snapped as he walked up to the young footman, scaring him into a jump. "Could you tell me where the young lady's maid, Mina, went? She left the other day."

"I-I don't kn-know, my lord," the footman gasped. "I wasn't here when he came to get her."

He? A "he" had come to get her? Jamie felt his heart harden.

"Who came to get her?" he practically growled down at the footman, who visibly shriveled, terrified.

"I don't know, my lord. It was my free day, so I wasn't here to see it with my own eyes. But John, the footman on duty, said the man didn't stay for long. He just chatted shortly with the duchess while Miss Mina packed, and then they left in a hurry."

"Did they mention where they were heading?"

"I don't know, my lord. John didn't say."

"Did she seem upset?"

"Her Grace? Isn't she always upset?"

Jamie took a deep, strengthening breath. "No, not my mother. Mina."

"I-I don't th-think so, my lord. John said she seemed reluctant to leave, but the man insisted, saying it was for the best."

"Is there a problem here, Master James?"

Jamie looked up at Ivanoff quietly closing in on them. The footman immediately seized the moment and scurried away to safety, as far away as possible from the crazy gentleman who had accosted him in the foyer.

"No, no problem," Jamie said, but Ivanoff just lifted his black eyebrows, clearly not believing him.

"Then, please, Master James, indulge me. Why were you hovering over poor Alan? He didn't seem to enjoy your closeness that much."

"I was just asking him—" Jamie started, but the butler interrupted him with a sigh.

"Please don't tell me this is about Miss Mina."

Should he lie, keep up his uninterested gentleman attitude, or should he give in to the fact that if anyone knew anything it would be the butler?

In the end his heart won.

"I was only wondering if he knew where she went. Alan said there was some man here to get her."

For being such a large Russian bear of a man, Ivanoff knew exactly how to look smaller as he stared at Jamie with an innocent gaze.

"We don't know anything, Master James. Miss Mina didn't tell us, and neither did the gentleman who came for her. The only one who knows anything is your mother. Why don't you go and ask her the same question?"

"I already have."

Ivanoff's eyes started to flicker as he couldn't hold back his amusement any longer. "Oh, did you now? And what did our lovely duchess have to say about it?"

"Nothing," Jamie growled, feeling more and more despair for every word that was uttered. Ivanoff clearly had no intention of giving him any information he might have, or even of letting Jamie know how much he knew.

The servants in this part of the house were a dead end. He had to seek information elsewhere. Like from Agatha. If anyone knew, it was she.

Not only had she been the one spending the most time with Mina, but she was his mother's constant companion and confidante.

Without another word, he left the smiling butler in the foyer and went in search of Agatha. Unfortunately she was another dead end.

"I would never betray my mistress by succumbing to gossip. Miss Anna knows what she is doing, so please just let this go, Master James. Your mother loves you, you know. She wouldn't do anything to harm your future happiness."

No, but she would quite happily interfere without second thoughts about the consequences if she could have her way, Jamie thought as he watched Agatha turn her back to him and briskly walk away. He loved his mother dearly, but sometimes…sometimes he just wanted to *do* something to her. Like put her in the dungeons and forget about her for a couple of days.

Or at least for an hour or two.

He didn't think his father would mind. And thinking about his father… There was one more source he hadn't tried yet. Hannibal Darling might seem elusive, but if anyone knew anything and would show his son mercy enough to spit it out, it would be his father.

Unfortunately, his father didn't.

"Why would I know anything about a maid?" Hannibal said without looking up from the ledger he had in front of him. "You should know by now that I don't listen to your mother when she rants about the household. I never have and never will. You know this, and she knows it, too. That woman just loves to talk; she is not interested in getting a response."

"Please, Father. This is important. I think the girl might have been taken from here against her will."

"Of course she was," the duke sighed, giving up reading his ledger to focus on his sixth son, who stared at him in dismay.

"You knew she was grabbed by force and did nothing about it? Father! I know she's a mere maid, but still… No one should be forced, and especially not from our house!"

Frowning, the duke held up a warning hand. "Calm down, my son. No one took the maid by force. She was sad to leave so soon, but like a good daughter she did as her father asked her to."

Her father? Jamie went to the large window overlooking the lake, his hands crossed behind him. She had mentioned her father, if his memory served him right. The poor businessman who struggled to make ends meet, and whose inability to care for his family was the sole reason Mina had to work as a maid.

Something flickered in his memory, something the footman had said about Mina not looking forward to her future, and something cold grew inside of him.

Was Mina's father about to give her away to another man, to save his own meager life? It had happened before—Penny was living proof. Not all fathers were as caring as the duke. Many fathers used their offspring as pawns to gain something: money, power, or social status.

And Mina's father was a poor man.

If Lord Nester, Penny's father, could give his highborn daughter away to a sadist, what wouldn't a lowborn business man do to his unimportant daughter to get some advantage?

"Did she seem…scared?" Jamie asked, holding his breath while waiting for his father's answer.

"Who? Your mother?"

Was the whole world centering around his mother here at Chester Park? "No. Mina."

The duke scratched his head. "Why are you insisting the poor girl left Chester Park against her will? It's just as when you insisted there was something odd about her and accused her of being a spy. I don't think I've ever seen your mother laugh so hard."

Jamie felt his ears grow warm. That had not been his best day, certainly. He could still hear his mother's hysterical laughter ringing in his ears. "So she left by her own choice?" he asked, to hide his embarrassment, but his father's twinkling eyes told him he'd failed miserably.

"She did. And before you ask me about it, she was very happy to see her father, as he was to see her. They both admitted to having missed one another very much, and the reason for the rush was that Mina's mother also missed her. Fine?"

Jamie nodded, dejected. "Fine."

"Now, please leave so I can have my morning nap before your mother comes barging in with her plans for the ball we seem to be throwing tomorrow."

"I just don't understand…"

"Everything is not for you to understand," the duke interrupted, rudely. "Just indulge me when I ask you to please cease your uncommon interest in a maid long gone. I'm sure your mother will explain it all to you when she's ready, but for now, please stop this nonsense. I can understand the attraction, James, because she's one sweet young woman, but it has to end there. The girl you met here at Chester Park is just a maid. Nothing more, nothing less."

"It was not like that."

"Oh, really?" The duke's bushy eyebrows became one with his just-as-bushy hair. "You could have fooled me. The whole house was gossiping about it, you know. Lord James Darling following a lowly maid around like a lovesick puppy. You even spent a night outside her bedroom door, for heaven's sake, almost tripping your mother when she tried to go downstairs for breakfast."

There was nothing more he could say, Jamie realized. Every harsh word his father had said was true. He had even thought it himself earlier the same morning, when he had planned to install Mina somewhere for his own satisfaction. She was just a maid. It didn't matter if she made him feel all warm and almost happy. She was still a maid.

"One day you will understand," the duke said softly, putting a heavy hand on his son's shoulder, as he walked him across the room. "Just as your mother and I hope that one day you will make us understand what you experienced when in France. No, you don't have to say anything now. But remember, when you are ready to talk, we will be here, listening."

The door closed in his face, and Jamie found himself standing outside his father's office, with the duke on the inside, locking it quite soundly. As he walked down the hallway, his father's words echoed in his mind: *She's just a maid. Nothing more, nothing less.*

But she had been more, at least to him. She had made him wake up and realize that he still lived and breathed. She had brought him back into his family's open embrace, and he would be forever grateful to her for that achievement.

One day you will understand.

Would he? Ransacking his heart, he knew he wouldn't. He didn't forget as easily as the rest of his family seemed to. It had been almost a month, but he could still feel her lips against his, her warm breath washing over his face as they said goodbye, and if he closed his eyes he could still smell her lovely red hair.

No, he would never understand. But he would give it time. If he hadn't heard from Mina in a week or two, he was literally going to sit on his mother until she spit out the truth and where he could find Mina.

He knew there was no future for them, but he had to know that she was doing well. He needed to see with his own two eyes that she didn't suffer in poverty or hadn't found herself trapped into marrying someone against her will just so she would have something to eat every day.

And if he was lucky enough, she would be tired of her poor circumstances and throw herself into his arms and beg him to take her to his bed. Or any bed, for that matter. His body needed closure, as did his mind.

And if it meant rescuing her from poverty and being able to secure her in a small cottage for his pleasure, then his life would be beyond perfect.

It would be complete.

If only he could find her…

"Master James, there was a letter for you." Ivanoff interrupted his thoughts, and absentmindedly he accepted the small, dirty square of paper, which seemed to have traveled a great distance. Hope, like none other he ever had felt before, surged through his heart as he ripped the letter open, and when he saw who had signed it he staggered to the closest chair, suddenly too weak from relief to stand up.

My dear lord,

I am sorry I had to leave before you returned, but my father came to get me and I had no option but to go with him. I will be going to London in the end of March, though, and I hope we can meet there so I can explain my actions to you.

I have missed you.

Mina

It was no explanation. It didn't say where she was at the moment. But it was hope. And it was the beginning of the rest of his life. With Mina.

With new determination, he went to look up his nephew Sinclair, who was the one in charge of the Chester Park holdings. Somewhere on the vast lands surrounding the castle there had to be a small cottage just waiting for Mina to move into in the end of March. It didn't have to be overly spacious; she was not such a large person, after all. All she would need was a small table, two chairs, and a bed narrow enough to force them to lie close to each other.

As he walked through the castle he whistled a happy tune, too excited to keep his emotions inside. Finally he would have Mina in his arms again, and this time she wouldn't be a part of the household. No, this time she would be all his to rule over, and he knew exactly what to do.

He was going to give her a fairytale ending.

Chapter Twelve

London, April 1815

The ballroom at the Eastons' house was filled with finely dressed peers as the *ton* assembled for yet another Season. Distinguished gentlemen with just the right touch of boredom moved slowly across the room, their lovely wives floating beside them in dresses ordered with the sole purpose of outdoing the other ladies with flair. Eligible bachelors hovered about, trying to avoid eye contact with the eager mothers standing along the walls with their daughters dressed in their best white debutante dresses and looking mildly green with nervousness.

Mina could hardly believe her eyes as she followed her parents across the floor. Hundreds upon hundreds of beeswax candles flickered all over the room, and over her head hung chandeliers which had her mother moaning with jealousy.

"Oh, this is so exciting!" she squealed, and Harold Aubrey laughed down at her.

"You like what you see so far, Mina?"

"I do," she admitted breathlessly, hugging his arm tightly. "I can hardly keep myself from skipping."

"You do *not* skip across a ballroom, and especially not *this* one," her mother wheezed from the other side of her father. "I told you about this ball, remember? It's here you are introduced to society and where you have one—and I mean only *one*—chance not to end up snickered at or as a wallflower. Misbehave here, Mina, and you will suffer for it."

Mina smiled reassuringly toward her mother, knowing how anxious Mrs. Aubrey had been for this moment.

"I promise you I will make sure to behave as properly as I can. I must admit I would not want to spend the rest of the Season on a chair in the back, watching everyone else dance."

"It is for your own good, mind you," Mrs. Aubrey stressed, keeping her voice low so no one would overhear her lecture. "I just want you to have a chance to shine beside all these titled young ladies. An untitled businessman like your father doesn't rank highly here, even though he is born into an acceptable family. It does help that I am the daughter of a viscount, but most of all your dowry will make you quite attractive to the eligible gentlemen."

"I would rather meet someone who finds my person more attractive than my dowry," Mina answered automatically for the umpteenth time, more interested in searching through the guests after a tall gentleman with unfashionably long white-blond hair.

"I know." Her mother sighed, dejected but unable to hold back a tender smile. "And I do too, Mina dear. It's just that I want you to enjoy the sensation of being popular. We will not force you into accepting anyone; I have promised you as much. But that doesn't mean you can't enjoy being surrounded by attentive gentlemen who fight about having the honor of the next dance."

"Leave the girl be." Mr. Aubrey gave his wife's

hand on his arm a jovial pat. "Let her enjoy her first social gathering without the burden of finding a husband. If she doesn't meet a suitable gentleman during the London season, rest assured that we have a certain gentleman waiting in Soberton who would most willingly take her off our hands."

"Oh, yes, indeed." Mrs. Aubrey sighed with relief. "I find it sad that Mr. Whyte prefers the peace of the countryside instead of joining us here in London. But his sense of responsibility to the people of our parish is highly admirable."

It was funny, really, Mina thought as she followed her parents to a group of empty chairs with a great view of the ballroom. She had disliked the Honorable Luther Whyte so immensely for so long that it was with much surprise she now realized that she liked him, once she had let go of her hostility. His angelic looks aside, he was a serious young man who firmly believed in caring for others and felt more compassion for his fellow man than anyone she'd ever met before.

Relentlessly he collected money and necessities of life, always there for anyone in dire circumstances. To him it didn't matter if it was a beggar or a peer; all men were created equal in his mind, and Mina admired him for his persistence.

She would never tell her mother this, but if she had learnt to like Mr. Whyte before her escape to Chester Park, she would probably have stayed behind, quite happy to marry him. He was a kindred spirit, and she found discussing all kinds of subjects with him highly entertaining.

He was open and honest and didn't hide the fact that he cared deeply for her. He had even admitted to her that it was her feisty outlook on life which attracted him the most about her. For someone who had to look upon dullness most of his days, her laughter and merry attitude lifted his spirit and gave him the strength he needed to continue his quest.

A small, small part of her almost wished she had never met Lord James Darling and been spellbound by him. Life with Mr. Whyte might not have been a dance, but it would have been interesting and rewarding. And with that in mind she had made a silent vow to herself: If Jamie couldn't leave the past behind him and see a future with her, she would agree to marry Mr. Whyte when she returned to Soberton in June. It was a curse, being this pragmatic, but in the end all she wanted was to live life to its fullest, not wasting it waiting for a man who might never come to his senses.

She might not love the Honorable Luther Whyte as she loved Jamie, but she respected the vicar deeply and knew he would take good care of her if she became his wife.

A murmur went through the room, and she woke from her thoughts, hearing excited whispers traveling from ear to ear. Something had happened at the door, and when she considered all the ladies' awestruck faces, she knew it had to be the Darling family. No other men could make a whole ballroom of women sigh simultaneously.

She took a step to the side to get a clearer view, and her breath caught in her throat as she looked upon the newcomers. Jamie's two oldest brothers, the Marquis of Newbury and Lord Henry Darling, led the group with their lovely wives on their arms. Behind them the rest of the family trailed, and she almost laughed straight out as she noticed Rake casting wicked grins to all the ladies he passed. His lovely wife, hung on his arm, didn't care, though. She was busy talking to her sister, the once Incomparable Queen of the *ton*, Lady Chilton, who now was married to Lord Newbury's oldest son and heir, Sinclair Darling, the Earl of Chilton.

Behind them, looking like they would prefer being anywhere but at this very ball, came a crew of reluctant Darling men, and in their midst walked Jamie.

Poured into a divine evening outfit, he looked absolutely magnificent in the midst of his handsome relatives. His tall body and broad shoulders made him look too large for the ballroom. With his striking white-blond hair hanging freely down his straight back and his wolf-like eyes narrowed under dark eyebrows, he looked more like a savage than a fashionable gentleman.

Breathlessly she watched him follow his family to the thrones where their hosts, Lord and Lady Easton, not too humbly sat and greeted their guests as they approached, one family at time. Oh, how she had missed him. Just looking at him made her knees feel weak, and all thoughts about the honorable Luther Whyte disappeared like dew under the morning sun. Unlike his twin brother, who thrived surrounded by his peers, Jamie seemed angry and frustrated, glaring harshly at anyone who dared greet him. As soon as he could, he disappeared into the gambling room, together with the other set of Darling twins, Andrew and Edward.

It was a bit disheartening, not being able to confront him immediately. But then again, she was in no hurry. She had the whole Season in front of her to engage with him, and even though they didn't socialize in the same circles, now and then they would undoubtedly end up at the same assemblies, and then she would make sure to corner him as often as she could.

And if all things went well, she wouldn't have to chase him; instead he would seek her out to court her. All she had to do was to let him know she was attending the ball too.

But that proved to be an impossible mission.

The Easton House was a huge townhouse, and its ballroom was enormous and filled with guests. For an unmarried young woman such as herself, it was completely impossible to move closer to the Darling family without dragging her unaware parents with her.

Mr. Aubrey wasn't interested in meeting the duchess's relatives when she wasn't a part of the crowd. Instead he preferred discussing business tactics with his friends, who had common interests. Mrs. Aubrey didn't know the Darlings and therefore couldn't introduce Mina to them. Instead she chatted with her friends and even with her Soberton archrival, Mrs. Primrose.

But it was not a completely hopeless situation. Looking at Rosalind, Mrs. Primrose's beautiful daughter, who stared, petrified, at the eager gentlemen closing in on her, Mina knew there was one way for her to be able to leave her parents, if only for a short while. Waiting for her mother to stop gossiping with Mrs. Primrose, she grabbed the first opportunity she got.

"Mama, I need to go to the dressing room," she whispered quickly as soon as Mrs. Aubrey had to breathe. Her mother looked duly disappointed, as did her companion, and Mina tried to look as innocent as possible as she continued, "Perhaps Rosalind and I could accompany each other?"

Rosalind immediately grabbed Mina's arm, turning her back to the approaching gentlemen. "Of course I will go with you. We will be back soon."

Gratefully the two loving mamas continued their dissection of the other guests, and Mina could hardly believe her luck. Now all she had to do was drag Rosalind in the right direction.

But her companion wasn't as obliging as she had expected when she came up with her escape plan.

"Mina, the dressing room is *that* way." Rosalind nodded toward an arched doorway. "You are moving in the wrong direction."

"I-I..." Mina stuttered, unable to think up some great excuse to move toward the Darling family instead.

Rosalind shook her head condescendingly and without mercy continued in the direction of the dressing room. All Mina could do was follow her lead, but she stretched her neck, trying to look through the crowd and find a face she recognized. But not one of the Darlings was to be seen, and soon she found herself in the lavish dressing room, waiting for Rosalind to refresh herself. Her friend took her time, clearly quite relieved over this unexpected sanctuary.

"Mina?"

Looking up, Mina met the surprised eyes of Penelope Darling, who had just entered the dressing room together with her sister, Lady Chilton. Scrambling to her feet, Mina curtsied politely.

"Lady Penelope."

"W-what are you doing here? Are you working

here at Easton House? B-but that is a ball gown… Are you *debuting*?"

Before the ball, Mina had pictured many different, mostly quite clever things she could say when she finally stood face to face with one of the Darling family, but now as she finally did, she hadn't a clue about what to say. The shock in Penelope's face, her complete surprise over finding Mina there as a guest, erased every last memory of well-prepared wittiness. Instead she started to stutter.

"I-I… Eh, yes."

"What is it, Penny?" Lady Chilton asked, a frown marring her beautiful face as she looked at Mina. "You look like you have seen a ghost."

"I think I just have." A smile erased the shock, and Penelope's vivid blue eyes started to sparkle. "A most welcome and wonderful ghost, too."

"I don't understand…" her sister started, but Penelope didn't listen to her. Instead she lifted one hand, thoughtfully placing it against Mina's smooth cheek.

"Who are you, really?"

"My name is Philomena Aubrey. I live in Soberton, a small village in the midst of Hampshire."

"Eh…" Penelope snorted surprised. "As in Philomena Aubrey, the wealthiest heiress anyone has encountered? The girl who has made all unmarried men jump with joy, eagerly awaiting her debut?"

"Well, I wouldn't say the wealthiest," Mina shrugged, uncomfortable as always when someone mentioned her dowry.

"Oh, dear me!" Penelope laughed out loud. "This is absolutely hilarious. Rake will love this when I tell him.

Oh, you must come with me so I can look at him when he recognizes you. He almost never loses his wits, but this will knock him over."

"You are *that* maid," Lady Chilton whispered, as she too recognized Mina. "The one who…who had Jamie running amok when he found out you were gone."

So Jamie had run amok?

Suddenly Mina didn't feel as awkward anymore. Instead she was practically gloating with satisfaction as she watched the two sisters giggling in front of her.

"Mina?"

Rosalind came up beside her, looking nervously at the two elegant ladies talking to her friend. Mina immediately introduced the ladies, and Rosalind paled, impressed, fully aware of the high social rank these two ladies possessed. Being acquainted with them could never be wrong for a young unconnected debutante from the country, and Mina knew Mrs. Primrose would probably faint with satisfaction when she was told of her daughter's new friends.

"You must come and meet the family," Penelope said, dragging Mina with her. "I know they will be so happy to see you."

Leaving Rosalind with Lady Chilton to be escorted back to her mother, Mina and Penelope made their way across the ballroom, in the opposite direction of Mrs. Aubrey and Mrs. Primrose. No wonder she hadn't been able to spot them, Mina thought, as they closed in on a man she would recognize any day of the week.

Lord Richard Darling took one look at the young woman his wife almost threw into his arms. Then he threw back his head and laughed loudly enough for the orchestra to hesitate a moment. As the music continued, Rake bowed and put a chaste kiss on Mina's knuckles, his wicked grin warming her.

"Well, well. If it isn't Miss Mina in person."

"Oh, not *just* Miss Mina," his wife informed him, gleefully. "Miss Philomena Aubrey."

Just like his twin, he was handsome, even when staring at her open-mouthed, Mina thought, as she met Rake's disbelieving eyes. What was it with these Darling men? Not even dumbfounded did they lose the tiniest part of their handsomeness.

"As in Philomena Aubrey, the heiress with a dowry to kill for?"

When Penelope confirmed that with a mischievous grin, Rake exploded again with laughter, and again the music paused for a second or two.

"Oh, this is absolutely hilarious," he groaned when he found his voice again, unknowingly repeating his wife's first reaction. "You have to let me get Jamie. Caroline is determined to find him a wife because she finds him too gloomy these days, and on her list of possible wives you are number one, due to the sensational stir you have created even before arriving on the scene. Unfortunately for Caroline, Jamie has been hiding in the gambling room ever since we arrived, much to her great frustration."

So that was why Jamie had looked like he was in deepest agony. Having an interfering sister-in-law determined to introduce you to every unmarried woman at the ball could easily do that to a confirmed bachelor.

Poor Jamie.

She knew exactly how he felt, since she'd had quite a hard time with her mother last year, practically being thrown toward every eligible gentleman in close proximity to their country estate. Of course, that had changed after they met the Honorable Luther Whyte. Then Mina had more or less been thrown at him constantly.

Meddling relatives were unbearable, no matter how good their intentions were. And that was why she stopped Rake just as he was about to stroll toward the gambling room to happily turn his twin's world upside down.

"Please." She put a hand on his arm, and he hesitated slightly. Lord Richard Darling had bent more than his share of rules in his life, but never the ones of a gentleman. She knew he would never insult her in public by impolitely removing her hand.

"Why not tell him?" One of Rake's eyebrows arched upward, an amused smile softening his handsome face. "My dear Miss Aubrey, don't you think my brother deserves the truth? He didn't take your disappearance well, I'm afraid, and especially not the fact that you left with a man."

Mina swallowed the smug purr which tried to escape her and tried to look as serene as possible. "It was my father who came to take me home."

"We were told as much. Didn't make Jamie less worried, though. And Mother has been uncommonly quiet about it, not even giving him a hint about your whereabouts. I think that made Jamie even more worried, as Mother is not known to not inform everyone of her thoughts."

"Jamie needs to be told," Penelope agreed with her husband. "But not in front of everyone. You go and get your brother, Rake, and I will take Miss Aubrey to the terrace. It is a bit chilly still, but that is as private as we can find here tonight."

"Can I tell him?" Rake sounded like a small child, begging for another piece of cake. "I promise I will be gentle."

His wife snorted, most patronizingly. "You don't have a gentle bone in your body when it comes to your brothers, so no, you may ask Jamie to come to the terrace, and then you stay behind, making sure no one else follows."

"Penny…"

"Rake…"

Looking just like that surly child who never got that other piece of cake, Rake left for the gambling room, quite aware he couldn't win when his wife had made up her mind.

"Come," Penelope urged Mina over her shoulder. "Now, as Rake finally is out of the way, let us find you somewhere private to meet with Jamie."

"I thought we were going to the terrace?"

"Oh, Lord, no," Penelope snorted. "The terrace would be too chilly with the cold weather outside, and besides, it would be too easy for the whole Darling family to stare at the two of you through the windows. It is much preferred to be behind a closed door. I will stay behind, though, as a chaperone, but I promise to give the two of you as much room as I possibly can without creating a scandal."

Leaving the crowded ballroom behind them, they dove into a hallway, and after passing a few doors, Penelope opened one and looked inside.

"Perfect," she smiled, relieved. "Lady Easton's parlor is empty, just as I thought. No one dares go in here for fear of stepping on Lady Easton's tender toes."

"Maybe we shouldn't..." Mina started, but found herself pushed into the quiet, dusky room.

"Oh, we most definitely should. The walls of this room beg to hear a less vile conversation than the normal poison its mistress spits out. Now, you wait here, and I will go and get Jamie. He will have to pass this corridor on his way to the terrace, and I want to grab him before Rake has time to alert the family about your meeting."

Mina stared at the door Penelope had softly closed, listening to her disappearing steps. Absentmindedly she straightened her already perfect dress as she went to one of the large windows, drawing the curtain to the side as she stared out into the dark garden.

She had never been this nervous before in her life. Recognizing the importance of this moment, she knew in a few minutes she would stand here as a winner or be left a loser. It was not always so easy to know how men would react, and Jamie was harder than most, something she had learnt while staying at Chester Park.

More than once he had lashed out his ridiculous accusations to her, always seeing something suspicious in how she acted or what she said. She had never known what he would react upon. Even the most innocent of conversation could tick him off, and completely without warning.

The darkness of the room didn't brighten her mood, and she let the curtain down again. Grabbing a stick from the cold fireplace, she removed the glass from the only candle lit in the room and watched as the stick began to burn. After putting the glass back on, she quickly moved around the room, lighting a few more candles, making the room much more cozy and inviting.

Meeting Jamie in the darkness wasn't such an alluring thought, especially as she desperately needed to see his face. She wanted to be able to read every last thought in his silvery eyes and give herself a chance to guard her heart when…

She shook herself mentally. *If* he would deny her.

This was not like her. She usually wasn't this unsure of herself. This nervous. But considering how emotionally unstable Jamie had been when they met last, she just didn't know what to expect, and it scared her, more than she liked to admit.

This meeting was all she had thought about since leaving Chester Park three months earlier, and now as it was finally taking place, she was practically shivering with the fear of being rejected. It was clear Jamie hadn't told his family about the agony he constantly carried around inside his heart, as Penelope and Rake both immediately thought this was a marriage about to happen.

But Mina knew better.

Maybe Jamie would surprise her by being able to look past her lies, and what he might consider her betrayal, but in her heart she knew he wouldn't. At least not at first. What had happened with Aurélie in France had scarred him more deeply than even he understood, and the question wasn't how long it would take him to get over her deception. The real question was—would he ever?

She was so caught in her confused thoughts that she missed the two sets of footsteps outside in the corridor. Not until the doorknob turned did she wake from her thoughts. Clasping her hands together, she straightened her back, watching the heavy wooden door swing open, and with a whimper she saw Jamie walk into the room, stopping abruptly as his eyes found her.

Behind him Penelope snuck in, closing the door behind her before going to the farther side of the room and turning her back to give them some privacy. Mina barely noticed the lady's discreet movements; her attention was completely centered on Jamie's face. Paling, as he recognized her, he looked like he had seen a ghost, and perhaps he had.

The ghost of a maid he once had known.

Chapter Thirteen

The only thing heard was his ragged breathing as he stared, stunned, at her, unable to grasp what he saw in front of him. But as his eyes narrowed and his hands turned to fists by his sides, she couldn't stay silent anymore.

"My lord," she breathed nervously in greeting, bobbing a small curtsy before she could stop herself, acting on how the situation had been when last they had interacted, when he had been the master and she the supposedly humble servant.

Still silent, he took a hesitant step closer to her, his wolf-like eyes penetrating her until she shivered with anticipation. Slowly he crossed the floor. When he stopped in front of her, she couldn't wait any longer. With a whimper coming from the deepest part of her soul she threw herself against him, wrapping her arms hard around him.

She felt him tense, his muscular body hardening against her. Closing her eyes, she buried her face against his elegant vest, feeling faint as she once again smelled the intoxicating scent that was his and his alone.

A shiver ran through his body, but he didn't move. She felt his arms twitch against her bare arms, as if he fought an overwhelming urge to wrap them around her, embracing her.

In the end, she lost.

Determinedly he grabbed her arms, forcing her to release him. Her immediate feeling was to refuse, to hold on to him as hard as she could and not let go. But as she opened her eyes, looking up at him, she met only cold rejection, and with sinking dismay, she let go of him, watching him take a few steps away from her again, as if he couldn't control himself when standing too close to her.

"Jamie…"

He held up a hand, silencing her. "Don't." He took a deep breath. "Just…don't."

Desperate to reach him before he closed the last door to his heart, she held out her hands toward him as if trying to hold on to his very being.

"Please listen to me," she begged, her voice a mere whisper. "You have to let me explain…"

"Explain what?" he interrupted hoarsely. "What could you possibly explain that would change even a part of what I'm feeling right now and what I have been feeling for the last four months? You left me, Mina. *You* did. Without looking back, you removed yourself from my life, not once considering what it would mean to me to come home and find you gone."

"I wrote you a note…" she started, but he snorted loudly, effectively silencing her.

"That note didn't say anything. All you did was inform me that you had left, that you were…gone…"

"I told you I would be in London," she cried out, unable to hide the fear of losing him, and he closed his eyes, as if he felt as much pain as she did.

"Which didn't help much, now, did it? You didn't tell me anything about your situation, about your life, or if you were suffering…" His voice trailed off as he glared at her, a painful laughter escaping him. "Hell, I don't even know if you're even called Mina. Is that a lie too?"

She shook her head. "No, that is not a lie. Mina is what most people call me, short for Philomena."

He stared at her silently for so long she started to squirm under the cold gaze holding her captivated. "Philomena… As in Philomena Aubrey?" he finally asked, quietly, and she nodded affirmatively.

His laughter surprised her. It wasn't a sound of joy or glee. It was too cold, harsh, forced. It humiliated her.

"Jamie, please," Mina tried, but he ignored her plea. Instead he turned to look at his sister-in-law, who stood awkwardly at the other end of the room.

"You knew about this, Penny? You knew that the heiress Caroline has been nagging me about was Mina?"

Penelope shook her head. "No, I only found out shortly before you did, this evening. I met Mina in the dressing room, and that's why I came to get you. I thought it best you would learn about this as soon as possible, without anyone else interfering."

"Like Rake," Jamie breathed, and Penny nodded.

"Like Rake. You know your brother; he wouldn't have been able to stay silent."

Jamie chuckled coldly. "No, he wouldn't have. But to be honest, right now I would have preferred him here, interfering, rather than having to face…her…myself."

Her?

Feeling smaller and smaller with every breath, Mina knew she had to get away from there. She couldn't stay one more second in his company, knowing she had lost before having a chance to begin. With a whimper, much like the one when he first arrived, she ran toward the door. Ignoring Penelope calling out after her, she dived out into the corridor and didn't stop until she reached her parents, who stood where she had left them, chatting with their friends.

"Ah, Mina!" Her father beamed as he noticed her standing silently by his side. "You have to meet my dear old friend Mr. Rodney. We have been friends ever since I was old enough to do some real mischief, and he was my constant companion."

The jovial gentleman laughed heartily, his big belly bouncing, and put a chaste kiss on her knuckles in greeting. "Pleased to finally meet you, Miss Aubrey. Your father has filled my ears with stories about you whenever we have met during the years, and I'm glad finally to have a chance to meet you in person."

When Mina bowed politely, Mr. Rodney beamed even more, if possible, and pointed toward a young man standing behind him. "I took the liberty of having my oldest son, Rupert, join me. Please let me introduce to you Mr. Rupert Rodney. Miss Aubrey."

The dowry again. Mina sighed silently as she curtsied politely to the haughty young man who barely bent his head in greeting. His father, losing his jovial attitude for a moment, glared meaningfully at him, and Mr. Rupert Rodney stretched his lips in something which she guessed was supposed to be a smile.

"May I have this dance, Miss Aubrey?"

"Of course you may!" Harold Aubrey agreed cheerfully before Mina had a chance to open her mouth.

Looking at the two beaming fathers, standing

beside her, Mina knew they had planned this a long time, probably since their childhood. Introducing their son and daughter and completing their friendship with their children tying the knot, the two men would thus finally become family.

Mr. Rupert Rodney didn't even hide his bored yawn as he swung her around in his version of a waltz, stepping on her feet whenever he could. Feeling sore, both in her heart and all over her feet, Mina wanted nothing more than to leave the assembly. Unfortunately, she knew her mother wouldn't be ready to go so soon. Mrs. Aubrey thrived when surrounded by her friends and acquaintances, gossiping about everyone and everything. Mina would have to be practically dying for Mrs. Aubrey to consider moving closer to the front door.

She had to endure.

It would be only a few more hours of twirling around the ballroom in the arms of eligible bachelors, looking like she enjoyed herself while slowly withering inside, before she could leave. A few more hours pretending she was happy and content while suffering as her crushed heart fell into hundreds of pieces all over the crowded room.

She must have seemed the most elusive and introverted debutante ever to step into a ballroom, but she didn't care. All she could think about was Jamie.

The one man who didn't want her.

As she and Mr. Rupert Rodney passed the corner where the Darlings held court, her eyes sought his tall and striking person, her heart somersaulting as she met his cold gaze. Instead of returning to the gambling room, Jamie had followed her into the ballroom. After he joined his family, his eyes had not left her once, following her every move with his cold, unreadable eyes.

It was exasperating.

And, she had to admit, quite exciting.

But mostly it was exasperating.

She wanted nothing more than to throw herself into his embrace, but that ship she had already burnt, thoroughly. Lord James Darling might still be in shock over her sudden appearance in his life and amongst his peers, but it was clear he wasn't particularly pleased about it.

"What did you expect?" Rake asked after quite rudely interrupting her and Mr. Rupert Rodney's twirling, unwittingly rescuing her toes from complete destruction. "You know Jamie; no one holds on to grudges better than he does. 'Never forget, never forgive' should be his personal motto."

"I know." Mina sighed, dejected, as Rake much less painfully twirled her across the dance floor. "I just wish he would listen to me and let me explain my actions, instead of glaring at me angrily."

"Right now he is angry with you for deceiving him, and considering it is Jamie we are talking about, it will probably last a while, so I guess you'd better get used to it."

Mina didn't know whether to laugh or cry. "If you are trying to comfort me, my lord, I must admit you are not succeeding very well."

He grinned, his lovely gray eyes sparkling with mirth, and she couldn't help but grin back. He was contagious, Lord Richard Darling. Like the plague.

"Don't give up on him, Miss Philomena Aubrey. I

know he will come to his senses if you just give him time to think things through thoroughly."

"Why should I give him time when he refuses to offer me even one minute?"

"Because you love him."

"I do not," she pouted, but neither she nor Rake believed a word of that statement. Of course she loved him. Why else would she be hurting like this because of his immediate rejection of her?

"And he loves you."

His voice was soft, like his velvety eyes, and she almost believed him. "No, he doesn't."

"He wouldn't act like this if he didn't."

"Oh, he likes me, I admit as much. But the road from finding someone interesting and to loving them is long and winding."

"You should know one thing," Rake said as he stopped twirling and instead led her to the section behind the elderly and the wallflowers, where they could talk in private yet in full view of the other guests. "Being a man deeply in love with his wife has made me quite sensitive to others feeling the same. Not for *my* wife, mind you, but for being in love. And Jamie is most definitely in love."

She knew she shouldn't say anything. Jamie had, after all, trusted her to keep the truth to herself. But the situation had changed, and knowing Rake wouldn't stop meddling in what he thought was a simple lovers' quarrel made her decision easier to make. She didn't have to tell the whole truth. This was Rake. Just hinting about it would make him turn into a full-blown bloodhound.

"I know he is," she agreed gravely. "But I'm afraid

I'm not the woman his heart wants."

For the second time that night Rake stared at her, openmouthed. "How… What… Who…"

"I have told you more than I should," she cut him off, using his confusion to end the conversation. "If you want to know more, you have to ask Jamie. I will not abuse his confidence. Now, if you'll excuse me, I would like to be taken back to my parents."

There was no end to Mrs. Aubrey's contented satisfaction as Rake, in the presence of all her friends, left *his dear family friend Mina* to her mother. Even Mr. Aubrey looked pleased when the younger man greeted him politely and told him his parents sent their best regards with a heartfelt wish that he must return again, as soon as possible.

"What a successful evening," Mrs. Aubrey sighed, content, as they sat in the carriage on their way home. "Did you see Hester Primrose's face when Lord Richard Darling in person made sure to give his parents' regards to us? Oh, I relive it over and over in my head."

"Rupert Rodney was a disappointment, though," Mr. Aubrey said, fatigued. "I had such high hopes for him, Mina, but he turned out to be quite as full of himself as his mother."

"Mr. Aubrey!"

"As long as it is the truth, my dear, I may as well say it out loud," Mr. Aubrey told his wife as he patted her hand compassionately. "I must admit I'm a bit disappointed. Mr. Rodney has always been such a dear chap. I didn't think his son could be anything but the same. But there you have a mother's influence."

"Mr. Aubrey!"

With a loving smile Mr. Aubrey put a hand against his wife's cheek. "Considering how perfect our daughter is, you should see this as a compliment."

Looking at her parents exchanging affectionate gazes, Mina knew this was what she wanted. She didn't need the overwhelming but painful love she felt for Jamie. What she needed was the comfortable partnership her parents had.

What she needed was the Honorable Luther Whyte, who would cherish her with warmth and compassion and show her the respect she deserved. So maybe she was giving up on love too easily, but remembering Jamie's cold eyes, she was sure she would never get what she needed from him.

His heart belonged to Aurélie, and that would never change. She had admired Jamie for his stamina and his stubborn loyalty from the first moment they had met. Expecting him to give up on Aurélie and love her instead would go against what she loved the most about him—his faith in others.

"Oh, I can hardly wait until tomorrow." Mrs. Aubrey yawned sleepily, leaning her head against her husband's shoulder. "After such a successful night as you just had, Mina, our home will be filled with flowers. Not to mention all the invitations we will receive. This will be such an exciting Season, Mina. I can hardly wait."

Three more months, Mina thought as she forced a seemingly excited smile. Three more months before freedom.

Chapter Fourteen

Just as her mother had predicted, the foyer was filled with flowers as Mina came downstairs the next morning. Vase after vase stood on all the flat spaces, and the stench was overwhelming.

"Not stench, Mina," Mrs. Aubrey lectured her as Mina joined her in the breakfast room. "Fragrance is the word you seek."

"No, it isn't. The flowers are lovely, I admit that. But all those joint fragrances make me nauseous."

Ignoring her daughter's disrespectful attitude toward the gifts bestowed upon her, Mrs. Aubrey held up a thick handful of envelopes, waving them with a triumphant smile. "And look at all these invitations we have received this morning. You are a success, Mina. Not even in my most secret dreams did I imagine this. We will have to look up a good seamstress; your wardrobe is too small for all these parties and dinners."

"Do we have to accept all the invitations?" Mina asked, and her mother gasped, outraged.

"Philomena Aubrey, how can you even suggest declining an invitation? Don't you understand how difficult it is to get even a few invitations? To receive this many is an honor. *An honor*, mind you. To decline would be an insult to the hosts, and we are not in a position to be able to risk our social standing."

Mina knew this, and with a sigh she agreed to go

with her mother later that day to have more dresses made for more parties than she wanted to attend. Her own feelings aside, she did enjoy her mother's enthusiasm. Mrs. Aubrey was in her element, and the *ton's* obvious demand for her daughter pleased her beyond measure. She would wring every last drop of enjoyment possible out of this, gratefully celebrating this unexpected treat while trying not to shove it too harshly down Mrs. Primrose's throat.

"I know we have your newfound friends from the Berkeley family to thank for this. The young man who brought you back to us yesterday was more than clear in front of everybody that he looked upon you as a success and us as friends. Is he…married?"

Mina bit back a smile over her mother's not-too-subtle inquiry. "Yes, he is."

"Oh, how wonderful," Mrs. Aubrey said with a disappointed grimace. "But there are many eligible gentlemen in that family, or so your father told me. When you stayed with them, there wasn't one of them who felt special to you?"

Her spontaneous reaction was to lie and say no, but then again, something inside her needed to confess to someone about her feelings. She needed someone to confide in. Someone who could tell her what to do. And who was a better confidante than her mother?

"Jamie," Mina confessed, and Mrs. Aubrey leaned closer. "I found him utterly special."

"Such an odd name," Mrs. Aubrey said. "Is it Scottish?"

"No, Mother. It's a nickname for James. His full name is Lord James Darling, and he is the most wonderful man I have ever met."

"Do you think he feels the same for you?" Her mother could hardly contain her excitement, probably already planning the wedding of the Season in her head.

"No, he doesn't. He lost his heart to a young French woman he met when he was on the continent with Wellington."

"What a lovely story," Mrs. Aubrey sighed, again openly disappointed. "Has the young woman joined him here in England?"

Mina shook her head. "She died during the war."

"How sad," her mother chirped, excited, not at all sad over the young woman's demise, and Mina didn't know whether to laugh or cry over her mother's obvious partiality for her daughter.

"Jamie still mourns her, though, and I'm afraid he always will. He has admitted as much."

Mrs. Aubrey's eyebrows disappeared under the edge of her turban. "He told you about this himself?"

"Yes, he did. Although I have to ask you to keep this to yourself, Mother. Jamie hasn't yet told his family about losing Aurélie, and I don't want them to hear it from elsewhere."

"No, of course not," her mother said slowly. "I will not say a word about it, but I must confess I find it strange that a man like that would give a confidence like this to a mere maid, which was what he believed you to be, wasn't it?"

Mina couldn't hold back a giggle. "Oh, no. He didn't believe me a maid at all. From the very first moment we met he thought I was anything but a humble servant. Probably because I wasn't behaving as such."

"I believe you." Mrs. Aubrey laughed. "Ever since

you were a little girl you have never been able to stay prim and proper and definitely had problems staying humble. I remember one time…"

"Are you not ready yet?" Mr. Aubrey burst into the breakfast room, his valet on his heels, waving a cravat. "The Green Park Picnic is about to start, and we should have been on our way an hour ago."

Mrs. Aubrey's shriek was deafening, and as she stood, the chair she had been sitting in tumbled backward onto the thick carpet. "I forgot about the picnic! What kind of mother am I?"

Making a quick sandwich of her toast, scrambled egg, and ham, Mina tried to ignore her dramatic mother, but to no use. Mrs. Aubrey had already worked herself up quite well and was more or less panting with distress.

"Oh, Mina, look at us," she moaned. "Look at *you*! My goodness, you still have your morning dress on!"

Mrs. Aubrey didn't listen to Mina's indignant protests about not having finished breakfast. With more strength than her fragile person seemed to possess, her mother dragged her almost bodily out of the breakfast room and up the stairs. In the end, the daughter succumbed, knowing it was useless to get upset.

Half an hour later, an achievement worth mentioning, the Aubrey family arrived at Green Park. The trees were still without their leaves, due to an uncommonly cold spring, and Mina pulled her shawl closer around her shoulders as she climbed out of the carriage. The winds were cold, and it smelled as if rain might be about to start falling.

It was not a good day for a picnic, but polite society was too set in their ways to even consider changing their social schedule because of something as banal as the weather. If there was a place you should be seen, then they all went there, even if it meant freezing in clothing too thin for the weather.

"There you are!" Mrs. Primrose called out as she closed in on them. "I'm so glad the three of you finally decided to join us this chilly morning."

Mrs. Aubrey didn't answer the badly hidden insult. Instead she put on her best tired face. "Oh, you know how it is, Hester. It took us most of the morning to write thank-you notes to the men who so kindly sent the most beautiful bouquets of flowers which filled our foyer. Not to mention going through all the invitations to see if there were any for this week that required a prompt reply."

Mrs. Primrose looked just the right amount of envious, and Mina had to turn away slightly so she wouldn't laugh out loud over her mother's triumphant stance.

"Yes, we had the same problem," Mrs. Primrose said between her teeth and, knowing she'd already won the competition, Mrs. Aubrey grabbed her friend's arm.

"Oh, I believe you. With such a beautiful daughter as Rosalind, your footmen must have had a most hectic morning."

With her pride sufficiently flattered, Mrs. Primrose waved her free hand toward the tables and chairs, where Rosalind stood watching the servants serve the picnic. "You must come and join us. Please, leave your seating arrangements behind; we have plenty."

"Oh, how very kind of you," Mrs. Aubrey beamed, very pleased she would not have to admit that she had only brought blankets to sit on—the Soberton choice of picnic seating.

The people of the *ton* obviously believed in a more comfortable way to enjoy an outdoor meal, as they had brought chairs, tables, and servants to handle them. Following the two older ladies, Mina stared at the picturesque scene in front of her.

Or almost picturesque. Mud had worked its way up through the wet winter grass, staining once-shiny boots and the lower parts of delicate dresses. Legs of chairs had sunk down into the lawn, and she had to look away from some of her peers who sat on chairs which had sunk down so deeply they almost sat on the ground.

"Mina." Rosalind greeted her with a friendly kiss on the cheek. "I'm so relieved you could join us. Mother threatened to invite a few eligible gentlemen to come and sit with us so I could mesmerize them with my wit. You know me, Mina. I'm not a witty sort."

Mina squeezed her friend's hand. "Yes, you are. Somewhere deep inside of you, a small witty person is resting, waiting for the right time to burst forward."

Rosalind laughed and sat on a chair, inviting Mina to sit beside her. "I wish I could be like the rest of them, able to entertain easily and chat about everything and nothing. But I am not. I would much rather go back to Soberton and my quiet life there."

"Don't you want to get married, Rosalind?" Mina asked, curious. "Have a home and children of your own? It is what most young ladies desire, after all."

With an uncomfortable grimace, Rosalind laughed softly. "I must admit I would much rather remain unmarried and be in control of myself. Mother is unfortunately showing unusual insight in the matter and seems to be aware that I am going to end up an old spinster if she doesn't have me at least engaged before this Season ends. She is desperately searching for an eligible bachelor to take me off her hands before we reach June and head home."

"My own mother has tried to push me into a marriage I don't want, so it is difficult for me to put myself in your place, but I do believe your mother only wants what is best for you."

"I know she does." Rosalind sighed deeply, dejected, a common feeling when it came to Hester Primrose. "At least she does sometimes. I'm afraid my mother is much more selfish than she might seem. I'm grateful she has my little sister Lizzie, too, so not all her prospects lie with me."

It was amazing that two young women of the same age, grown up in the same small town, surrounded with the same people, could feel so differently. Rosalind would rather spend her life alone, enjoying the silence and solitude of her own company. For her, it was pure hell having to socialize with men, or worse—talk to them! She mostly found men tiresome and their interests too violent or too loud.

For Mina, it was quite the opposite. She had always wanted a large family, probably because she was an only child herself. She had always looked forward to meeting the man she would spend the rest of her life with. She had loved her months at Chester Park just because of this. Watching the large Darling family and their endless love for each other had made her long for her future even more.

Unwillingly she scanned the crowd, searching until she found the colorful group that contained everything she'd ever wanted. As her gaze locked on Jamie, her heart started to beat faster.

Lord, he was a handsome man.

He stood with the other set of twins, Edward and Andrew, giving them condescending looks as they discussed something quite intensely which, if she wasn't mistaken, had to do with a stack of chairs. He looked utterly urbane and manly, his long hair neatly bound at his neck under the gray high hat. His long cloak was in the same light color, and she knew his eyes must shine more silvery than ever.

He was the picture of a perfect gentleman, and she wanted to…rub some mud on him. She most definitely didn't like him perfect. And as he smiled in greeting to two young starry-eyed debutantes who looked ready to faint out of sheer delight, she wanted to tear that stupid hat off his head and stomp on it.

It pained her that he looked so comfortable and as though obviously enjoying himself. Lady Newbury, his matchmaking sister-in-law, kept introducing new young women to him and his brothers, and every time the bloody gentleman had the ladies giggling, with rosy cheeks.

She wanted her elusive Viking back, the one who had growled at everyone but her. But to be honest, that hadn't been her; no, it had been Mina the maid. If she had arrived at Chester Park as Miss Philomena Aubrey, he wouldn't have looked at her twice. Or even once. Knowing Jamie, he would probably have stayed as far away from her as he possibly could. But the strange maid who had laughed at him and treated him as though she was his equal had intrigued him and kept him interested enough to pursue until they got to know each other.

And then it was too late for her.

But to him it seemed to be a new beginning. *The era of Lord James Darling, the flirtatious bachelor.*

Another young lady was pushed in front of him, and Mina had had enough. Watching Jamie flash his gorgeous smile toward other women made her miserable, and she didn't want that. This was her debutante season; she wanted to be happy and have fun, not sit around waiting for something which would never happen. "Do you want to take a walk?" she asked Rosalind as she stood up.

Surprised, her friend looked up at her. "Of course, if you want to. I'll ask Mother for permission."

After listening to Mrs. Primrose's and Mrs. Aubrey's lecture about what they could and could not do, the two young ladies strolled down a pathway lying in open view of their anxious mamas, a chaperoning maid trailing along behind them.

Shivering in the beautiful but terribly thin dresses their mothers had forced them to wear, they hooked arms to catch a bit of warmth from each other.

"I tell you," Rosalind said, her teeth chattering so loudly Mina almost couldn't hear what she was saying, "it's only the second day of the Season, and I can honestly say I wouldn't mind returning to Soberton this very day."

"How can you not enjoy this?" With as much feigned excitement as she could muster, Mina swept her hand toward their surrounding peers, who all failed miserably to look as if having the best of times. "Shivering ladies trying to hold on to the gentlemen's shaking arms. Everyone staring at their carriages, wishing they had the courage to be the first one to leave. As this is my first Season, I can't compare it to earlier years, but my guess is there have never been so many freezing people of the *ton* in Green Park before."

"Mama thinks this is very exciting." Rosalind sighed, revealing her diverse feelings in the matter. "She is certain I will become the most sought-after debutante of the Season, especially since you introduced me to your friends from the Berkeley family. For some reason, my mother thinks we are the best of friends, and therefore my success is indisputable."

Mina glanced at her friend's exquisite profile, secretly hoping Mrs. Primrose's not-so-secret wish would come true. Rosalind was as sweet on the inside as the outside and deserved to be recognized for it. Unfortunately, her mother was a bit too pushy and forward, sometimes neglecting to behave as she was supposed to according to all the social rules.

If there was anyone Mina wanted to find peace and quiet in life, it was Rosalind. But Mrs. Primrose had other plans, quite the opposite of her daughter's, and Rosalind might not have as much time in freedom as she thought. If her mother found a suitable gentleman who wouldn't mind taking her oldest daughter off her hands, Rosalind might find herself married before she'd had a chance to refuse.

"I didn't know you knew the Darlings," Rosalind interrupted her thoughts. "They are quite the subject here in London, aren't they? Mother has not stopped talking about them since we met them yesterday, and she is delighted to be able to call them acquaintances now, all because of you."

"The duchess is an old friend of my father's," Mina

admitted, watching her words so she wouldn't blurt out the truth without thinking. "I met her for the first time this winter, when I was away visiting friends."

"The two ladies we met yesterday at the Easton ball seemed very nice. Lady Chilton, who walked me back to Mother, was very amiable and more than gracious. Mother told me she was called the Incomparable when she made her debut, and it is rumored that she has received more requests for her hand in marriage than the rest of the debutantes combined. Of course Mother then continued with a tedious lecture regarding my cautious attitude toward gentlemen and how it aggravates my chances of becoming married."

Mina's heart went out to her friend. Having a mother who had more than overdone the matriarchal part of finding her daughter a husband, she knew more than well what Rosalind went through. But where Mrs. Aubrey had learnt her lesson, Mrs. Primrose still pursued a husband for her daughter. And listening to Rosalind, Mina guessed it probably didn't matter who the gentleman was, as long as he was eligible.

"I'm sorry, Rosalind." Mina hugged her friend's shivering arm. "Please let me know if there is anything I can do to ease the situation for you. I can be quite resourceful, and Father always sighs and says I am a force to reckon with."

Rosalind let out a small, pained laugh. "Perhaps I could have them fill your dance card instead of mine and thus manage to escape an awkward moment."

"I think your mother would notice if I danced with all your suitors."

"I'm afraid you are right. Mother never misses

anything." Rosalind sighed. "I find it so unfair. It is so easy for the rest of you, to engage with men. You flirt and laugh and always seem to know what to say. I…I get too nervous… I forget what I was talking about, and it always ends with me warm and blushing, while the gentleman escapes my clutches as soon as he can without compromising etiquette protocols."

"I think you put too much importance on the matter," Mina said as they turned around at the end of the path, heading back toward their peers. "The only one who expects you to excel socially is you. You are a debutante, Rosalind. No one thinks less of you if you don't show the self-confidence of a matron or a young woman who is attending her second or third season. We are supposed to stumble and behave awkwardly—we are debutantes!"

Rosalind's light laughter traveled over the wet grass. "Oh, Mina. Thank the Lord that you are here to share this with me. Without you, I think I would be a complete disaster, a shivering shadow of a debutante, hiding behind my mother."

"And they say *I* am dramatic…"

"Isn't that Lady Chilton's sister walking our way?" Rosalind changed the subject, squinting toward the couple approaching them, clad in much more proper coats for the weather than the two debutantes were.

"There you are, Mina. We have been searching all over for you." Penelope let go of her husband's arm and put a friendly peck on Mina's cheek. "Miss Primrose, your mother asked me to ask you to hurry to her side. You have some obligations to fulfill."

Rosalind let go of Mina's arm and waved her maid closer. "She never gives up," she mumbled, dejected.

"Do you want to come with me, or would you prefer to stay with your friends?"

"Mrs. Aubrey has given us her permission to keep Mina for a little while. We will have her back by your side soon," Penelope said kindly, and Rosalind sighed deeply.

"You are lucky," she whispered to Mina as she passed on her way toward her mother, the maid following her closely.

"Mina, you are shivering," Penelope said, putting a hand on Mina's muslin-clad arm. "Come, let's go to our carriage and find you a coat. I think Caroline has one in there in case of emergencies."

"So how are you enjoying London so far, Mina?" Rake asked as he offered the two ladies his arms to hold. "Is it like you have pictured it to be?"

With a hand lightly resting in the crook of his arm, Mina started to walk beside the married couple. "It is wonderful. Last night's ball was divine. I could never have imagined such flair, not even in my most vivid fantasy."

"I agree." Penelope laughed. "My first time at the Easton ball I spent with my mouth wide open, overwhelmed beyond my every expectation."

"And there I thought you were just mesmerized by my handsome person," Rake drawled, and his loving wife hit him lightly on the chest.

"Oh, stop it. You know I thought you were magnificent, just like the rest of my gender. You just want me to repeat it now and then because you like to hear it."

Rake's grin deepened. "Guilty. But who can blame an old married gentleman when he tries to relive the highlights of his roaming days?"

"Your roaming decades, I would say," his not-so-humble wife snorted and turned to Mina. "He was the most infamous libertine ever to have set foot in a ballroom before he realized I was all he needed. It's lucky for him that I am such an understanding woman and let him dwell in his past now and then without punishing him for it."

"I wouldn't mind a little punishment if you were the one giving it to me," Rake practically purred, and his wife blushed prettily as she caught the hidden message.

They were such a lovely couple, Mina thought a bit enviously. Anyone could see how unfashionably they loved each other. But what was more important to her, they trusted each other completely. Few women of her acquaintance were as fortunate. Most women had to agree to an arranged marriage, or a husband who wouldn't have been their first choice, all because of wealth, connections, or titles.

Love was seldom an option. Love was a luxury few could afford.

Mina knew her situation was uncommon. She might not be titled nor have the best connections, but she did have two things which gave her the power of her own future—money, and parents who would let her choose her own spouse without restraints or conditions.

Penelope and Rake might be the perfect couple nowadays, but Mina knew about the rocky road they had traveled before finding their joint happiness. It had been painful, and with too many misunderstandings. But all in all, it gave her hope. Hope that she too would be able to find happiness.

"Here's the carriage." Penelope interrupted her thoughts. "Now, let us find that coat I'm sure Caroline hid here somewhere."

A minute later, Mina was clad in an elegant and warm coat and starting to feel more like a human again and less like a piece of ice. Without asking, Penelope and Rake started to steer her toward their family, and she knew what their game was. They wanted her to reconcile with Jamie. An impossible mission, Mina thought as they closed in on the Darlings.

Jamie was standing in the middle of a gaggle of unmarried young ladies and their gloating mothers. She knew he had seen her join his circle of family and friends, but he stubbornly refused to acknowledge her presence. Instead he gave the surrounding ladies a smile which had them waving their fans madly.

Well, if he was going to ignore her, she might as well follow his lead. With a radiant smile of her own, she turned her back to him and instead chose to greet the lady in charge, Lady Newbury.

"Miss Aubrey."

"My lady."

"I am so pleased to finally meet you," Lady Newbury said kindly. "Your name has been on everyone's lips, ever since you changed from a maid to an unknown but very welcome family friend."

"Thank you so much, my lady, for your kind acceptance of these odd circumstances. The duchess helped me and my father with a situation otherwise difficult to see through."

"I hope your initial problem is solved?"

Ignoring the chorus of exhilarated giggles from behind her, Mina forced a polite smile. "It is, my lady.

Thank you so much for inquiring."

Lady Newbury frowned toward the commotion. "Why don't we move over to the fire by our carriage? It will offer us much less disturbing surroundings, I assure you."

Secretly relieved to be able to leave the ruckus behind her, Mina nodded and followed Lady Newbury through the crowd, Rake and Penelope right behind her. The servants had lighted a warming fire and set chairs around it, and with a blanket over her legs, sipping on delicious hot broth, Mina was quite warm.

"Rake, you have to talk to your brother," Lady Newbury said as soon as the four of them were alone and out of earshot.

As Rake and Penelope leaned forward, Mina knew she had fallen out of the ashes and into the fire. These three weren't going to sit idle at the side, silently waiting for what the outcome would be. No, they seemed determined to interfere as much as they could, and with desperation Mina looked toward her unsuspecting parents, who had not a clue about what their daughter was about to endure.

"He is making a fool of himself with this outrageous flirting," Lady Newbury continued. "If he's not careful, he will end up married to one of those giggling debutantes before he knows what happened. Marriages have been forced before; Sinclair and Charmaine are an excellent example."

"Why do you think he will listen to me?" Rake snorted with just the perfect amount of rakish disdain. "Jamie has not confided in me for years, and even though I have been literally sitting on top of him, ordering him to tell me the truth about what happened in France, he still refuses. The man is simply too bloody stubborn."

"I think it runs in the family," Lady Newbury confided to Mina, who had a hard time staying serious. This family was beyond ridiculous. Oh, she knew she was one of the few persons who were honored to see this side of them, and she knew she was blessed, sort of. The Darlings were already infamous for all their libertine men and uncommon closeness between family members.

"I can't understand why he insists on acting as oddly as he does." Sending his aloof brother a frustrated frown, Rake lost his usual mirth. "One day he is behaving like a hermit, shutting everyone out, and we have to practically beg for an opportunity to look him in the eyes. And now he collects hearts like a madman. I wonder why that is?"

All three stared expectantly at Mina, as if they all thought she would offer them an easy solution to their problem. But she couldn't help them there. She didn't know what went on under that silky blond hair.

Ever since their first meeting Jamie had been a mystery to her. Oh, she did like mysteries, always had, which was exactly why she had been drawn to him. But the man wasn't consistent in his actions, and that was a bit frustrating. Or a lot. The most innocent of words could set him off, change him from warm to cold in a second.

To be frank, she had been called too dramatic most of her life, which was not entirely untrue. But compared to Jamie she was as serene as fresh milk, because, in her humble opinion, he was as stable as a quagmire.

"Why not leave him be, and instead rejoice in the

fact that he is no longer avoiding you?" she tried, but all three Darlings snorted loudly at that suggestion. "Or perhaps you could ask him?"

"Ask him?" Rake chuckled, an amused eyebrow arching upward. "Don't you think I have? We all have. Over and over again. He's like a clam, and there's just no way to get him to open up."

"He told me I was nosy," Lady Newbury said, her voice filled with hurt feelings. "Me! As if I ever have been nosy. Rake, you irritating man, stop laughing immediately. If you are not careful, you will choke to death. One way or another."

Ignoring the threat from his sister-in-law, who stared at him with murder in her lovely green eyes, Rake dried his eyes before pointing toward Jamie with his cane. "It's interesting, though, how the man can't stop staring at you, Mina. There he stands, surrounded by almost every marriageable woman in the *ton*, and all he can do is stare at the only one who isn't there. It is very interesting, indeed."

Mina's heart beat faster, and she wanted desperately to turn around and see with her own eyes that Rake was right, that Jamie was staring at her. But she forced her unwilling body to stay still. It might be childish, but she didn't want to give him the idea that she was as interested in him and his actions as she really was.

"Wouldn't it be interesting if we offered him some competition?" Penelope mused. "Nothing can be as annoying as watching the one you love engage with another eligible person."

"Jamie doesn't love me," Mina interrupted the conversation, secretly hoping they would continue with persuading her he did, and preferably with hefty arguments. Unfortunately, her company wasn't as interested in that direction as she was.

"I think you are right," Rake said, his smile more rakish than ever. "No one ever died from a little friendly competition. I sure as hell found myself quite disturbed when you insisted upon marrying Saint Thomas."

"Just don't do to Jamie what you did to Hereford." Lady Newbury shook her head toward Mina. "My dear daughter nearly got her husband killed, and all because she made him think she preferred Tristan Knightley to him."

"Why not?" Rake looked surprised. "That was quite effective. It made Devlin realize how crazed he had been, and they ended up almost sickly happy thereafter. You see, Mina, Devlin had abandoned Fanny at the beginning of their marriage, for reasons so stupid I will never reveal them to anyone else. Poor Fanny fought desperately to make him realize that she was all he needed, but the situation came to its final conclusion when she had Devlin think she had an affair with one of his friends."

"It was too much," Lady Newbury interjected sternly. "If Fanny hadn't been able to stop the duel, they could both have been killed. At least Devlin would have died, as he had made up his mind not to shoot. Do you really want to hurt your brother so badly?"

"Of course not." The former infamous libertine looked like a hurt little puppy. "But I think fighting Jamie requires more than just dangling Mina in front of him. He is trying very hard to ignore her and pretend disinterest, which tells us just how interested he really is in her. There is lots of love in those silvery eyes when he thinks no one notices him staring at her."

"Jamie doesn't love me," Mina said again, this time with more force, as she knew this was the truth. It was not that she didn't like the thought. If Jamie had loved her as much as she loved him, she would be the happiest heiress ever to have set a foot in London. But the truth was that Jamie's heart belonged to Aurélie.

"Of course he does." Lady Newbury brushed Mina's faint input aside with an elegant wave of her hand. "He wouldn't behave as if he didn't, otherwise."

Mina didn't know whether to laugh or cry. How would she ever be able to make them understand her point of view when they didn't listen to her? Or worse, when they used that strange illogical logic most of the Darlings had? It was like hitting her head on a stone wall over and over again.

"No, he doesn't," she said, using her sharpest voice, and was awarded the threesome's attention. "I think I told you this earlier, Lord Richard Darling: Jamie's heart belongs to someone else."

"It does?" Lady Newbury and Penelope squealed in unison, staring angrily at Rake. "Why haven't you told us about this?"

Squirming under his blanket, Rake tried to look blasé. "Because I asked Jamie about it, and he denied it completely. Didn't even blink. How could I not have believed him?"

"You think *I* lied?" Mina was starting to feel a bit annoyed.

"No, of course not. I think it is what *you* believe it to be." Rake tried to soothe her upset feelings, gently patting the blanket where he thought she kept her hand.

"My brother might be stubborn and secretive, almost ridiculously so. But he has never been a liar."

She wanted to scream with frustration. Or just hit his bloody loyal head with something hard. His cane, for example, looked sufficiently hefty enough. And if she happened to hit the meddling ladies too, while she was at it, then that would be just a lucky coincidence.

"What if I don't want Jamie?"

She had thought nothing could infuriate her more, but as she watched the threesome laugh hysterically over her question, she knew she was becoming angrier than she ever had been before.

"Of course you do," Rake said matter-of-factly as soon as he had calmed down. "How could you not? It's Jamie we are talking about."

Closing her eyes tightly, Mina took a deep, calming breath. Then she took another one. At the fifth, she managed to open her eyes again and look at them without biting their heads off. "Has it never occurred to you that I have someone else whom I am thinking of marrying? Someone who I know wants me as his wife?"

"As if you would," Rake chuckled. "Who could beat Jamie?"

"The man I'm going to marry as soon as the Season is over."

"Y-you have someone else?" Penelope stuttered in disbelief, and Mina nodded, feeling pretty pleased with herself. Thanks to all the hours she had spent with the Soberton Dramatic Society, she was able to look serene and honest. Or maybe her company was too busy digesting what they'd just learnt and didn't pay enough attention. Either way, they bought it.

"How could you not love Jamie?" Lady Newbury spat. "What is wrong with him? Isn't he the most gorgeous of men? So his hair might be a bit too long, and you already know he can be a bit…peevish. But underneath it all, he is quite the catch."

"Is it the eyes?" Penelope stressed. "I know some people find them cold and narrow, but if you love the man, I think you can overlook the ice and instead enjoy the heat in his heart."

Rake turned toward his wife, staring at her as though outraged. "There is nothing wrong with Jamie's eyes. They are perfectly fine, thank you."

"I didn't mean…"

"He might be a fashionable disaster in the eyes of his fellow gentlemen, but there is nothing wrong with his eyes."

Mina wanted to roll her eyes until they popped out of their sockets. These people were beyond odd. They were ludicrous. And furthermore, they were insane.

"My suitor, who does exist, mind you, is an intelligent and composed man," she enlightened them with pleasure, "who has given his life to the church, and I couldn't admire him more for his devotion."

For the first time since they had sat down by the carriage, the Darlings were quiet, staring at her with unreadable eyes. Squirming uncomfortably, Mina cast a longing eye toward her parents, who stood with Hester Primrose at their carriage, chatting with their passing peers. Pretending to have been waved at, she waved back and nodded brightly.

"I'm so sorry. I see my parents are calling me over. If you'll excuse me, it seems I must go and join them." Looking as innocent as she could muster, she offered them her most radiant smile, made to stun.

“Of course you shall.” Rake jumped up from his chair and elegantly managed to not trip on the blanket which fell to the ground from his knees. “Penny and I will accompany you.”

Knowing their company would mean further interrogation and more arguments about why Jamie was the perfect man, Mina curtsied quickly in the direction of Lady Newbury before walking briskly toward her parents, succeeding in her effort to reach them without the married couple being able to talk to her. Or even catch up with her until it was too late.

After thanking them profoundly, Mina waited until they were out of earshot before asking her parents to take her home. Unfortunately, Ophelia was enjoying herself too much and denied the wish.

“Not yet, Mina. Why don’t you grab a sandwich and a hot beverage? It will make you feel much better.”

Sighing deeply, Mina followed her mother’s command and grabbed an almost frozen sandwich, nibbling at it while her eyes automatically searched the crowd for a special blond head. But as she couldn’t find Jamie anywhere now, she sighed again before moving closer to their carriage, longing to climb into it and the slight warmth it offered.

She never saw him coming. One second she was standing there sulking, and the next she was dragged behind the carriage, away from all eyes. With her back pressed against the carriage, she stared up into Jamie’s cold, silvery eyes.

Chapter Fifteen

His warm hands held her arms firmly, making sure she had no possibility of escape.

Not that she wanted to. The sudden welcome closeness to him sent a tumbling heat through her being, and suddenly she wasn't as bothered by the cold weather anymore. As she looked up into the handsome, frowning face hovering above her, her heart pounded erratically, and she felt out of breath, as if she had been running across Green Park like a maniac.

Jamie didn't notice her reaction to him. Or he simply ignored it, as he was too busy glaring at her.

"Is it true?" he said between his teeth. "Are you getting married?"

They had worked impressively fast, Lord Richard Darling and his lovely wife. As soon as Mina left them they must have dragged Jamie away from his admirers and informed him of her news. That she had a suitor. That she was getting married.

And he clearly didn't like that at all.

Trying her best not to gloat, Mina opened her eyes as widely as she could, offering him her most innocent face. "Yes, my lord, it is true."

For once he didn't see through her acting, and that lack told her more than anything how worked up he was about her removal from the marriage market. "Who is he?" he snapped, unable to hide his anger.

"You don't know him, I'm afraid. He is not a part of your acquaintance."

"What's his name?"

"I can't tell you who he is, as our engagement has not been officially announced yet. But you will be able to read about it in the paper as soon as I'm back in Soberton, when the Season has come to its end."

His eyes narrowed into thin slits, piercing her icily, searching her face for the truth. "I don't believe you."

She shrugged as daintily as she could, which was a struggle, considering he still held her arms. "You don't have to. It's not your prerogative."

"*You are mine*," he hissed, and she had to bite her lip hard so she wouldn't howl out of pure happiness.

"I am? Why, I haven't noticed you showing any particular interest in my person since I arrived in London. One could rather say you have been more interested in anyone *but* me."

"Are you jealous?"

"Yes," she admitted before she could stop herself, and then cursed silently as he sent her a victorious smile, releasing her arms, apparently now feeling much better about the situation.

"Jealous enough to lie about being engaged, perhaps?"

"I have never said that I am engaged."

"But you said you were getting married."

"I did."

He leaned closer again, and her heart started to race again as she looked at his full lips so close to hers. If she leaned forward only a little bit… Memories from before, when they were still at Chester Park, overwhelmed her, and she felt faint with the need to kiss him again.

"Mina," he purred softly, luring her deeper into his irresistible web. "Were you lying about having a suitor back home?"

Mesmerized, she shook her head, unable to pronounce one syllable. All she could think about was kissing him.

"Don't stare at me like that," he whispered, leaning closer again with a painful grimace, as if acting against his own will. "If you don't stop, I can't help myself. I must…"

"Kiss me," she murmured, forgetting she stood quite in the open, in Green Park, with the whole *ton* on the other side of the carriage. Lifting her hands, she grabbed his cravat, forcing his lips closer to hers. His valet would never forgive her for destroying the intricately folded piece of cloth, but she didn't care. All that mattered was the tall man in front of her, staring down at her with hot amazement in his silvery eyes. She felt his trembling hands grab her waist, and with a groan she pressed her body closer to his, rejoicing over the familiar feeling of him.

As his lips touched hers, her knees buckled, and she would have crumpled to the ground if he hadn't held her tightly. His groan as she deepened the kiss was like manna for her yearning heart, and her hands let go of his cravat, instead finding their way around his neck to press his mouth even closer to hers.

"Oh, my Lord!"

The gasping voice shot through the hot fog clouding Mina's mind. Jamie's lips and hands left her mouth and waist so quickly she stumbled backward, hitting her head against the carriage behind her. With a groan she lifted a hand, caressing the tender spot as she looked up at Jamie, who stared with horror at the two women who had interrupted the precious moment. His handsome face had lost all its color, and his lovely dark eyebrows, so different from his blond hair, looked like two dark lines on a white piece of paper.

"Philomena Aubrey," Ophelia whispered, her hand grasping the cloth covering her ample chest as if her heart hurt too much for her to bear. Beside her, Mrs. Primrose stood, her face showing an odd mixture of feelings: triumph, amazement, and a quite hefty pinch of jealousy.

"Mama…" Mina started, searching for the right words to say, but her mother let go of her chest, instead leveling a trembling finger in front of her, effectively silencing her daughter.

"Don't. Simply…don't. There is nothing you can say, my dear. The damage is done, and now you have to face the consequences of your actions."

"Madam…"

This time the trembling finger shook toward Jamie. "You'd better be quiet, my lord. You can remove your person from my sight, thank you very much. We will expect your official visit tomorrow. Dinner at eight. Be there."

Jamie took a bold step closer to the formidable matron, squaring his broad shoulders in anticipation of the confrontation, but something had him hesitating. Mina's mother looked ready to weep, tears filling her eyes as the shock settled in.

Instead of lashing out at her, trying to convince her nothing had happened, he bowed his head deeply and, without looking back at Mina, walked away, leaving her alone with two quite hysterical women.

"Oh, I can't believe this," Mrs. Primrose shrieked in excitement. "I can hardly wait until our friends hear about this! What were you thinking, Mina? Kissing a man? And in the open, too… Why, Mina, one hardly kisses one's husband in the seclusion of one's own home, or in one's private chambers. But to find you—you, a supposedly innocent debutante—in the arms of a man… And not any man. No, you had to be found in the arms of Lord James Darling, one of the infamous Darling men…"

"We are not going to talk about this to anyone," Ophelia prompted harshly. "Please, Hester. You can talk all you want about this later, but let us reach some sort of agreement with the Berkeley family before it becomes known to our peers."

"Oh…do I have to?" Mrs. Primrose looked like a small, sad puppy. But as she met Ophelia's sharp gaze, her shoulders slumped in defeat. "All right. I will not say a word until you have had your chance to meet with him again. But then you will not be able to stop me. This is a much too sensational bit of gossip for me not to tell. Mind you, everyone will talk about it anyway, so please let me be the one spilling the crumbs."

Ophelia gave her friend a warm hug. "Thank you, Hester, you are the best of friends. I will tell you when we have come to an agreement, and then you will be free to whisper as much as you want. When Mina's future is secured and her married status saves her reputation, she deserves to have the tongues of the *ton* wagging about her."

Married?

Mina's knees buckled, and she stumbled to a

nearby chair. Her head had been spinning too fast for her to be able to think straight ever since she and Jamie had been interrupted. She hadn't had a chance to think it through, to analyze what actually had happened. But as she stared openmouthed at the two women now discussing the best way to start the rumors, she realized her dream had come true.

She was about to marry Jamie.

Ignoring her celebrating heart as it made somersaults in pure and ecstatic joy, a feeling of desperation spread throughout her soul. The thing was…it still was not by his choice. It was a forced marriage, just the thing she had decided against long ago, when she first met him at Chester Park and fell helplessly in love with him.

Even then she had played with the thought of forcing him to marry her, to give herself the rest of their lives to make him love her. But she had decided against that, as she knew without a doubt she wanted him to marry her because he loved her. But now that ship had sailed. Judging by the determined looks her mother kept sending her, she would be Lady James Darling before she could muster arguments against it.

As if there were any…

She, a virginal debutante, had been found in a man's arms, kissing him as if this was the last day on earth. There was no way around it. No extravagant explanations could save her.

Not that she wanted to be saved now. If she was going to be forced into a marriage, she could at least be glad it was with Jamie. Thinking about all the stalking fortune hunters who probably wouldn't have minded staging the same scene if it granted them her hand and dowry, she knew she had at least made a scandal with the best man.

With *her* man.

Ophelia and Harold Aubrey didn't say a word on the way back to their townhouse. They simply sat on the opposite bench in the carriage, staring at her with disappointment, and she felt smaller by the minute and grateful the tortuous trip was short, as the distance between Green Park and their humble home wasn't far. It would probably have taken them less time to walk the distance.

"I am so disappointed in you," Ophelia muttered as she ushered Mina toward the stairs. "I know we would probably have had the same outcome in the end anyway, but still… I wanted to enjoy your first season. Most young women only have one season before they marry. After that you would not be mine any longer. Then you would belong to a man. To another family. But much more importantly, I wanted you to enjoy it, too. A woman doesn't get too many chances in life to shine, and for a young lady of our acquaintance, her debut in the *ton* is probably her only chance. And now you will be whisked away, married to one man before you've had a chance to be courted properly by others."

"I don't care about other men, Mama."

"I know."

As they reached Mina's bedroom, Ophelia sat down on the chair in front of Mina's small desk, her foot tapping against the wooden floor. Quietly Mina sat down on the bed, waiting for the motherly reprimand she deserved, now that they were alone. But when Ophelia finally spoke, she surprised her daughter. Her mind had already left the unfortunate occurrence in

Green Park behind, and instead she was planning ahead.

"You could wear that gown we had made for the ball next week. It is really pretty, white muslin with silk flowers embroidered all over. It would look stunning together with the new silver-colored bonnet and the matching cashmere shawl we bought at Bond Street the other day. You would be a very lovely bride."

Mina felt torn between the lovely picture her mother was painting and the forlorn look on Ophelia's face. "I'm so sorry, Mama. I wish I could undo what happened today so you wouldn't have to face this scandal."

"What were you thinking?" Ophelia sighed deeply. "I have not brought you up to throw away your whole future on a…a whim… You know better. I know you do."

Feeling like the worst daughter ever to have set her foot in London, Mina hung her head over her tangled fingers. "I do," she whispered with tears in her voice.

The small bed creaked as Ophelia sat down beside her daughter, tenderly embracing her. "Don't feel bad about this, Mina dear. What is done is done, and now we have to make the best of the situation. I am correct when I assume you have favorable feelings toward this man?"

"I do."

"Well, at least I can be relieved you are marrying someone you feel warmly toward. It would have broken your father's heart, and mine, if we'd had to give you away to a man against your will. You are lucky, you know. What if it had been a man with a much less favorable agenda who had forced this marriage? A man who only wanted your dowry, not you? I…I don't think

I could have lived with that, giving you to such a man. No, I have to confess I am grateful that it was that Berkeley son, the one you have been talking about. At least I know he's not after your money. That family has more money than the rest of England combined."

"I just wish…" Mina stood up and walked over to the window, looking down at the lush square outside. "I just wish he would have asked me, so that I would know he loves me as much as I love him."

"It certainly looked like he loved you quite a lot when we came upon the two of you."

"Mama, this is not a joke!"

Ophelia dried her eyes with a handkerchief, trying to compose herself again. "Oh, I'm so sorry, dear child. But you never cease to amaze me. Here you have what you wanted, served to you on a plate made of gold. And yet you still are not satisfied. Still you want something more. Mina, you must appreciate what you have and stop looking toward the horizon for something better."

"I just want him to love me."

"He does. And if he doesn't, he will. No man can withstand you, Mina. You are a bundle of love and happiness. Before he knows what happened, he will find himself being a very happy man."

Ophelia made it sound so easy. So reachable. Unfortunately, there was that little thorn named Aurélie. The sad truth was that Jamie would never love Mina as much as she wanted him to, not as long as his heart was buried somewhere on the continent.

Oh, she knew he liked her very much. Probably even loved her a little.

But not as much as she wanted.

Not as much as she deserved.

Chapter Sixteen

"You lucky bastard."

Jamie didn't look up at Rake, who had joined him, uninvited, in front of the crackling fireplace of the library in the Berkeley townhouse. Instead he continued to watch the wine swirl around in his glass, hoping his twin would hear the silent message and leave.

But not Rake.

If Jamie had screamed at the top of his lungs at him to leave, the cad would probably still sit there, his amused grin firmly in place. What had happened in Green Park and the consequences thereof was just too much for Rake to leave alone. Without mercy, he just had to rub it in as much as he could.

"When Penny told me what happened, I could hardly believe it at first. You, who last night most angrily repudiated all interest from a certain Miss Philomena Aubrey, were today found kissing her in the middle of the Green Park Picnic by her mother and that awful friend of hers with the constantly wagging tongue. If I didn't know better, I would have thought you had planned it."

"Perhaps it was she who planned it?"

"Mina?" Rake arched an eyebrow. "No, she doesn't have it in her. She's as innocent as a newborn child when it comes to lies and deception. We were all witnesses to her horrible attempt at pretending to be a maid. No, if someone planned this, it had to be you. And the question is, why?"

Jamie snorted disrespectfully before going back to ignoring Rake. But his twin didn't care about the obvious cut. He was too busy telling Jamie what he thought, without regard to his listener's unwilling ear.

"Why would an eligible bachelor, such as you, lure an innocent little debutante, like Mina, into marriage? It is not as if she would have said no if you had asked her, nor would her parents have refused you as a suitor. Even our parents would have thrown a party out of gratitude for your good choice. So why force the marriage?"

Dejected, Jamie closed his eyes. "It wasn't forced; it wasn't planned. It just…happened."

"So you just *happened* to kiss Mina in front of all polite society?"

"It wasn't in front of everyone. We stood behind a carriage, and if Mrs. Aubrey hadn't walked around the carriage right then, no one would ever have known. And besides, if you have to know, it was Mina who kissed me, not the other way around."

"My, my, my…" Rake almost purred. "James Howard Darling, you sit there and try to look fooled, yet you can't hide that smug smile from me. You like this."

"I am not smug."

"Oh, yes, you are. You are as smug as the kitchen cat after catching a mouse."

Jamie shook his head, giving a loud, frustrated snort. "Really, Rake. Why would I be happy that I am forced into marriage? I think you are missing the meaning of the word *forced*."

“You are not more forced than I was when I married Penny, and we practically ran toward the altar, hand in hand. No, you couldn’t have planned this better if you had organized it yourself. I am awed. It is the perfect solution for you. You don’t have to apologize to her for your behavior. You don’t have to court her and compete against all the other suitors surrounding her, drooling over her vast dowry. No, you can just lean back and watch as her parents most happily deliver her directly into your life.”

Rake was uncomfortably close to the truth. An unfortunate habit of his, one for which Jamie should have been prepared. His twin was not known for leaving anyone wondering what was on his mind. If Rake didn’t find you and bother you with his thoughts about things that were none of his business, you could just put on your best clothes and head down to the church for his funeral.

Rake cared, and therefore he interfered. Constantly.

“Poor Mina,” Rake continued with an exaggerated sigh. “All those glorious plans she had for her future are now gone forever. Instead of marrying that vicar of hers, which she seemed quite happy about, she now has to marry you—the one man who doesn’t want her.”

Jamie clenched his jaw, hard. Rake was after blood, and he hated to admit it, his twin was succeeding. What plans? *What vicar?* What if Mina hadn’t been lying when she said someone was waiting for her? What if she had met someone during those months after leaving Chester Park?

Oh, agony… What if she had fallen in love with someone else?

Desperately Jamie ransacked his memory for what

Mina had said exactly, in Green Park, but all he could remember was her delicious lips when she whispered, "Kiss me." He pushed aside the memory of the kiss and tried to remember her reply to his jealous outburst, but all that came to mind was that he had decided that her engagement was only a lie meant to provoke him.

Maybe it hadn't been a lie. Maybe Mina had found a man worthy of her beautiful heart. A man who loved her enough to stand back and let her have one Season in London before she would become his wife.

"Why, your face is almost as pale as your hair," Rake mused beside him, waking Jamie from his devastated thoughts. "One could almost believe you care about her."

Jamie couldn't take it anymore. He sent the chair crashing backward as he stood up in anger, glaring at his amused twin brother. "Of course I care. She…she is perfect, and I couldn't…" His voice trailed off as the image of Mina, smiling with love toward another man, seared through his mind.

"Perfect, you say? I must admit this is an interesting truth to come from you, especially when one considers the small but very interesting fact that you are the man who told this particularly perfect young woman that he loves someone else."

Fighting an overwhelming urge to strangle Rake with his bare hands, Jamie stalked over to one of the windows of the library, where he looked out into Berkeley Square lying dark in the late evening hour. The mere mention of Aurélie sent the same awful feeling of betrayal through his body.

What kind of man was he, really? A young woman had tragically died because of him. Because of his misdirected trust. A normal man would have mourned her until his last day on earth, punishing himself for what he had done.

But not him. No, he had found himself mesmerized by a pair of sparkling blue eyes and a laughter which made his heart feel light and happy, and without a second thought he'd turned his back on Aurélie and what had happened on the continent.

He was the lowest of men, not worthy of either woman. He had never considered himself a shallow man. Not when it came to emotions. He had to admit he had been a bit shallow about women with his bodily needs, but that had ended when Aurélie came into his life. She had been different from all the women he had met before.

Aurélie had been very French from head to toe, sophisticated and flirty at the same time. Her directness had been refreshing in the middle of the war, where lies and treason were more common than the truth. She had led him in a merry chase, and he had willingly followed her every whim until he won the ultimate prize—her.

He had always had a thing for forward women, being the son of a woman who knew exactly what she wanted and never once hesitated going after it. Aurélie had fit the image of a perfect woman to him.

Almost.

She'd had a habit of acting a bit too condescending toward other women. If she could ridicule her gender she did, without mercy and sometimes, in his opinion, ruthlessly so. Men she loved, on the other hand. She flirted outrageously with all men, wrapping them around her petite little finger until she had them in her hand.

Ned Beckett, one of his closest friends when in France, had once made an innocent joke about Aurélie's success with men, and Jamie could still remember the searing anger he had felt then. Wave after wave of jealousy and, to be completely honest, insecurity. He hadn't acted upon it, leaving his friend unaware of the tumult of feelings he had whipped up.

A few days later, Aurélie had been called a spy, and stubbornly he had decided to act as her champion, to leave all his lesser thoughts about her behind, and he had dragged her to the court. And he had lost everything. Their future. Their child.

Mina was a completely different story. He didn't know why, but after his first initial suspicions regarding her character he had found himself trusting her, completely. Why, he had even told her about Aurélie and what he had done which led to her death. He had never been that open to anyone, not even Rake. But something with Mina just made him trust her.

Something about her made him feel like he had come home.

It was weird, though; she was the sort of woman he would never have looked at twice, before. She was young, a debutante, innocent of the darker side of life. She had spent her childhood in a small, quiet country village and never met anything but love and friendship. She was a pretty girl, even with her fiery red hair, but not as beautiful as many other women he had met and flirted with, including Aurélie.

But her heart was beautiful. And her sweet soul was divine.

She made him feel whole again. She made him feel safe and settled. He loved her laughter, her open mind, and her awful acting. No one had been able to make him so happy and so angry at the same time, and that without breaking a sweat.

He knew he had to marry her, as he couldn't envision a life without her. He wished he possessed the ability to make her as happy and content as she deserved to be. But unfortunately he had already destroyed his chances to accomplish that, the moment he told her about his love for Aurélie.

When he first found out who she really was, he had been so angry. She had betrayed him. Betrayed his love. Betrayed his trust. Coldly he had cast her away, turning his back to her when they met with Penelope's help. But as soon as he'd had a chance to think things through, especially after watching her dance with other men and wanting to torture every last one of them, he knew he was lost without her.

Unknowingly she had presented him with the perfect solution for his initial problem, though: how to marry a maid. His initial reaction to the truth had made it impossible for him to start over without crawling a bit, and he didn't want that. He wanted her to do the crawling, to ease the road for his wounded pride. Loving Mina the maid had been easy; begging Philomena the heiress for forgiveness was harder, because she had never told him how she felt for him. Oh, he knew she liked him. Her sweet, innocent, and incredibly enticing response to him told him as much.

But did she love him?

His promise to himself to wait for her had proven harder to hold on to than he had thought. All it had taken to unleash his insecurities was one rumor of her marrying someone else and he had thrown himself all over her. But then again, that interrupted meeting had worked out splendidly from his point of view. Now she would become his and his only. All other men could forget her. Especially that vicar of hers.

"Do you love her?" Unnoticed, Rake had joined Jamie at the window.

Sighing in weariness, Jamie rubbed the bridge of his nose. "Of course I do."

"Then why are you looking this gloomy?" Rake asked softly, for once leaving all amusement and wicked jokes aside. "I thought marrying the woman you loved meant the perfect ending for you. And yet you still look like you would prefer to be anywhere rather than here."

"You don't understand…"

"No, I don't," Rake interrupted harshly. "I wish I did. I wish you had respected and trusted me enough to tell me what's been bothering you. You act as if you are all alone, but you aren't. You have a large family who loves you and wants nothing but to help you. But instead of letting us, you have acted like a bloody hermit, hiding in the darkness, licking your wounds and growling whenever someone dares to come too close to you."

"It's not that easy…"

"That's where you are wrong. It is, Jamie. It is that easy. You don't have to fight your wars by yourself. We are here for you, every last one of us. It doesn't matter if it's a splinter in your finger or a kidnapped wife; we stand by your side, armed to our teeth."

Looking at his twin's angry face, Jamie found to his surprise that he didn't mind his interfering brother's harsh words. Rake was right. He had been avoiding them, unable to admit his actions openly, his gruesome part in Aurélie's death.

A murderer, Raphael had called him.

"I killed her," he whispered before he could change his mind. "The woman Mina talked about, the one I loved. Without mercy, I sent her right into death's embrace."

Silently, with unreadable eyes, Rake stared at him, and unable to continue standing, Jamie walked back to the fire, collected the chair he had sent crashing, and sat down on it. He refilled his glass of wine, waiting for his brother to join him. When Rake sat down beside him, he braced himself, knowing this was not going to be an easy conversation. But it would be a much needed one.

"I don't believe you."

"It is the truth."

Rake snorted loudly. "You are *not* a killer, Jamie. I know you."

Jamie couldn't hold back an amused chuckle. "Rake, now you are being silly. I have killed more men in war than you have fingers and toes. Calling me unable to kill is as far away from the truth as calling you a virgin."

"Well, there is a difference between killing and killing." Rake grinned, his normal amused face in place. But there was seriousness in his gray eyes which told Jamie the jokes were just a sidetrack. "Killing another soldier in war, when it is you against him, is one thing. But to coldly plan and murder an innocent woman… *That* is not you."

"You weren't there. You don't know what happened."

"Then enlighten me."

Jamie lifted the glass to his lips, emptying it quickly, searching for some false strength in the wine. Strength to admit what he had done. What he had lost.

"I met Aurélie Delon at a party held by the noblemen of a small French town near the Spanish border to honor us English soldiers. She was the most beautiful woman I've ever seen, with long black hair framing a heart-shaped face and lovely brown eyes. Her coyness and husky laughter drew me like no other before, and I knew I had met my future wife. The only problem was, she didn't fancy me at all."

He smiled softly, remembering how tiresome she had found him, but he had prevailed, and in the end he had won her over.

"She sounds like a wonderful woman."

"Oh, she was horrible." Jamie laughed. "Spoiled rotten and too aware of her own importance. But underneath all that she was the best friend a man could have. Stoically she stood beside me through everything, listening to me ranting about my fears and the horrors of war. Some of my stories must have given her nightmares, but she never flinched. She just held my hand, knowing I needed to get it out of my head."

He looked down at his hands, trying to remember the feeling of her touch, but it was impossible. Too much time had passed, and the memories had become less, leaving him with the fear that he one day wouldn't remember her at all. Her sacrifice needed to be savored. Her life couldn't end as a dim memory in his mind.

"Sounds like you found a gem just as special as Penny."

As Rake shifted in the chair, stretching his legs in front of him with a groan, Jamie frowned slightly. No, he hadn't.

Aurélie had been much, but she most definitely hadn't been of Penelope's kind. She had been there for him, he would give her that, but only to listen. She had never interfered or helped him in any other way. Neither for him nor against him. She had stood behind him, yes, but never beside him.

Not like Mina did.

"It was only rumors at first, rumors that someone in our midst was a spy, informing the French of our plans. But after we spread falsified information, which the French acted upon, we knew the rumors were right. Someone was a traitor. It didn't take long before Aurélie's name was mentioned. Another young woman had seen someone who looked like her talking to a strange man in the shadows, a man who most definitely didn't belong to our acquaintance."

Leaning forward, Rake couldn't hide his curiosity. "She was a spy?"

"Of course not," Jamie said icily. "Aurélie was completely innocent. The other young woman was acting out of envy because the man she loved didn't want her, he wanted Aurélie. It didn't matter to the young woman that Aurélie wasn't interested in her young man; all that mattered was that he wanted her."

"What happened? It must have been an awkward situation."

"Oh, it was. I have to admit it was really awkward. Whispers and looks mixed with more rumors and a few hateful anonymous letters. Aurélie couldn't stand it. She wanted me to bring her here with me, to the safety of England. But I couldn't. I was there to fight for my country; I couldn't simply leave everything I had come for because of her. And besides, I knew the rumors weren't true. I told her it was cowardly to sneak away, that it was better if she stood up and convinced the foolish men and women that they were wrong. But she refused. In the end, I'd had enough and dragged her to the court, sure they would free her of any charges. But they didn't. Instead they had witness after witness telling stories and lies about how they had seen her sneak around, and some even said they had overheard her having secret meetings with men, sexual meetings."

"Oh, dear Lord," Rake breathed. "Jamie, it must have been a horrible situation for the both of you."

"They had men stepping forward, confessing to having had sex with her and without thinking telling her things just because she was such a good listener…" His voice broke, and he had to take a few breaths before he continued. "There were even men I called friends who took the stand, lying about how they had made love to the woman I loved. We had no chance. It didn't matter that she was innocent, not when so many claimed the opposite. And in the end they sentenced her to death."

He hid his face in the palms of his hands, unable to meet Rake's compassionate gaze as he continued his gruesome story.

"They let me see her once, before the…execution… She sat in the corner of the dungeon they had thrown her into. She was so dirty, Rake. She had wounds all over her small body, badly hidden beneath her torn dress. But the worst was how they had broken her spirit. She was so small, crying in my arms as I held her until the guards decided the visit was over and dragged me out of there. I…I tried everything I could to get her out of there. Talked to the men who had accused her, but not one of them took my side, and in the end I had no choice. I knew I had to get her out of there with force. But I was too late. When I burst into her cell, I found it empty. The guards laughed as they told me she was gone. They had already taken care of her. She was…dead…"

"Jamie…"

"And that was not the worst of it," Jamie interrupted, forcing himself to spit it all out at once now that he finally was talking about it. "When I held her in my arms in the cell, the last time I met her, she told me she was carrying my child."

"Oh, my God."

"She begged me to rescue the child," Jamie cried, unable to stop his body from shaking as the sobs tore through his heart and soul. "Sh-she said that as long as the child grew up with me she knew it would be happy. She knew it would be…safe."

Rake didn't say a word, but he moved closer to Jamie, embracing him hard as his twin cried out his grief against his shoulder. The fire slowly grew smaller as they sat together until Jamie's sorrow was spent.

He had thought sharing wouldn't help, that he would be stronger if he saw this through by himself, but as the calm after the storm arrived, Jamie realized how much lighter his heart felt now that he had shared the burden with his brother.

"My back," Rake groaned.

Jamie straightened his and groaned too.

"Mine too. Ouch, it feels crooked."

Rake held up a new bottle of wine, and Jamie nodded, holding up his glass to be refilled. He most definitely needed something to calm his nerves, something that would put some spine back into his back. Right now he felt worn out and empty. Almost ravished.

And it didn't end here. Now he had to endure Rake's reaction, and knowing his brother, he knew he would react. A lot.

"Thank you for telling me this," Rake began. "I'm still angry with you for keeping it to yourself for this long, though. If you had told us when you arrived home, I think things would have been much easier for all of us. We are your family, and even though it is hard to stand us sometimes, we do love you. But that aside, Jamie, there is something in your story that doesn't make sense to me."

"I'm sorry?" Jamie frowned, not knowing how to respond.

"Don't become angry with me for asking this, but Jamie, is there any possibility that everyone told the truth, that Aurélie really was a spy?"

It was so strange. Before, he would have rushed up and forced Rake to take back those words, but somehow…somehow telling the whole truth he found he had some sort of distance to it all. Or maybe it was the way Rake had held him. With love… Somehow he could take a step back and look at the situation, not coldly, but at least with a bit less emotion.

"I…I don't know. It was such a surreal time. Words against words. I believed her, I truly did. But when my friends admitted that they had…"

"If it had been only one…"

Jamie sighed, his shoulders slumping in defeat. "But they were many. Honest men with whom I had fought side by side. Men I had known since childhood.

Men I *knew* were my friends. Why would all of them tell such an outrageous lie about one French woman if it wasn't true? They didn't gain anything by it. Instead they lost…me."

His befuddled mind tried to understand what his mouth was saying, but it was too much too soon. "I'm sorry, Rake, but I can't think about this right now. I will consider it in time, and I promise I will end this conversation with you. But not now. I'm too tired."

With a whack on the shoulder worthy of their father, Rake stood up and stretched with a yawn. "I hear you. And I will stand back. For a while. I will tell the family, though, as I guess you will not. No, don't you stare at me like that, like you dislike me immensely. You know they have to know. Either I will tell them or you will. Your choice."

The mere thought of going through it all again, enduring the questions and comments of the rest of the family, made him feel faint. "You go ahead."

With Rake's amused laughter trailing behind him, Jamie left the library for his bedroom. He most definitely needed to sleep. Tomorrow he would meet with Mina and her family, and hopefully soon he would be able to gather that stubborn redhead in his arms and call her his wife.

It was a happy thought, thinking of Mina as his wife. He knew, without a doubt, that she would make him the most contented husband in England. But the question still remained—would he be able to make her just as content? He had already destroyed one woman's life. What said he wouldn't do the same to Mina's?

And if he succeeded and won her love, was he worthy of it? After destroying someone else's life so completely as he had Aurélie's, could he deserve happiness?

Could he deserve love?

Chapter Seventeen

"Good evening, Wife."

Mina's heart skipped a beat as Jamie's smooth voice cut through the silence of her new bedroom at Chester Park. To hide how much her hands trembled, she grabbed her hairbrush and started to yank her way through her hair, nervously watching his reflection in the mirror in front of her as he made his way across the room.

Lord, he was gorgeous.

Clad only in tight-fitting breeches and an airy white shirt, he looked more like her Viking than a nobleman. He had left his hair loose, falling like a blond waterfall down his broad back, framing his strong, handsome face. He carried a bottle and two glasses, and without a word he put them down in front of her, filling them nearly to the brim with wine.

"Thank you," she whispered, accepting one of the glasses as he held it out to her.

"Here, let me." He took the brush from her hand and let it slide through her hair with slow, sensual movements. "Your hair is so soft, it feels like silk against my fingers."

He dragged his fingers through her hair, slowly, and she met his gaze in the mirror, unable to move away from the heat blazing from him. Her heart beat faster as she watched him lean down and lightly touch her ear with his lips, his dark, burning eyes not once leaving hers.

She lifted the glass of wine and took a large sip to steady her jumpy nerves. And then she took another one. And another.

"I guess I'd better take that." Jamie grinned as he reached forward and took her glass from her. "I don't want you to fall asleep in the middle."

"In the middle of what?" she asked before she could stop herself, and with a low chuckle he knelt down beside her, taking her arms lightly and turning her toward him.

His hands moved slowly, sensually, along her arms as he leaned closer, so close she could feel the warmth of his breath against her lips. "In the middle of making you my woman."

She ripped her arm from his hand, grabbed the glass, and poured the rest of the wine down her throat.

"Are you nervous, Mina?" His eyes smiled warmly at her.

She nodded, staring longingly at his glass, which stood a bit farther down the dressing table. He was quicker, though. Just as she leaned forward to grab it, he hauled her up into his arms and stood to carry her over to the bed.

"It's nothing to be nervous about, Mina. It's just you and me, and we have done most of it already, remember?"

Of course she remembered. His lips against her breast, his hands finding their way to places no one else had touched her. His tongue moving inside her mouth until she whimpered with an unknown need of him.

Her heart beat faster as he laid her down and then

lifted one of her feet, removing the dainty shoe. "Such a lovely shoe."

"I love those shoes," she confessed groggily and watched it fly across the bedroom and land somewhere on the other side, soon joined by its companion.

"Such lovely feet," he purred as his hands followed her leg up under the skirt until they found the edge of the stocking. By the time he had removed both stockings, Mina felt herself burning up. His hot hands and his just-as-hot eyes had her weak with need of him, and the nervousness started to ease a bit.

He was right. It was just the two of them. She and the man she loved.

Her husband.

He must have sensed the transformation inside her, because with a wicked smile he lifted the hem of her skirt and disappeared beneath it. She giggled as his hair tickled her bare legs, but she lost all giddiness as his lips touched her knee, tracing its shape with his tongue.

"Oh, my," she breathed, and another chuckle was heard from underneath her skirt.

His hands worked their way upward and landed quite resolutely on her breasts. Another giggle, spiced with a lot of large-eyed surprise, came from her as she looked down her neckline and saw his fingers emerge in the décolletage. "You are in my dress, my lord."

With a yank as harsh as the ones she had given her hair, he lifted her dress upward, freeing her from it. It joined the shoes on the other side of the room, soon followed by his breeches and shirt. He hovered above her, his strong hands resting against the pillow, one on each side of her head. She looked up into his face, the face she loved more than life itself, and with a whimper she lifted her arms and grabbed his neck, dragging his head down closer to hers so that her lips found his.

"Mina," he moaned as his body lay down on top of hers, covering her like a soft, muscular blanket. Even though her thin chemise still separated their bodies, she shivered with delight at the feel of him. It was such a strange feeling, to be this close to another human being, let alone to a man.

Hidden behind the curtain of his hair, the kiss deepened even more, and Mina could hardly breathe as their tongues danced intimately. But who needed to breathe? Not she. No, she would be perfectly satisfied to spend the rest of her life in this bed, with this man, kissing.

Jamie wasn't as satisfied with the just-kissing part, though. With a grunt he lay down beside her so his hands could leave the pillow. One hand dived in under her neck and forced her mouth to stay pressed to his while the other started to explore her body.

It was heaven.

His hand created a hot, shivering trail all over her body, and she pressed herself closer to his hand, not wanting him to miss a spot with the sensation he created. She grabbed his shoulders and held on as hard as she could as his hand found its way down to the junction of her legs, pressing softly against the thin fabric of her chemise.

She hadn't thought she could get any hotter, but oh, how wrong she had been.

"I'm burning," she moaned, breathless.

"Are you burning for me?" His voice was a mere whisper.

She couldn't even answer, losing her breath as he

slowly began moving his fingers in circles. It was like her whole being became only one thing—that tender spot under his hand which throbbed almost painfully until she couldn't think about anything but the convulsing waves overtaking her mind, her body, her soul.

Caught in the aftermath of passion, she almost missed him as he put himself between her legs, but the prick of pain as he slowly entered her brought her back to earth again. She opened her eyes and looked up into his face, taken aback as she noticed his look of torment as he lay still after joining them. She caught his face in her hands, forcing him to meet her eyes.

"Are you in pain, Jamie?" Her voice trembled with fear.

"God, no…"

"You look like you're in pain… You don't have to do this if it hurts you."

The laughter which escaped him sounded more like a groan than an actual chuckle. "It doesn't hurt me, Mina. Believe me."

She stared at him, bewildered. "But… I don't understand…"

Letting go of his face, she let her hands travel down his shoulders, down his back, enjoying the feeling of him. To feel his smooth skin under her palms and how he trembled as she touched him made her want to touch him even more. Everywhere.

She squirmed slightly as she let her hands travel down his back, and a new sensation sent her almost into a faint as she suddenly realized that he was inside her. It was not only she that was throbbing deliciously between her legs—he was too.

"You are inside me!" she gasped, and he groaned as she squirmed again, trying to see.

"Oh, God, no," he groaned, forcing her to lie down again. "Keep still. I can't hold back if you don't. This feels too good. I just want to…"

Suddenly she understood. He wasn't in pain because of something she did. He was in pain because he was trying to stop himself from feeling the same passionate satisfaction he'd just given her.

Her mother had, with a fiery red face, told her that she would encounter a new phase in a relationship now that she was a married woman, and that it would hurt at first, but if she trusted her husband it would become better in time.

Mina did trust Jamie. Completely. She always had, right from the first moment she laid her eyes on him and fell madly in love with him. He was her Viking. He was the love of her life. And now he was her husband. If she'd still had any fears about her wedding night, they all blew away as she watched him restrain himself from hurting her.

Not that it hurt that much. Not at all, really. It had at first, which had made her come back to her senses. But not now, now it just felt ..good. She shifted her hips again, and they both moaned.

"Stop it," he hissed, his face twisted as he tried to stop himself from moving.

"No."

The groan which left him as he pressed deeper into her to keep her still was like manna to her heart.

"Stop wiggling, Mina. I-I can't hold myself any longer…"

She just had to feel the sensation of him moving

inside her again and wiggled a little bit more and gasped as she felt that wonderful compulsion build up inside her again.

"Mina?"

She looked up into his pained face and grabbed his hair again. "Please don't stop," she begged, and with a gasp he started to move, slowly at first, but as her body answered his movements he became more forceful, thrusting deeper and deeper until he pinned her hard with a growl.

"You have to learn to obey me, woman," Jamie whispered into her hair as he lay down beside her, stretching his body with a satisfied groan.

Without answering him she scooted closer, resting her head against his shoulder and her hand on his chest, feeling the hastened pounding of his heart against her palm. She put one leg over his, slowly dragging her toes against his bare leg, enjoying the feeling of the soft hair covering his calves against her ticklish skin.

Her hand against his chest jumped when he laughed, unable to hide his amusement as she pressed herself even closer to him. "If you don't stop pushing me toward the side of the bed, I will fall onto the floor. Probably I'll drag you with me, as entangled as we are at the moment."

She lifted her head, meeting his silvery eyes and the warmth of his smile. "Do you mind?"

"Falling to the floor?" He kissed her on the tip of her nose. "A bit, I guess. It's a very hard floor. It would hurt. But then again, if you are in my arms I might change my opinion."

She just had to roll her eyes, trying her best to mimic his mother, who was an expert when it came to dramatic eye rolling. "Do you mind that you have ended up with a disobedient wife?" she clarified. "I am not very good with following orders and rules, I'm afraid."

He sighed dramatically. "Well…it is a bit late for second thoughts now, so I guess I will have to endure being married to a woman with a mind of her own. Even though that mind sometimes scares me. Ouf…"

She looked down at him where he lay flat on his back on the floor beside the bed. She tried to stop the laughter which filled her, but even though she bit her lower lip hard, a giggle escaped her, and she was immediately rewarded with a dark look.

"You pushed me out of the bed!"

"I did not," she puffed, trying to sound outraged.

"Yes. You. Did."

"I am just a small, weak woman. How could I ever push a large man such as yourself anywhere?"

Groaning, he sat up, a hand on the back of his head. "Small and weak? Bah…humbug. There is nothing small and weak about you, even though you look like a delicate little flower. You're the devil in disguise, and you should thank me for marrying you before the rest of the men caught your game and ran screaming the other way."

"I should thank you?" She laughed as he climbed back into the bed with a wicked grin. "I was the one who kissed you in Green Park, remember. If anyone should be grateful, it should be you for ending up married to me without having to lift a finger, and for being awarded my quite hefty dowry, too."

"I don't care about the dowry," he said as he started to kiss her toes on the foot closest to him, one after another. She almost forgot what they were talking about as she felt that new sensational feeling overwhelm her again. She closed her eyes and let the waves of heat he created wash over her. She was so caught in the ocean of passion she almost missed that he continued softly, "You can keep it. Do what you want with the money—save it for our children or give it to charity. I can take care of you, nonetheless."

It really should annoy her that he so easily brushed her dowry aside.

It really should.

Such a hefty sum would have most men drooling, but not Lord James Darling. Born into a wealthy family, he'd never had to worry about where the food on the table came from or how he would make ends meet.

But then neither had she. She had been blessed with a home which had not suffered the need of money. Everything she ever wanted had been given to her as soon as she mentioned it. If she had wanted to renew her wardrobe every other month, her mother would probably have clapped her hands in excitement while her father would have paid without a word. After a sufficient time of heavy sighing, that was.

The thing was—she had never cared about money. It was the persons who had none that thought about money. Or obsessed about it. Not the person who had more than enough. So she decided to let his indifference pass. Besides, if their future would be blessed with more than one child, the money could go to them. The firstborn was the only heir and therefore the one who would inherit whatever estate and wealth Jamie had.

The bed creaked as Jamie climbed farther up,

slowly kissing her calf, her knee, and then her thigh as he moved. His soft hair brushed against her delicate skin when he created delicious patterns with the tip of his tongue on her belly, her breasts, and her throat. When he finally reached her face, she didn't hesitate. Eagerly she pressed her lips against his smiling ones, kissing him until both of them were laughing breathlessly.

****

The warm morning sun found them lying in the middle of the bed, their limbs entangled and their hearts beating as one. No one could have prepared her for this, Mina thought, groaning lightly as her body ached in hitherto unknown places. It had been a wonderful night, filled with sensations and a passion she never could have envisioned beforehand. Opening her eyes, she looked at Jamie's sleeping face, so peaceful and handsome now when he wasn't on his guard.

Poor man.

He had not had the easiest road so far when it came to love, considering his loss of Aurélie and the child. But now he had her, and she wouldn't rest until he was as happy with her as she was with him. Lightly she touched his face, watching him wrinkle his nose in response.

The love in her heart for the handsome man resting in her arms overwhelmed her for a moment, and she blinked away a few tears.

Jamie flew up, almost knocking her chin with the top of his head. The transformation from handsome man sound asleep to frowning Viking looking ready for war was done in a fraction of a second, and for a moment she could only gape, astonished.

"A-Are you hurt?"

She caught herself with her mouth wide open and closed it firmly, shaking her head at the same time. "No, my lord."

"You are crying!" His voice was high-pitched and worried as he stared at her accusingly. "What happened? Did someone hurt you?" He took a deep, shaky breath. "Did…I…hurt you?"

"No…"

He grabbed her hands, dragging her upward until she sat beside him. "Then what is the matter, Mina? Please, tell me."

His thumbs caressed the palms of her hands, and she was starting to feel all warm and breathless again. "I was just admiring you."

"What?" He hadn't expected that explanation.

"You are one quite beautiful man, you know."

He was his mother's son for sure. Those silvery eyes rolled with perfection. "Mina," he sighed, dejected. "Are you telling me that you are sitting in our bed and crying because you think I am beautiful?"

She nodded with a small, happy sob.

He snorted softly. "You are a strange woman."

She didn't mind him calling her strange, not when he looked at her with so much warmth and love while caressing her cheek with his large, warm hand. Unable to withstand the love filling her very soul, she opened her mouth and, with a shaky voice overflowing with emotion, admitted the truth she couldn't deny any longer: "I love you."

He froze, a marble statue sitting in her bed, staring at her with horror as if she had told him she'd killed his whole family instead of admitting what was in her heart. It felt like eons of time before he moved again, slowly letting go of her face and hands as he stood up, leaving her alone on the rumpled bed.

He took a deep, ragged breath. "No, you don't."

"Eh? Yes, I do."

"You can't."

She stared at him in bewilderment. "I can't?"

"No." He dragged a hand through his hair as he walked to and fro over the wooden floor of the bedroom, unable to stand still. "I'm just not a loveable person."

He was ridiculous. She didn't know whether to laugh or cry over his idiotic conclusion, but as she was an understanding woman who knew he had a…thing…when it came to emotions, she clasped her hands in her lap and gazed at him with her best serene expression. "Yes, you are. I love you, remember?"

"Stop saying that!"

She was an awful woman. Really, she was. She was actually enjoying this, which was sort of bizarre, considering she'd just told him she loved him and he denied it altogether. But then, she *knew* he loved her. He was just too scared of getting hurt again to dare to admit it. And with that knowledge, she didn't mind him fidgeting a bit. In fact, she wouldn't mind him feeling too much for a while. She had for the last year and knew how confused one could become.

"And you love me." It was a brazen statement, said in the sweetest tone of voice. His eyes narrowed as he glared suspiciously at her.

"No, I don't."

"Yes, you do. You are just too afraid to say it out loud."

"Mina…"

"Yes, my love?"

He stalked across the floor until he stood in front of her, hovering. "Stop fooling yourself. I don't love you and never will. I do appreciate you, though, for the wonderful, caring person that you are, but I don't love you. My heart was lost in France, and I'm afraid I will never be able to find it again."

"If you say so."

He threw his hands up in the air out of despair. "You are just as simpleminded as Rake. Why can't the two of you just accept the truth as you are told? He thinks Aurélie was a spy even though he wasn't there to see her innocence, while you think I love you even though I say I don't. You both are out of your minds!"

And with a last frustrated growl in her direction, he barged out of the room to his dressing room, leaving her gaping at his back.

So Rake thought Aurélie a spy?

What wonderful and exciting news. She had to go find him and hear for herself on what grounds he rested that conclusion. She dressed as rapidly as possible with no maid in attendance. Luckily, as it was early in the morning and most of the Darlings were still in bed, she found her new brother-in-law sitting at the breakfast table alone, as the early bird that he had become since marrying Penny and preferring to spend his evenings in bed with her instead of roaming the town all night.

"Well, if it isn't our blushing bride," he drawled as she walked into the room. "Where is that new husband of yours? Still in bed, exhausted?"

Yesterday she wouldn't have understood his wicked jest, but after spending a passionate night in

Jamie's arms, she knew exactly what he meant and felt her cheeks growing warm, awarding her a rich chuckle from her new brother. Ignoring Rake's grin, she sat down on the other side of the table, facing him.

"Do you really think Aurélie was a spy?"

He was not a man caught easily by surprise, but this time she had managed it.

"What…Why…"

"Jamie admitted you had told him as much."

Rake leaned back in his chair, slowly folding the paper he had been reading. "We had a talk before your wedding, Jamie and I, when he told me about what had happened in France. How the woman he thought himself in love with had been accused of being a traitor and a spy and that he was the reason she died. I was so thankful for him finally opening up, sharing with me why he was in such pain, that at first I didn't really listen to *what* he said. But then there were things in his tale that didn't make sense. Small things, at first, which made me wonder, and then in the end…"

Rake's voice trailed off as he stared out into the air, collecting his thoughts. She watched him while he frowningly tried to find the right words. The man in front of her was clad in utter elegance, the superb gentleman from his dark hair down to his shiny Hessians. But where most other people saw only a wicked libertine who never seemed to take anything seriously, she saw a warm and caring man, one she knew loved her for the person she was to him, to Jamie, and to his family.

Lady Penelope was a lucky woman.

"How much has he told you?" Rake asked, interrupting her silent declaration of love to him.

"Not so much," she admitted. "He told me about Aurélie and that he was the reason she, and the child she carried, died."

"Did he tell you about the other men?"

Ooh… "No, he most definitely didn't tell me about any other men."

Rake chuckled, his amusement obvious. "You don't have to sound so happy about it, Mina. One could get the impression that you want Aurélie to be the villain in your fairytale."

She made a small grimace, unable to hide her mirth. "I'm afraid a small, weak part of me would be quite happy if the perfect Aurélie wasn't as perfect as I've been told by Jamie."

"Well, then, send a grateful prayer, because I most definitely think she was a villain, and quite a perverse one. The only person who thought of her as innocent is Jamie, and he is blinded by his guilt."

"May I ask what men you mentioned?"

"According to Jamie, the other Englishmen, the ones he called friends, all stood up and admitted she had seduced them and tried to lure information out of them. All of them. And even though Jamie insisted that they lied and begged them to reconsider, they still, unanimously, held their stance. Now, tell me, Mina. What friends would knowingly and cold-bloodedly send a young, innocent woman to death, especially one their friend insisted he wanted to marry? If anyone of them had swayed or changed his mind, I might have believed in Aurélie's innocence. But not one did, which Jamie was quite clear about. He was the only one who believed in her. No one else. Not even the villagers stood up and declared it all a lie. No, they all knew what kind of woman she was, and that was why she was sent to prison and then sentenced to death."

It made sense. Every last word Rake spoke made perfect sense, and Mina felt tears run down her cheeks as she cried for Jamie and his utter belief in love and chastity. "I only wish she hadn't been carrying his child," she sobbed and accepted the handkerchief Rake offered her. "I think that is what hurts him the most—his child, which he made sure never had a chance to see daylight."

"Well…" Rake drawled from the other side of the table. "I think she made up the child."

She had not been prepared for that conclusion. "Why…What?"

"Jamie said he slept with her once, only two weeks before she was killed. Two weeks, Mina. According to the doctor I spoke with after Jamie told me about Aurélie's pregnancy, it is far too early to know after a mere two weeks. It takes at least one more month until you can be sure you are pregnant. The doctor was most confident that Aurélie lied. She lied to hurt Jamie as much as she could in her last hours, in revenge, because he had forced her to go in front of the court even though she begged him not to."

"What if she was speaking the truth?" Mina couldn't help but muse, stoically trying to find Jamie right, to stand by his side even though it went against all her own wishes. "What if Aurélie was only an innocent pawn in a greater game?"

"She wasn't."

Shocked, Rake and Mina looked toward the doorway where Jamie stood, his normally tall body seeming small and frail. Slowly he walked over to them, so slowly it seemed he dragged his feet in deepest mud. As he sat down beside Mina and lifted her hand to his lips, kissing it lightly, his handsome face looked worn and old. For once the normally vibrant and forceful man was tired. Broken.

"Jamie…" Rake started, but Jamie held up his other hand, the one which didn't caress Mina's most tenderly.

"You are right, Rake. You both are, with your rash assumptions about me and about Aurélie. I have been hiding myself so deeply in the guilt I've felt over her death that I've not once even considered what everyone else was telling me. But listening to you now, Rake, made me finally understand that there is more to this than what I first thought. Aurélie was not the innocent, sweet young woman you seem to think, Mina, and I am so sorry to have led you to that belief. She was typical French, forward, flirty, and sending passionate glances to all the men surrounding her. After surviving the ghastliness of war, meeting Aurélie was like manna for my wounded soul. She was the complete opposite of a bloody battlefield, and I walked blindfolded into her lair. My friends tried to tell me she was no good, but I didn't listen. I needed her beauty so I could forget the gruesomeness I'd been part of until then."

Mina dabbed her eyes with the soaked-through handkerchief. The pain in Jamie's voice was devastating, yet she couldn't stop herself from feeling that the large wedge which had been parting them had been removed at last. Now she could help him relive the past and leave it behind. Together they could face their future, their life with each other.

"I'm so relieved," Rake said hoarsely and shook

his head with an amused, yet tearful smile when Mina offered him the soaked handkerchief back. "If you knew how much this has pained me. Knowing you hurt and not being able to be there for you. To mend you."

"It is not your chore to mend me."

"I am your brother. Your twin, for goodness' sake! I love you, Jamie, and if you ever leave me outside of anything again *I* will personally drag *you* to Gentleman Jackson's, and this time it will be me knocking you out."

The gentle love, filled with a silent promise of trust, flowed over the table and had Mina crying even harder, and the tension eased as the two brothers chuckled with manly superiority over her emotional outburst.

"She is a bit dramatic, isn't she?" Rake grinned. "Even Penny with all her daydreams and beliefs in eternal happiness isn't this emotional. Bloody hell, she's almost as dramatic as Mother."

"I know," Jamie sighed, his face overly dejected. "I should have run the other way as fast as I could as soon as I noticed this flaw. But now she is my wife, and I have to live with her the rest of my life. Nothing to do but to endure. Ouf…"

"You are a horrible man." Mina laughed, teary-eyed, as her husband rubbed the sore spot on his side where her elbow had hit. "And you are just as dramatic as I am."

"He sure is." Rake chuckled and elegantly managed to avoid the bun his twin sent in his direction. "Which leads me to ask you a favor, Jamie."

Mina felt Jamie tense beside her, but his voice was light. "Yes?"

"I want us to go up to Lancashire and visit your old friend Ned Beckett, so you can hear his side of the story. He was there with you, and if I'm correct, he was one of the men accusing Aurélie of treason."

"How did you…?"

"You haven't seen him or spoken of him since you came back. Before you went to France he was always here, avoiding that cold manor of his as much as he could when not in London. But since you came back from France, he has been nowhere in sight. It's not hard to assume why your friendship suddenly was lost."

Mina looked from one serious brother to the other, silently rejoicing over Rake's plan. Jamie might finally see things as they really were, no longer blinded by his feelings, but he still needed the truth confirmed. And who could better confirm it than someone who had been there and a part of the whole thing?

"All right." Jamie sighed in defeat. "Let's go and visit Beckett and hear his side of the story. Even though I think Lancashire this time of year must be awful."

Rake didn't waste any time. Without another word he stood and left the breakfast room, and soon they heard him holler for Ivanoff.

Jamie didn't waste any time either. As soon as his twin left them alone, he turned slightly and grabbed Mina's chin lightly, forcing her face upward so she could meet his serious eyes.

"You don't have to say anything," she lied and was awarded a small but warm chuckle.

"Oh, I know I have to. You will never leave me be until I have admitted that you were right."

"Thank you."

"I love you."

"I know."

Tears filled his eyes as he grinned again. "Thank you."

Rake chuckled as he watched his brother race up the stairs with his wife in his arms, in a hurry to start their life together now that everything was said and done.

Or almost done. First they would have to travel through England and visit an old friend, and then their happily ever after could begin.

Chapter Eighteen

"Oh, dear, Lancashire is so cold this time of year," Mina moaned as Jamie lifted her down from the cozy warmth of the carriage. "It's almost May, and yet it feels like January."

"I can't feel my toes," Penelope whined behind her, as she let her husband help her down. "I lost them somewhere in Derbyshire, I think."

Rake pulled her coat close under her chin and kissed the tip of her shiny nose softly. "It was you who insisted upon joining us. We all thought you should stay behind at Chester Park and concentrate on bearing our child instead, but not you. No, you more or less threatened to follow in a carriage of your own if we didn't let you come with us."

"I want to be there for the people I care about," Penelope sniffed stiffly. "I happen to love both Jamie and Mina very much, and if you think I will stay put for another five months because of your child, you are sadly mistaken, my lord."

Rake's shoulders slumped in a heavy sigh, and Mina exchanged an amused look with Jamie. He might have been the libertine of his time, the most eligible bachelor to ever walk a ballroom, but those days were long gone. Now Lord Richard Darling lived and breathed for one thing only—his pregnant wife.

And she ruled his world with a swollen fist.

"Let us not stand here and freeze." Like a master and commander, Penelope marched up to the front door of the decayed manor before them. The place looked like it wanted nothing more than to fall into a pile of tired stones as she knocked briskly on the frayed wood. The footman who opened it took a terrified step backward as Lady Penelope Darling, with the force of a steamboat, entered the house. "Please let Mr. Beckett know that Lord James Darling and company are here to see him."

Petrified, the footman disappeared, leaving the foursome alone in the dark and damp foyer. It felt like they had walked into a crypt instead of a nobleman's home.

"My God," Jamie breathed as he looked around. "What has happened to this place since last I was here? I have to admit this house had seen its best days back then too, but not like this. Paintings used to cover the walls over there, and a thick rug lay on the floor. Now it's all empty and cold."

"Like my life."

The man joining them in the foyer was tall and slender, carrying a cloudy glass with some brown fluid in it. He was clad in a worn robe, and Mina could see he wore his nightshirt underneath. At lunchtime.

"Beckett," Rake drawled politely, "such a long time since I saw you last. Please let me introduce our wives, the Ladies Darling."

"Delighted," the somewhat frayed gentleman said with a wobbly bow. "Such lovely ladies. You are lucky men, old chaps."

It was hard to imagine that the man in front of them was as young as Jamie and Rake. With his uncombed, greasy hair and dirty nightclothes, he had certainly lost the stylish elegance which normally identified a noble gentleman. But what made him look older than his late twenties were the smudges under his bloodshot eyes and the deep wrinkles covering his face. Wrinkles a man of his age shouldn't have, but she guessed he had lost quite a lot of weight. His body was quite thin, dwarfed by the oversized robe.

Jamie stood silent, a twitching muscle in his face revealing his jaws were clenched tightly. He and Rake had told many tales from their youth, during the journey to Mr. Beckett's home, and they had spoken of him as a not too clever but very funny and charming man.

The man in front of them was anything but.

Beckett waved his hand toward a dark hallway, almost falling over in the attempt. "I would invite you in, if I had something to invite you in to. A storm last year had a tree crashing into the formal area, and now we spend our days in our private chambers."

"Our?" Rake arched an inquiring eyebrow. "You are married?"

"I am," Beckett said with a hateful grimace. "Bloody bitch. She's up there, you know, hovering in her bedroom with all the valuables she could find throughout the house. With her greedy fingers nipping everything worth anything. I will soon be out of money to buy necessities."

His glance at the cloudy drink in his hand told what those necessities were. Not food. Not servants. No, he was talking about alcohol.

"Bloody bitch," he repeated with a whisper. "I should have let you have her, you know. My life would have been so much better. But no, I was too caught in her game and wanted nothing more than to pin her down in my bed. My apologies…"

The last was directed toward the ladies, and both Mina and Penelope nodded, their faces flushed with embarrassment.

Jamie didn't hear the last part of the outrageousness his former friend spoke. He looked shocked, his hands shaking as he took a step closer. "A-are you talking about…Aurélie?"

Mina's heart stopped a beat as she caught Jamie's sudden urgency. Was this true? Was the woman Beckett so hatefully spoke of…Aurélie? Was she…alive?

"Who else?" Beckett spit out. "Who else would have you, me, everybody fooled like this? Oh, she thought she had won the highest prize when she decided I was worth snaring, as I was the only one who had an estate of my own. Little did she know she was drawing the greatest blank anyone had ever seen. She wanted you, you know." A bony finger pointed hard into Jamie's chest, but he didn't blink. "Found you so attractive, and liked that chivalrous attitude of yours. But you are the seventh son…"

"Sixth," Rake and Jamie unanimously interrupted, both unaware of their rude input, too caught in trying to make sense of what they were being told to stop themselves from replying automatically.

Ignoring the twins' irrelevant correction, Beckett staggered over to a wall and leaned against it with a sigh of relief. "If she had known that you came from one of the richest families in England, and had a personal wealth most men envied, she would have discarded me as fast as she possibly could. But I fooled her." His laughter was hollow and filled with self-contempt. "Told her all about my mansion and my vast lands. And the bitch bought every word. But in the end it was me that was the one fooled. She didn't want me. She only wanted to come to England and become a part of the *ton.* Endless parties and an overfilled wardrobe. Well…it didn't go as she wanted, now, did it? Bah! Instead I took her here under the pretense that we had to fill my pockets a bit before we joined polite society. Then I sold the carriage… Bloody bitch…"

Eyes rolling back into his head, Beckett fell with a thud, the glass breaking into pieces as it hit the cold stone floor. Jamie rushed to him but stopped dead when a loud snore escaped his former friend's drooling mouth.

"This is so exciting," Penelope squealed beside Mina, hugging her arm tightly. "I am so glad I endured the ride here. I wouldn't have wanted to miss this for the world."

"*You* endured?" her loving husband said, his smooth voice filled with astonishment. "Please do correct me if I'm wrong, but in my world—our world—you were the one who turned what should have been an easy journey through the countryside into living hell. You never stopped complaining, my love. Never…"

Ignoring her whining brother-in-law, Mina turned toward Penelope with shining eyes. "It is, isn't it? Oh, I can hardly wait until we meet her. Oh, Jamie, this is the best thing that ever could have happened to me. Truly, it is. Not only will I be able to meet the not-as-perfect-anymore Aurélie, but I will also be able to rub in that you are all mine."

Raising her hand, she called to the shivering

footman, who had tried to hide in the shadows of the hallway leading to the back part of the house where the kitchen and the servants' quarters lay. "You there. What is your name?... Alan? Then, Alan, could you please inform the lady of the house that she has guests waiting for her in the foyer? And please, Alan, don't let her know exactly who these guests are."

Aurélie wasn't well liked by the servants, Mina assumed, as the footman named Alan stopped shivering and with a triumphant nod ran up the stairs, his giddy laughter trailing behind him.

"Ladies, you should be ashamed of yourselves," Rake frowned before turning toward his brother. "Jamie? How are you?"

There was an odd blank expression on Jamie's face where he stood, looking down on his former friend, who lay snoring at his feet. "I'm fine," he almost whispered, his voice vaguely astonished.

"Don't mind the ladies," Rake said, casting another murderous glance toward their wives. "Their unspeakable rudeness is beyond childish."

"Oh, I don't mind." Jamie looked up, his silvery eyes sparkling with mirth, and Mina sighed with relief, finally aware of the tension she had felt waiting for his reaction. "I truly do not mind. At all. You are, as always, right, Mina. I have spent the last two years feeling miserable and unworthy of happiness because of the woman upstairs. Why, she almost had me give up you, Mina, just because of the guilt I felt over something that never happened." He walked up to Mina and put his hands gently against her cheeks, placing a chaste kiss on her forehead with so much love she almost started to cry. "I have to confess that one petty part of me feels maliciously satisfied that *this* is her life. This damp, moldy house, on the verge of falling apart, is the castle she wanted. That man on the floor, the one I thought was my friend but who chose to let me believe I had killed her, is her hateful husband, who does anything he can to spite her. No money. No parties. No luxury. Truly, Rake, this couldn't be a better outcome if I had thought it up myself."

Rake laughed and whacked Jamie on the back, which would have had him sprawled out on the floor beside Beckett if he had been smaller man. "Bloody hell, Jamie. You are turning more and more into me every passing day."

"Oh, good Lord, no," Jamie gasped with feigned fear, and Rake sent a clenched fist his way, pretending to become upset.

As Jamie laughingly lifted his hands, Mina joined the eye-rolling Penny at the front door, watching the twins as they sparred lightheartedly.

"They are just like small children sometimes," Penny said with a patronizing sigh, and Mina couldn't help but agree, but quite happily. Seeing this new Jamie, this playful man, sparring with his brother, she couldn't ask for anything else. Gone was his pain and the attitude of the frowning hermit. Instead a happy man stood there, openly laughing, without shadows in his heart.

"Ehrm." Alan the footman interrupted the commotion as he came down the slippery staircase. He stopped at the last step, turned, and with a sweeping, dramatic gesture, he announced solemnly, "Madame Beckett."

The laughter left Jamie's eyes as he stared at the

woman who came floating down the stairs. Mina felt her eyes growing larger and larger as one of the most beautiful women she'd ever seen halted halfway, her elegant hand flying to her throat as a shriek left her rosebud-like mouth when she recognized the tall man standing in the foyer.

Aurélie.

She was an astonishing vision, a true diamond of a woman. If it hadn't been for Lady Chilton, Mina would easily have been able to declare her the most beautiful woman she'd ever seen. Aurélie's hair was thick and black, her eyes large, with the most delicious chocolate-brown nuance. Her small nose was perky and very French, her unbelievably red lips pouty and seemed to be made for kissing. She was clad in a deeply red dress that drew all the attention to her very ample breasts, which seemed to want to burst out of their confinement. All in all, Aurélie was a seductress, and she made sure to dress as one.

"Jamie!" Aurélie gasped, and even that gasp was sensual, made to lure her prey closer. "I thought you were dead! Ah, mon ami!" Floating down the rest of the stairs, she threw her voluptuous body against Jamie's, slipping her hands around his neck to force his lips closer to hers. "Ah, my wonderful man! You have returned to me!"

"Does she really pronounce every last sentence as if it has an exclamation mark at the end?" Penny whispered, looking just as mesmerized as Mina felt.

"I think so," she whispered back. "And she pronounces Jamie as Hameee."

"Extraordinary," Penny breathed.

Mina nodded, just as fascinated. "Indeed."

“Look at her,” Rake said as he joined them, his voice filled with amazement. “She’s rubbing herself all over him. My God, she is one spectacular woman.”

She really should feel a bit jealous, Mina thought, as she watched her husband stand there with another woman practically climbing onto him, but it was impossible. Aurélie was a fascinating woman, yet she had already lost any grip she’d ever had on Jamie. That gloriously handsome man in his light gray clothes and thick winter coat, his blond hair hanging down on his shoulders, looked too uncomfortable in the seductress’s embrace for Mina to even begin to feel uncomfortable too.

In the end, it was Jamie who broke their closeness. “Enough,” he said coldly as he lifted her hands from his neck, releasing them by her sides as if they were filthy rats. “You lost your right to touch me when you made me believe you were dead.”

Aurélie’s hands flew up to her swan-like throat. “Mon Dieu, Jamie! I was told you were dead!” She pointed her hand toward the still-snoring Beckett. “*He* told me you were dead! If I would have known… Oh, mon ami…”

Big tears left her large, chocolaty eyes, running slowly down her peachy cheeks, and the threesome at the door sighed simultaneously in response. A small smile grew on Jamie’s full lips when he heard, and Aurélie, who obviously thought he was falling for her tears, immediately took a step closer, her arms stretched out in front of her, inviting him back into her embrace. When Jamie’s face hardened again, her arms fell and her eyes darted all over the room, searching for something which would give her some leverage, something which would make her able to sway Jamie her way. As her gaze stopped at Beckett, a triumphant shadow washed over her face, and if they all hadn't been watching her so closely, they would have missed it.

"You have to save me, Jamie," she whispered, her face turning into a mask of fear. "Monsieur Beckett is forcing me to stay here against my will."

Jamie wasn't so easily turned, though. "He is your husband. He can keep you here for the rest of your life if he wants to."

"But look at this dungeon of a house! There is no furniture, no warmth, *no servants*! Just that useless footman, who even refuses to go inside a lady's bedroom!"

Alan, the useless footman, leaned forward. "I am *married*," he informed them with a weary voice, before jumping backward as Aurélie, with a shriek, came after him.

"You-you liar!" she squealed with vengeance after his disappearing back. "I wouldn't touch you with a stick! A stick!"

Shaking his head, Jamie turned and strode to his family at the door. "Come. I have had more than enough of this. Let us go home."

"Oh, no," Penelope said, disappointed. "I am enjoying this. Can't we stay for a little while more?"

Rake chuckled as he opened the door. "No, my love. Jamie is right. Let's go home and concentrate on bearing that baby of ours, instead. And besides, I am desperate to touch you without a constant audience."

With a contented smile, Penelope grabbed her husband's arm and followed his lead out the door, leaving Jamie and Mina alone with the distressed Aurélie and her snoring husband.

"You can't leave me here, Jamie! Please, take me with you. I will do anything you want. Anything!" The sultry look in the seductress eyes told exactly what that anything would be, and Jamie snorted, disgusted.

"I wouldn't touch *you* with a stick," he said, using her own words against her. "You made your choice in France. You chose Beckett because you thought he was a wealthy man just because he has a mansion of his own, and now you have to live with that choice. Come."

The last word was directed to Mina as he offered her his arm and turned toward the door, heading out to the awaiting carriage. In the doorway he hesitated slightly, looking back at the furious woman who looked ready to rip the hair of her head. "I guess I should thank you, though," he said, almost as an afterthought. "If you had chosen me, I would never have met Mina here. Because of you, I am now married to the woman I love, and I couldn't be happier or more grateful for the love she bestows on me. I am one of England's wealthiest men, but that means nothing to me. Nothing, compared to Mina."

"B-but you are a seventh son," Aurélie spat. "Beckett told me that."

"Sixth, but who's counting," Jamie said, turning back to Mina. "Besides, I have my own wealth, inherited from generous relatives without offspring. I now receive about ten thousand pounds annually, and since all I have to spend money on is Mina here, I guess I will die even wealthier. Goodbye, Aurélie. I hope your life will be long and pitiful."

The ghastly shriek behind them was cut off when the door closed, and Mina couldn't help but laugh. "Did you see her face when you told her how much money you have? Oh, it was hysterical!"

"I can't believe I thought myself in love with her." Jamie laughed. "My God, what an awful woman. I should send some money to Beckett just to thank him for rescuing me from her greedy claws."

"I can send a part of my dowry," Mina teased. "You said I could use it for charity if I wanted to."

They halted outside the carriage, in which Rake and Penelope waited for them, but instead of opening the door, Jamie dragged Mina close, and without caring about who could see them, he kissed her until they both were breathless.

"Let's go home and make babies of our own," he whispered in her ear, and she nodded, in full agreement.

"Let's go home and be happy."

Epilogue

It was common knowledge that a reformed libertine was the best husband, but Mina had to disagree with that saying because she knew, without a doubt, that the best husband was a reformed hermit.

After twenty years of marriage, she still sent a grateful prayer to her mother for so strongly wanting her daughter to marry the alluring Soberton vicar. If it hadn't been for the Honorable Luther Whyte, Mina would never have come to Chester Park and would never have met, in the stable there, an angry man with a broken heart, a man who accused her, quite ridiculously, of being a spy.

Sitting on a blanket outside Chester Park, enjoying the warmth of the sun, she laughed as her one-year-old granddaughter, Ophelia, fell down into her lap with a triumphant grin so much like her Great-Uncle Rake's. The baby was precious, just like Mina's beautiful daughter, who sat down beside her, kissing her mother on the cheek with love.

"I can't believe how fast she has learnt to walk," Isabel said proudly. "It seems only yesterday she was born, and look at her now!"

With her gaze following Ophelia's stroll back toward her grandfather, who stood waiting for her with open arms, Mina shook her head, laughing. "I was just thinking the same about *you*. Sometimes it feels like you are still a toddler, driving Ivanoff crazy with all your antics, and yet you already have one of your own."

"I am so grateful I married a man who loves his child as much as I know my father loves me. It has always been my strength, knowing that I have the two of you behind me, carrying me with your love."

"Oh, stop it." Mina grinned with teary eyes, and met her daughter's equally teary eyes. "You make this old woman all mushy, and I need my strength for tonight. Anna has decided, quite spontaneously as always, that she wants to hold a masquerade for your younger sister's debut, and as she is still too weak to leave her bed, she is determined that I shall be her hands and feet. But we are leaving for a prolonged Soberton visit tomorrow, you know, and I will have to tell her to set her plans aside."

"Good luck with that." Isabel laughed as she stood up and followed her daughter's trail.

"Lord, that child is lively," Jamie sighed as he sat down beside her. "I'm sure neither of us ever will gain any weight having to follow her around constantly."

"All the little things," Mina said, caressing his long blond hair which now had definite shadows of silver in it. "Do you look forward to our trip tomorrow? I know one person who is desperately waiting for you."

"Luther," Jamie snarled with contempt. "If he thinks I am going to let him win over me in chess again, he is sadly mistaken. That man will finally have to succumb to becoming the loser instead of me."

"In his eyes, you are the real winner, because you won me," Mina teased, and he rolled his eyes as all the Darlings did with such ease. "He did want to marry me, remember?"

"I remember, and I guess I should thank him. He was, after all, the reason for us getting married."

"He was?" Mina frowned, trying to remember what Jamie meant.

"Indeed, he was. If Penelope hadn't told me that you had a vicar back home who wanted to marry you, I wouldn't have become jealous and sought you out at Green Park all those years ago. You would never have kissed me, which was what forced us to marry."

Lying down with her head in his lap, Mina closed her eyes, enjoying the warmth of the sun and the heat of this husband of hers. It was amazing. All these years, and he still had the ability to make her heart beat faster simply by touching her. She guessed she should be grateful to all those people who in one way or another had interfered and caused her to change the path of her life in the direction of Jamie.

She really should be. But she wasn't.

Jamie was her fate, and she believed with all her heart that in the end she would have ended up here on this blanket with him regardless. Only by another path. After another choice.

She opened her eyes and looked at his handsome face, almost untouched by age, and felt her heart burst with love. As if he felt her looking at him, he met her gaze with just as much love.

"I love you, my love," he whispered, his voice hoarse with emotions.

"And I love you, my fate."

A word about the author…

Mother of kids.
Writer of romance.
Addict of coffee.

jenniferwenn.com

www.ingramcontent.com/pod-product-compliance
Lightning Source LLC
Chambersburg PA
CBHW060523260626
47161CB00003B/740

9781509215294